A Child for the Devil

By Conrad Jones

Detective Inspector Braddick Series
Brick
Shadows
Guilty Until Proven Innocent
Deliver Us from Evil

Detective Alec Ramsay Series
The Child Taker
Criminally Insane
Slow Burn
Frozen Betrayal
Desolate Sands
Concrete Evidence
Thr3e

Soft Target Series
Soft Target
Soft Target II 'Tank'
Soft Target III 'Jerusalem'
The Rage Within
Blister
The Child Taker
Unleashed

Hunting Angels Diaries
A Child for the Devil
Black Angel
Blood Bath
The Book of Abominations

Dedicated to Evie Jones

PROLOGUE	5
CHAPTER 1	25
CHAPTER 2	31
CHAPTER 3	44
CHAPTER 4	83
CHAPTER 5	92
CHAPTER 6	98
CHAPTER 7	107
CHAPTER 8	117
CHAPTER 9	144
CHAPTER 10	147
CHAPTER 11	162
CHAPTER 12	180
CHAPTER 13	187
CHAPTER 14	192
CHAPTER 15	200
CHAPTER 16	204
CHAPTER 17	218
CHAPTER 18	224
CHAPTER 19	227
CHAPTER 20	239
CHAPTER 21	251
CHAPTER 22	269
CHAPTER 23	272
CHAPTER 24	275
CHAPTER 25	278
CHAPTER 26	282

CHAPTER 27 301

PROLOGUE

Malcolm Baines woke up with a banging headache. He was disorientated and confused. There were murmuring voices in his head; he couldn't make out the words – they were almost whispers. A sickly, rotten smell filled his senses. As he opened his eyes, his vision was misty and blurred, and he decided never to mix vodka shots with cider again. It wasn't the first time he'd said, 'never again'. Malcolm often made resolutions in the haze of the previous night's alcohol, but he rarely stuck to them. He was weak when sober, but after a few drinks his willpower was virtually non-existent. If he combined alcohol with cocaine, he was partying into the small hours of the morning.

His job was his life. He found investigating the bizarre – and writing news stories about it – exhilarating, as did his colleagues. Headlines about government U-turns and the global financial meltdown were not for him. He was an investigator and proud of it. Malcolm buzzed off searching the Internet for unusual happenings, weird deaths, persons missing in unusual circumstances, and when he focused on a storyline, his tenacity to seek out the truth was unrivalled. His headlines were sculpted by him alone, not picked up from international news sites. His colleagues were a mixed bag of sports writers and mainstream columnists, but Malcolm considered himself different. He was special. When one or more of his workmates cracked a new headline, it was party time and the cocaine and alcohol flowed. 'Work hard, play hard,' Malcolm repeatedly told people.

At twenty-six, he'd climbed the ladder of success quickly and he was fiercely proud of his achievements thus far. His Facebook page sported a scanned picture of his Young Journalist of the Year award, instead of a picture of himself. He knew that he wasn't good-looking; in fact, he was overweight, his sweat glands caused him endless embarrassment and his ginger hair was thinning fast. Although he spent a fortune on cologne and designer clothing, women found him arrogant and physically repellent. His infrequent sexual encounters usually cost him money and they didn't last very long. Still, he knew that his success at work and financial status would attract a woman one day. Probably a gold-digger, but as long as she was compliant in the bedroom, it was all good. He was in no rush.

The whispering became louder and snapped him back to reality. Malcolm blinked and tried to focus on the room. Candlelight flickered in the darkness, casting shadows and distorting the faces around him. He wasn't in the nightclub, of that he was certain. He blinked again as fragmented memories of the night before returned to him. A woman had invited him to a party. She was black and she was hot. He could remember that much. As he focused on the people around him, he recognised her face, but it was distorted by the flickering yellow glow. He had no idea who the others were.

The woman he had been with in the club was stunning. He remembered her perfume was thick, almost cloying, and her eyes were so dark they were hypnotic. She'd approached him near the end of the night as his friends dwindled and headed off home in different directions. At the time, he couldn't believe his luck. Women never chatted him up, especially beautiful women. He had noticed her earlier in the evening talking to one of his workmates, and although he noticed how attractive she was, he didn't pay her much attention. At the end of the night when she introduced herself, she said that she knew his name and was a fan of his articles, especially the stories about missing people.

Malcolm had a talent for investigating the lost, and writing stories about reuniting families, pulled at the heartstrings of the nation – and sold newspapers. She said that she was studying journalism at university and aspired to be as successful as he'd been. Malcolm was flattered by her attention and bought half a dozen drinks, attempting to weaken her resistance to his sexual advances. All he succeeded in doing was getting himself blind drunk. She appeared completely sober, suggesting vodka shots near the end of the night. They tipped him over the edge. He recalled her inviting him back to her place for a party before he blanked out.

Malcolm felt rough and he couldn't move. He guessed that the alcohol had numbed his motor neurons. 'I'm out of my brains here,' he slurred. The faces stared at him blankly. 'Where am I?'

None of the blurred faces responded. Malcolm tried to wipe the sleep from his eyes, but his arms wouldn't move. He tensed the muscles in his arms and opened and closed his fingers repeatedly. Everything was working, so there was another reason why his limbs wouldn't move. He looked down but his neck was stiff and trying to move it was painful. His head wouldn't move. From the position he was sitting in, he could tell that he was in a chair. It had arms and a high back, but he could feel ridges of cold metal beneath his skin, which seemed odd.

'What is going on?' he mumbled, realising that his arms were tied to the chair. The sickly smell of incense drifted to his nostrils and tendrils of smoke from the candles hung lazily in the air. 'Hey, has anyone got a joint on the go?' Malcolm joked. His voice was still thick and slurred. He couldn't see the edges of the room; the darkness beyond the candlelight was impenetrable. The flickering yellow glow couldn't illuminate more than a few yards from the flame. The incense was making him feel nauseous. There was something else in the air that seemed familiar. It reminded him of the hot summer days of his youth when the local council workers went on strike and refused to empty the bins; black refuse sacks were piled high on the streets and maggot-riddled food spilled out of them where dogs and rats had ripped them open. It was the smell of rotting meat. As his senses sharpened, he realised that he may be stoned at a party full of strangers, but something told him that he wasn't. His instincts told him that something was wrong – very wrong.

He looked to the only face that was familiar. His mouth was dry, and his tongue felt furry as he spoke. 'Hey, Janine, sorry I blanked out. Where are we?'

'My name is not Janine.'

'Jackie?'

'Some call me 'she' some call me Fabienne, I like that.'

'Whatever your name is, what is going on?'

'You can call me Baphomet for now. Does that name ring any bells with you?' she replied calmly.

'It's unusual but I don't think I've heard it before.' Malcolm swallowed hard and his throat prickled. He had heard the name before, and it caused the hairs on the back of his neck to stand on end. 'Look I'm not in any fit state to think straight. Any chance of a drink? I'm parched.'

'You've heard the name before, Malcolm Baines. Now tell me what you were going to publish about us.' Her black skin glistened with perspiration, and in the dull light her eyes looked like circles of oil speckled with yellow jewels as the candles reflected in them. She neared him and put her hands either side of him on the arms of the chair. As she leant towards him her perfume smelled the same, but her breath smelled rancid. 'What were you going to publish about us?'

'I don't know what you're talking about, Fabienne.'

'I'm not Fabienne here, mundane one,' she whispered. 'Call me Baphomet.'

'Baphomet.' Malcolm snorted. He was tiring of the game, and his muscles ached. He needed to stand up and clear his head. The name sent prickles of fear along his flesh. He could feel goosebumps rising on his arms. 'You've had too much vodka, darling.'

'I didn't drink any vodka you fool.'

'What do you mean?' Malcolm nodded, laughing. 'You were pouring it down your throat. Are you having a giraffe?' As he looked into her dark eyes, he answered the question himself. She wasn't having a laugh at all. He swallowed hard and felt a raging thirst coming over him. He tried to smile and cock his head to the side, but it was held fast by something. 'Look. Let's stop messing around. You've had a laugh at my expense and now I need a beer and a piss, not necessarily in that order.'

'Shut up, you fat pig, and answer my question.'

'Come on love, I'm gasping for a drink here.' Malcolm laughed nervously. 'If you want to tie me up and play rough, I'm game, but I need the loo first.' He struggled with the bonds around his arms, but they wouldn't budge.

'What were you about to publish about us?'

'About who exactly?' he asked angrily. 'Let me out of this chair before I piss myself.'

'About the Order of Nine Angels.' She stared into his eyes and he sensed the contempt she felt for him. The name Nine Angels sent a shiver of fear through his brain. He'd been investigating their order for months. At first, he thought they were just another cult with delusions of grandeur, but the deeper he looked, the more his initial impressions melted away. The evidence proved that this order was far more powerful than any other he had investigated. It was also far more dangerous.

'This is bullshit, lady.' He laughed, although there was a touch of panic in his voice. 'Let me out of this chair and I'll tell you whatever you want to know. I'm busting for a pee and gasping for a drink and you're beginning to wind me up now.'

'You've been snooping around us and we don't like that.'

'It's my job to snoop around people, that's what I do for a living.' Malcolm tried to keep his voice strong, but his words were thick and slurred. 'Let me out of this thing and I'll talk to you.'

'You're not moving from the culling chair until you've told us what we want to know. How long you spend in it before you talk is up to you.' She leant close to his face, her nose inches from his. He could feel her putrid breath on his cheek. He realised that he couldn't move his head at all. It wasn't the drink that stopped him from moving, it was a clamp of some description. As he regained the feeling in his body, he felt cold metal encircling his skull.

'I don't know what type of game this is but it's not funny.'

'This is no game, Malcolm Baines, Young Reporter of the Year, and be assured that you will die here.'

'What?'

'You heard me. You will die here. The manner of your death is determined by you. Tell us what we won't to know now and it will be quick, lie and you will know suffering as you could never imagine suffering to be.'

'Don't be ridiculous. Stop this right now.' Malcolm kicked out his legs in a blind panic, but he realised that they were fastened to the chair too. 'Do you think I'm an idiot?' He thrust all his weight backwards in an attempt to tip the chair, but it hardly moved. 'Get me out of this contraption.'

'Contraption,' she said, smiling. 'It's the culling chair, where we cull nosey reporters and writers and other snoopy mundane people. You're just another one to add to the list.'

'Culling chair my arse; is this thing screwed to the floor?' he shouted at the staring faces around the room. 'This has gone too far. You've had your fun and scared the shit out of me, now let me go. I've had enough.' He was enraged, but the use of the name Baphomet and the term 'culling chair' sent bolts of fear through him. He had learnt about both in his search for a missing girl. He had found no definitive proof that either truly existed - until now.

His research had shown him that satanic groups or 'nexions' were widespread and powerful, and that such groups advocated 'culling' – the sacrifice of any who dared to expose them. The discovery of the abused bodies of two young girls in the nineties led Belgian detectives to uncover a satanic sect whose membership included government ministers and relatives of the royal family. At the time, the Benelux news agencies ran a huge campaign to seek out nexions, and the size of their organisation and the depravity of their actions had shocked the world. Malcolm was touched by the media hype and he'd studied the cases in detail. Some of their victims were murdered by new recruits as part of their inauguration into the group. Murdering a victim in front of other members secured their silence for life and proved that they were truly willing to leave the shackles of civilised values behind. Once in the group, only death could release them. At first, he thought they were a small group of wasters dabbling with the occult, but as he delved through case after case, their shadowy form gained weight.

Malcolm first encountered them when the mother of a young woman contacted him about her disappearance. Although he had researched hundreds of cults abroad, it was the first time he'd seen evidence of their existence here. She knew that her daughter had joined a cult and she appealed to Malcolm to help find her. That was the first time he heard of the Order of Nine Angels. It appeared that the group had emerged from older cults. That particular investigation uncovered nothing, and the girl remained on the missing list. Over the years he followed several lines of enquiry into the group, but their Internet profile gave no clues to their whereabouts. He'd specifically followed the disappearance of the young woman who joined their sinister ranks but then a few months later decided that she wanted out. She made several short phone calls to her mother and one panicked emergency call to the police, then disappeared off the face of the earth. Her family and the police were convinced that she'd been murdered, but they had no proof, no body and no idea who the nexion's members were. If this woman was a member of the order, then he was in terrible trouble; he thought it wise to tell her something credible without incriminating himself.

'Look, I was following a missing person case and stumbled upon the fact she'd joined a cult, that's all.'

'Carry on.'

'There' not much to tell. Her mother said that she thought her daughter had joined the Hell's Angels, but she was old and confused.' He laughed nervously and looked around at the faces. 'No one here has a Harley, do they?' The faces remained blank, so he carried on. 'Her friends told me she wasn't involved with any biker gangs, so I looked deeper into other groups and touched upon a website belonging to a group called the Nine 'Angles' not Angels.' Malcolm shrugged and licked his lips. 'I need a drink, please.'

'You know more than that.'

'Look, my head is cabbaged, and my gob feels like the bottom of a parrot's cage. I need a drink.'

'Let him drink.'

She laughed and pushed herself away from the culling chair, and he sighed with relief as a man stepped forwards. Malcolm thought that he looked expressionless as he approached. He was hoping that he'd have a tall glass of cold beer. As the man neared, he realised that everyone in the room was naked. The dark shadows had hidden their forms from his view. The fact that they were naked panicked him further. It added to the eeriness of the whole scenario in which he found himself.

'You can drink from him. We have nothing pure down here.'

'Whatever, I've had enough of this crap.' Malcolm licked his parched lips, not realising what she meant. The man stood in front of him and held his penis between his forefinger and thumb. 'What is he doing?' Malcolm shouted a second before a stream of hot urine hit him in the face. Two pairs of strong hands grabbed his head from behind, pulling his forehead backwards, pinching his nostrils and forcing his jaw downwards. Malcolm gagged. 'You people are nutters. Get off me.'

As his head was released, his stomach expelled its contents and vomit spewed from his mouth. The acidic liquid burnt his nostrils and the back of his throat. He gagged at the taste of cider and urine. 'You're sick. You're all sick.' He coughed and spluttered once the deed was done, and he tried to settle his breathing. He closed his eyes and took a deep breath. There was no doubt in his mind now that this woman was part of the group he'd investigated. He was intelligent enough to know that his situation was dire. His eyes were watering, and tears ran down his cheeks. He began to shiver uncontrollably as his mind raced, searching for a way out.

'Are you still thirsty, fat, mundane man?' She smiled for the first time. Malcolm noticed that there wasn't a line on her face. It seemed odd to him to be attracted to a woman who was responsible for him being strapped to a chair, but then the entire night had been freaky.

'I might be fat but at least I'm not crazy.' Malcolm spat his words and globules of vomit flew from his lips. He was terrified but defiant. 'You're bang out of order and you have no idea who you're messing with. I'm connected to some very serious people.'

'that's an interesting choice of words because some of our friends would be happy to mess with you.' There were chuckles from the dark corners of the room. Some of the laughter was guttural, almost animal-like. Malcolm couldn't see who was laughing and he found no humour in her words.

'I don't know what you mean by that, but no one is coming anywhere near me. You'll have to kill me first.'

'That's fine. We can do that.'

Her demeanour sent another wave of fear through him. Some of the cold cases he'd investigated in the US showed the victims had suffered violent sexual trauma.

'Get me out of this chair.'

He gritted his teeth and rocked violently in the chair, but his bindings were too tight to escape.

'They like to do things like that, but I don't think you would survive it and I need you to talk. Some of them would prefer to do it once you're dead anyway.' She touched a manicured finger to her full lips and licked it suggestively. 'Maybe later when you have told us what we want to know. Then we could have some fun tearing you apart.'

Malcolm sighed loudly. His situation was hopeless. 'Okay. You've got my attention.' Malcolm spat onto the floor. The salty taste of sweat filled his senses. He was in deep trouble. Nine Angles or Nine Angels, it didn't matter. Whoever these people were, they meant him harm. 'What do you want to know?'

'It's simple. We want to know exactly what you were going to publish about us.' Her eyes burnt into his, looking for signs of deception.

'About the Nine Angels?'

'Yes.'

'There was nothing of any substance, basically.' Malcolm spat again. 'I couldn't find out much more than the odd ranting on the Internet. There were some old sites about the Nine 'Angles', mostly in America and Canada, but they haven't been updated for years.'

'We aren't interested in history,' she said. 'I'm talking about the article you were writing.'

'Look, I'm not the first reporter to delve into this.' Malcolm scanned the faces for a response. 'The Yanks had a field day with cults, but there was nothing solid here in this country. There is no story.'

'You're lying.' She turned away. 'Strip him.'

Several men moved at once, helped by others that he couldn't see behind him. Malcolm opened his mouth to protest, but a hand was clamped over his mouth as his designer clothing was ripped from him painfully. Within seconds he was naked, and he could feel metal ridges beneath his skin. They felt curved, like pipes. Being naked in public was terrifying. He hated his body; it was pale and bloated; his tiny penis was nestled in a clump of ginger pubic hair, hidden by a heavy fold of fat. Humiliated and frightened, he decided to use his considerable negotiating skills to levy a way out.

'Okay, look, if you want the full details, then I'll start again.'

'This is your last chance.'

'Okay, okay. I found out that a missing girl called Pauline Holmes joined a satanic cult in Plymouth.' He paused as he made up the lie in his mind. 'That was all the information that I had so I began with the Internet and came up with the Church of Satan – which I'm sure you all know about – and then I tried to find her that way, but the people that I spoke to were jokers and potheads. After a year or so, she contacted her parents and the police and said that she wanted to go home, but she disappeared before anyone could actually talk to her face to face.' He paused for effect, but his story wasn't gaining any reaction in the room. 'I found out that she bought a ticket to Manchester with her credit card and hasn't been seen since. I looked into her case and found nothing but dead ends. There's no substance to the story and that's the truth.'

'You said that she joined a group called the Nine Angles?'

'I have no idea what they were called.' Frustration and helplessness were creeping through him. 'No one knows anything about her or who she was with. Like I said, there is no story. I don't print speculation and there were no hard facts to go to print with.'

'Come on now, Malcolm.' She smiled again. 'Malcolm Baines, up-and-coming, award-winning writer; you focused your attention on this Pauline Holmes girl and that's all you could come up with?'

'It's impossible to know who she was hanging around with. She stopped having contact with her friends and family. She didn't sign on the dole and she didn't pay any taxes. She never signed on the electoral register. She no longer existed.' He shrugged and tried to sound sincere. 'She could have gone back to the order she joined or done a runner up north with the ticket that she bought. There is no evidence that she boarded the train, but I couldn't find any that she stayed either.' He appealed to the other faces but there was no response from them. 'Who knows, and frankly no one will care because up until now, there has been no crime committed. Unless she makes a complaint or a body is found, there is no story, honestly.'

'So, the mother never mentioned that her daughter joined a nexion of the Order of Nine 'Angels'?'

Malcolm hesitated and his eyes flickered left as he manufactured an answer. He knew that the mother had mentioned Nine Angels. 'Like I said before, her parents said something about the Nine 'Angles', not Nine Angels, but the detail was so sketchy, I didn't follow it up. The police in Plymouth did some digging, but they turned up nothing. It was another dead end.'

'He's a liar,' a man's voice spoke this time. The voice came from the shadows at the back of the room. Malcolm heard footsteps as the man stepped into the light. The footsteps sounded like he was walking on gravel, and the sound echoed as if the room beyond the candlelight was cavernous. 'He investigated the girl's disappearance far deeper than that, and the police in Plymouth were convinced that she'd joined a group calling themselves Nine Angels.'

'The police knew.' She stared at Malcom and shook her head. 'You're lying to me.'

'They knew but they were doing nothing about it. I told you, it's a dead end.'

'The police have left the case open. Malcolm even went down there himself, didn't you Malcolm?' The man showed himself.

'What are you doing here, Clement?' Malcolm's eyes widened with surprise as the man stepped into the light. He was shocked by the man's presence, but it also gave him some comfort momentarily. 'Help me, Clement. Get me out of this thing, mate.'

'I have no authority here, Malcolm. Fabienne is in charge here. I'm merely a source of information.'

'Information?' Malcolm repeated. Stark cold fear gripped him. His breathing was shallow, and his heartbeat reached epic levels. Tears formed as he realised how much they would know already. 'What have you told them?'

'I've told them everything Malcolm.'

'Why would you do that?'

'Why do you think?' Clement answered with a smile. He reached out and touched the woman's face. She chuckled at Malcolm and kissed Clement. She pulled away quickly and glared. 'The rewards for helping out are generous, should we say?'

'You've set me up?'

'Well, I never liked you much, Malcolm. I can't think of anyone who does, if I'm honest.' The woman grew bored of toying with him and Clement looked disappointed as she stepped towards Malcolm. He looked at Malcolm with distaste. 'You're a fat, arrogant wanker at best and I was going to release you from your contract on your next review, but by meddling in our business you've saved me the time and the severance pay.'

'You were going to let me go?'

'Yes. You're past your sell-by date.'

'I wasn't staying anyway. I had job offers queuing up, Clement.' Malcolm rocked his head back against the clamp and laughed hoarsely. 'He's my boss. He's my tight-arse editor and supposed to be my mate.' Malcolm shook his head and looked at the blank faces in the room as if they should appreciate the betrayal. 'So, that's how this bunch of lunatics knew about the story, eh, Clement? You arsehole. You turned me in to this lot for lunatic; you wait until this comes out; you'll never work in the industry again. I'll see to that.'

'Do you think it will come out, really?' Jason Clement chuckled. 'To quote you, "You have no idea who you're messing with". We are also connected.'

'If anything happens to me, the police will come down on you like a ton of bricks. I worked closely with them on this. They'll find you. They're already looking into it across two forces,' Malcolm ranted. Saliva dribbled down his chin. 'One scratch on me and you lot are heading for the loony bin.'

'Who is looking into it, Malcolm?' Clement neared him.

'Never you mind,' Malcolm sneered. He felt a little glimmer of hope in the knowledge that he'd contacted the police during his investigation. 'They're all over the cases I highlighted.'

'Poor, deluded Malcolm.' Clement shook his head. 'Is it your friend Inspector Woods who is leading the hunt?'

'I'm not telling you, Clement.' Malcolm hissed. 'If anything happens to me the police will come directly to your desk. They know that I was keeping you updated.'

'I don't think the police took you seriously.'

'Oh, they did, you arsehole.' Malcolm sounded like a petulant child. 'Inspector Woods was well into it. He was all over the disappearance of the girl. It's only a matter of time before his detectives come knocking on your door, darling,' he sneered at the black woman. 'Bloody lunatics,' he barked at the expressionless faces around him. The woman smiled and seemed to look through him. She was looking at something behind him.

'They're not such a bad bunch, once you get to know them, Malcolm. The benefits of the sinister way are far greater than you can comprehend,' a man's voice came from behind. Malcolm thought he recognised it, but he couldn't be sure. He tried to twist his head, but the clamp held him. 'I was interested in your findings because I wanted to know how much you know about us.' The speaker stepped from the side into view.

Malcolm swallowed hard and his lips quivered. 'Inspector Woods? Don't tell me, you're with this bunch?'

'The Nine Angels are not what you think they are, Malcolm,' the Inspector spoke calmly. Malcolm almost laughed at the sight of his naked body. It seemed comical that the detective was speaking to him with his pot belly and bandy legs exposed. His testicles dangled ridiculously low from an unkempt bush of grey pubic hair. 'We offer a different way of thinking, a different way of life. We're not bound by the same rules as you. Society isn't ready to embrace our alternatives yet, but it will.'

Malcolm closed his eyes as all hope disintegrated before him. He swallowed and shook his head as he spoke.

'Okay, fine, I believe you,' he said, deflated. 'If I've pissed you all off, then I apologise. Do whatever you like, just let me go. No one gives a toss what you lot do anyway, and I won't tell them. I have no evidence and you haven't hurt me, so who would believe me anyway?'

'Society's ignorance and fear of something different makes us pariahs, Malcolm. If we are to maintain our normal roles in the mundane world, secrecy is essential to our existence. You threaten that. We can't let you go.'

'Okay, I get the message.' Malcolm chose to ignore the last line. He clung to the hope that this was a warning. 'I need to bin the story and forget all about you lot. Fine, I'll delete everything.' Malcolm looked from the woman to the inspector to his editor. They looked at him, their eyes full of contempt and something else – pity. 'Come on, no one will believe this shit anyway.'

'Where is the story stored?' The woman leant forwards. Her voice was stern but calm. 'Lie and we turn the dial.'

'What dial?' Malcolm panicked. He thrashed about in the chair, but it was useless. 'Please don't turn any dials,' he pleaded, despite having no idea what she meant. 'What do you want to know?'

'Everything that you know,' she whispered.

'Okay, the story and all my research are on my laptop. Let me go and I'll give it to you. I can get another one. I'll leave my job and work somewhere else, just let me go and you'll never hear from me again.'

'He's lying,' Clement spoke. 'He deletes everything from his laptop so that none of the other journalists can steal it.'

The woman nodded her head. 'Turn it on.'

Malcolm felt movement behind him, and the chair seemed to vibrate. There was a faint hissing sound and he felt a cold draft against parts of his skin. 'Don't turn anything, I'll tell you where my research is.'

'You had your chance, Malcolm.'

'I've stored it on a memory stick, don't hurt me please,' he begged; but his plea went unheeded. He heard a *click*, *click*, *click*, which reminded him of his gas cooker igniting at home. His eyes nearly popped out of his head as nine gas rings ignited beneath him, burning his skin simultaneously. The crackle of sizzling hair and blistering flesh was audible, and the strong odour of burning skin filled the air. He screamed and his body twitched, trying to escape the pain, but the more he moved, the worse it became. 'Stop, stop, stop.'

'That hurts, yes?' She smiled and watched the tears running down his face as the blue flames seared his flesh and boiled the body fluids as they wept from the sizzling wounds. The veins in his neck looked like they would burst, and his lips curled back to expose his teeth. 'Each turn of the dial releases a stronger flame. The pain you're feeling now is nothing to the agony we can make you feel if you keep lying to us. Where is your memory stick hidden?'

'Please stop,' Malcolm wailed. His brain couldn't compute the amount of pain it was processing so it focused on the nerve endings which hurt the most. 'Stop it or you'll never see it.' His words were almost inaudible.

'I'll never see the research?' she hissed as Malcolm writhed in agony. 'Then you'll never see daylight again, Malcolm Baines.'

Malcolm screamed for help and the scream turned into a sickening wail. No one but the nexions heard his screams. Eventually, Malcolm told them where all his research was stored, and he gave them the personal details they needed to make his death look like suicide. The dial was turned up many times before his heart finally stopped beating.

CHAPTER 1

They're Coming

I didn't meet Malcolm Baines before he died, but I'd read some of his stories. We had a mutual interest in the spread of organisations that were linked to the disappearance of homeless people. People trafficking is something that we all know about, but we choose not to look at the facts in detail because it frightens us. Google 'missing persons in the UK' and check out the websites. Did you know a child is reported missing every three minutes? Every three minutes, yet our newspapers lead with celebrity crap day after day. Over two hundred thousand names are on our missing person lists, and that can be multiplied by ten in the US.

Malcolm researched traffickers across the globe in his search for the lost. He had a knack for seeking out missing persons, even those who didn't want to be found. When they found his body in a burnt-out car, suicide was suspected. At the inquest into his death, the facts indicated that he had taken his own life. During the last twenty-four hours of his life, he'd apparently gone to a nightclub with his workmates, consumed a large amount of alcohol and cocaine, then signed up with three Internet gambling sites and lost every penny that he owned. His bank account was taken from a healthy balance to its overdraft limit within the space of a few hours, and his credit cards were maxed out shortly afterwards. According to the evidence presented at the inquest, after losing his fortune overnight he'd taken a five-litre can of petrol and driven his Porsche to a secluded spot in the New Forest, where he'd covered himself in the fuel and ignited it with his Zippo.

At the time of his death, I thought it very sad that a man could sink so low that burning himself to death was the only option that he had remaining. Now I know differently, although proving my theory at the time was impossible. The wreck wasn't found for four days, so the charred remains of his body had been further ravaged by the forest wildlife. Murder was never suspected. His body was cremated before the inquest was finalized, thus making it impossible to request a second, more-detailed autopsy; apparently a mistake made at the morgue led to his body being released to an undertaker who disposed of the corpse at the expense of the state. The documentation handed over at the cremation identified the body as that of a John Doe; a homeless man who had no family. The mix-up made a few headlines at the time, but little was truly known about what really happened. In my opinion he was investigating the 'Niners' and they killed him for that. Then they made his death look like a suicide. It was over a year before anybody listened to me.

This is the hardest book that I've written so far. Why? Simple: because it's true. And the knowledge that they're coming for me piles on the pressure to write it quickly. How would you start a book about real evil and hold the belief of the readers? All I can do is give you the facts, the names and the Internet links for you to follow. Then it's up to you to decide. I'm used to telling stories, but not like this one; not the truth. I've written biographies, but they're somebody else's truth, not mine. I write fiction, but this story is real. They say that fact is stranger than fiction, and it is true in this case. You only need to watch the news to realise there is more evil in the real world than in any fictional one. The evil that man can inflict upon fellow man knows no limits. Little surprises me anymore when it comes to the pain and suffering humans inflict upon each other. Where shall I begin my story? At the beginning, I guess.

The night it all began I was researching the novel that I was writing at the time, *The Child Taker*. It was inspired by the abduction of a young girl from an apartment in Portugal. She was on holiday with her parents and the story touched me so much that I wanted to write a novel where the abduction ended with the safe return of the child and all the bad guys died. Researching that book opened a window into a world that few would have the nerve to see, especially if you're a parent.

One of the most shocking stories that I read surfaced in Charleroi, Belgium in August 1996, when a local man named Marc Dutroux was arrested and confessed to abducting two young girls. Newspaper reports alleged that he ran a business in which girls were kidnapped and sold. They were confined in cells in the basement of his house and then sold for tens of thousands of dollars. He admitted that he transported them out of the country for a life of child prostitution. Pornographic videotapes were found and used as evidence to support the case against him. Google his name and you'll be saddened and amazed; dozens of links appear.

I often find disturbing stories during research, but this one rattled me more than most. The story of his arrest caused a public outcry as Dutroux was a convicted paedophile and had served time for the rape of five young girls. He was released after serving three years of a thirteen-year sentence. As the investigation came under the spotlight, accusations of satanic worship, rape and human sacrifice bubbled to the surface. This new slant on the twisted individuals involved baffled me. I simply didn't believe organised groups gathered to worship the devil, engage in the rape of women and children and be a party to murder. This was the not the stuff of seventies horror films when Christopher Lee and Vincent Price were world-famous vampires. Those films were tame compared to the gory effects we see on screen today, but even the most warped imaginations wouldn't have imagined this. The fact that it was real, sickened me, and sinister cults were firmly on my radar. I delved deeper into the story looking for the proof that this wasn't just one depraved individual acting alone. I needed to see proof that large numbers of people could meet and indulge in activities that would make most of us vomit.

When they searched Dutroux's home, they found a dungeon built in the basement from which they rescued two young girls – I won't put their names in here. I see no need for that, as the story is easily accessed on the Net. Can you imagine what those girls had suffered? Although traumatised by their ordeal, they told police that they'd been tied up, transported to ritual gatherings, and raped repeatedly by numerous men. At least three hundred child pornography videos were taken as evidence; some featured the two survivors being abused by Dutroux. Where was the evidence of a satanic cult? Read on, because I need to explain where it all began for it all to make sense.

The day after finding the two survivors, police dug up the bodies of two eight-year-old girls – again, I'll omit their names. They'd been missing for over a year. Two weeks later, they recovered the bodies of two more missing girls who had been buried deep under the floor of a shack in the garden. Dutroux confessed to raping and killing them. My question at this point was that if Dutroux was trafficking young girls for tens of thousands of pounds, then why was he burying their bodies beneath his property? Surely, they had a monetary value if he kept them alive. The truth is terrifying; obviously, they were being used for another purpose.

Dutroux was unemployed and receiving state benefits, but he regularly received deposits of tens of thousands of dollars in his bank accounts. After tracing the money trails, five additional people were arrested. Some were charged with abduction and illegal imprisonment of children. Others were arrested on suspicion of criminal association. One man was a Brussels born businessman, Jean-Michel Nihoul (I don't mind naming him. I hope he rots). He confessed that he had organised satanic sex parties in various Belgian castles with many VIPs as guests, including the judge who led the initial investigation. Judge Connerotte was dismissed from his position as a judge on 14th October.

In December of the same year, Belgian newspaper *La Derniere Heure* published a guest list of the attendees at a satanic gathering in a Belgian chateau. The orgy included judges, senior politicians, lawyers, police officers, and a former European Commissioner. There it was in black and white. My proof was there. It wasn't supposition or idle gossip; it was hard evidence used to convict a murdering rapist and his associates.

My interest in the sinister way began there, and in hindsight I wish I'd never stumbled across Dutroux. The thing is, I still wasn't convinced that their gatherings were about worshipping Satan or any other evil deity. I believed that it was about perverted sex. I thought that it was a group of paedophiles indulging themselves with others who shared their sick fantasies. My initial assessment of the whole thing was that it wasn't about religion, it was about child abuse. I was wrong about them. I underestimated them as just sexual deviants, but I was to learn quickly that my initial assessment was wrong.

CHAPTER 2

Nine Angels

The first time I encountered the occult in person was two years after *The Child Taker* was published. The book wasn't about the occult, but I did allude to them when talking about child trafficking and organised paedophile rings. It hadn't occurred to me that the book would bring them unwanted attention and make me a target. Anyway, that night, when I looked outside, a thunderstorm was brewing. The moon was shining and illuminated the clouds with hues of silver as they floated silently across the night sky. Does that sound like I'm writing teenage horror? Probably, but this is not a pale imitation of those books about handsome vampires and beautiful virgins which plague the bestseller lists. If you're expecting fur and fangs, tales of vampires and werewolves battling for the heart of a sullen teenage beauty, then you will be disappointed. There is no happy ending here, no wooden stake to drive through their hearts while they sleep, and no silver bullet. The evil I've encountered is real; its insidiousness has spread through society and its reach is truly shocking.

When it all began, it was a dark and stormy night, but there was no howling in the distance, just the sound of traffic drifting from the harbour and the occasional whine of an ambulance siren. It was a night like any other. It might not be the ideal way to begin a horror story or a book about zombies, but this is not fantasy; the victims and their murders are well documented. The perpetrators are human but monsters, nonetheless. They appear normal; they bleed and they breathe. They have families and they go to work every day. The good thing is that they can be killed like us, but they are many and because of exposing them in my books, they're coming for me.

Those of you that have read my books before will know my name. I'm Conrad Jones, author of fictional thrillers. I'll be fifty-four years old in July, if I live that long. I genuinely do not believe that I will. They cannot let me live because I brought them so much attention and many of them were arrested. I know their secret and I'm prepared to tell it. I know what they do, and I'm going to write this book about it and tell the world. People will look for them on the Internet and find them in seconds. Be careful not to abuse them in their chat rooms they monitor them and trace IP addresses; their websites are written by intelligent, articulate people and that makes them dangerous enemies.

They call us 'normal' people, the 'mundane', and in their minds we are sheep that can be abused, slaughtered, or sacrificed as they choose. Their websites describe in detail how to live the sinister way and avoid detection from their neighbours and friends. The more chaos they cause, the greater their standing within the group. If they commit evil, then it has to be proven. That's where the Press comes in. If their crimes are reported, their status is elevated. Their sites teach how to acquire a subject, slaughter them for ritual and make the body disappear. If the victim is random, that's fine, but if it's someone who has turned away from them or tried to expose them, then that has added kudos.

By now you will be wondering if I'm a rambling fruitcake or whether you have bought a fantasy book. If you're unsure, then google them now before you read on. I challenge you to; google O9A.org right now and you will see this is fact. You will find them as 'Nine Angles' and 'Nine Angels', and you will see they're spread across the globe and they use the Internet as well as any international organisation does. There are even some Facebook pages dedicated to them and their followers, although I would question the intelligence of those who openly affiliate themselves with such dark arts. The Facebook members are wannabees in my opinion. None of the hardcore nexions would be stupid enough to link their profiles with such nonchalance. It would be akin to joining a paedophile fan page. The Internet is an amazing place to meet people of a similar ilk, whether looking for customers, friends or, in their case, other evil folk, and for the majority of the time it's anonymous. They will try to stop me finishing this book, and if they find me, they will kill me. It's just a matter of time before they track me down; you see, you cannot hide from them forever, because they're everywhere.

I found the Nine Angels by accident that first night. At the time, I was writing my tenth book and watching the clock tick by between chapters. Time seems to warp when I write a story. I go into my mental bubble and time flies by at speed. I look at the clock, and then write. When I look again, the hands have whizzed around as if I've been sleeping. I can only describe creating a book as dreaming while awake. Have you ever had those dreams that feel so vivid that you can feel real emotions during them, even when you're almost awake? If you have, then that's the place I go to when I write. It can be a dark and lonely place.

I like to watch thunderstorms, and on the night in question I had the curtains open so that I could watch the lightning flash across the sky, as thousands of volts forked towards the earth. I went to Jamaica once with an ex-girlfriend, and at about two o'clock every afternoon it rained without fail. Not great for sunbathing, but the tropical storms at night were incredible to watch. The power of Mother Nature is astounding.

Sorry, I'm drifting again, but these minor details all add credence to the story. As I said, I loved watching lightning back then. It's different now, though, because I know they're out there. I know they're searching for me, and storms make me feel uneasy now; I associate the start of this nightmare with the thunderstorm that night. Anyway, as I was writing, I was tapping away on my laptop when there was a huge flash. It was as if a giant firework had exploded outside the window. Seconds later, there was a second flash and I counted in my mind as I waited for the imminent thunder to follow. One, two, *bang*, and I could feel the deep rumble vibrating in my chest. The storm was directly overhead, and Evie Jones was shaking like a leaf. She is a beautiful, brindle Staffie with a white throat and chest. In the summer, her stripes are gold like a tiger's. She sits next to me when I write, her head on my thigh, waiting for the odd tummy tickle between chapters. Fireworks and thunder are the only things I've seen which make her tremble with fear.

As the storm roared overhead, I was stuck on a chapter of my book and I needed to research something on the Internet. I decided to top up my red wine before logging on and searching for the information I needed. I walked into the kitchen, which is a long room with fitted cupboards on either wall. Two huge windows look out over Craig-y-mor and Trearddur Bay and the mountains on the Llyn peninsula. The windows and the view make it a bright, happy room in the daylight hours. I looked at the clock on the wall and it seemed as if it had flown round again. I topped up my glass of merlot and thought about having a cigarette at the back door, but my partner at the time hated me smoking and she could smell my indulgence from a mile away, so I decided against it.

Anyway, with a full glass of wine I went back to writing my thriller. I was writing a chapter about a prostitute murdered by her pimp and I wanted to look at some real cases on the Internet. Factual events inspire all the books I write. As I searched for murder cases similar to my imaginary scenario, a photograph loaded, which took my interest immediately. The piece I found was a newspaper article from a few months earlier and it contained a black-and-white photograph of a murdered girl. It looked innocent enough, but my nightmare began with that picture. The article said that there were signs that the murder was ritualistic.

The picture was a close up of her face. She had the most striking looks: her skin was black; she had full thick lips and pencilled eyebrows that gave her a surprised look; her hair was ebony, almost jet, and she tied it up over her ears as if she wanted to keep it under control. Because the photograph is black and white, you can't tell what colour her eyes are, other than that they're dark, nearly black. At first, I thought the picture quality was poor, but they were not dark brown. They were pure black, as black as the night. I've been to Africa many times, but I've never seen eyes so black or a woman so pretty. The murdered girl had been incredibly beautiful. Her eyes stared out of the screen straight at me, accusingly. In my memory of her, she still accuses me; of what, I can't be sure.

The name of the girl was Pauline Holmes, but in the following weeks I found out that she was not born with that name. She was nineteen when she died. I've put her picture and a copy of the story onto a memory stick. If they find me before I finish this book, the location of all the files and my diaries are in my computer and stored elsewhere on file-sharing websites. I've tagged them all with auto-send. If I disappear and don't cancel the send commands, they'll automatically go to dozens of reputable reporters. It's the only way to be sure the story is told.

The original article has disappeared now. They removed it from the Internet and the newspaper initially denied that they ever printed the story. The truth came out in the end, but that was an example of how powerful they are. They're everywhere, in every walk of life and in the halls of power across the planet. That's why I know they'll find me eventually. I'm now a fugitive from the law, but I can't turn myself in. I would be a sitting duck. People died at my house and others have died since. Would anyone believe it was self-defence? I doubt it. They blame me.

As I said, it was raining, and a storm was overhead. After reading about Pauline Holmes, I wanted to know more about the case as the report was vague and the details sketchy. I wanted to find out as much as I could about her background. I knew that if I went to bed, I wouldn't sleep because the book was on my mind. That's what happens when I write. The next chapters are lining up in my mind while my body screams at me for rest, but my brain won't allow it to. Sometimes when I wake, the next few chapters of a book are there in my mind. That gift may stop one day, until then, I'll write.

I looked out of the window as I scrolled through the phonebook on my Samsung. The trees were bending, and the wheelie bins were being blown across the car park. Trearddur Bay is the windiest place on the island, yet Anglesey council insists we use recycling trolleys. I would lose at least three trolleys a year to the wind.

Anyway, I text-messaged an old friend, Peter, to see if he was working. The display on the screen said it was three in the morning. Peter is a local police detective with whom I'm friendly. Before I became a writer, I was an area manager for McDonald's, and Peter was a young assistant manager when we first met. In his early twenties, he left the burger giant and joined the North Wales Police. Peter married his teenage sweetheart, Susan, who was the sister of three brothers, who all worked for McDonald's at the time, and we would see each other frequently at christenings and weddings, stag dos and birthday parties.

We often talked about my books and I used to quiz him about police procedure, if I needed to add clarity to a chapter. I'd talked to him earlier in the week to enquire about her case as the article mentioned she was killed on the island. He told me she'd been found in a, secluded woods close to the inland sea. At that point, he didn't mention any signs that it was a ritualistic murder. He said that he was working late and that if I had any questions to get in touch. Peter messaged back and said he was free to talk. Excited, I rang him.

'Hi, Peter, I know it's late, but you said to call you back about the Holmes girl.'

'You're up late or is it early for you?' Peter yawned. 'I'm just finishing, so it's late for me.'

'I've been working all day, so it's late for me too.'

'What do you want to know?'

'Well, whatever you're prepared to tell me, really.' I knew there were limits to what he could tell me. 'I'm interested in her background. I want to understand how a young woman like her ends up working the streets before being murdered in a woods.' Of course, I really wanted to ask about the ritual side of the murder, but I didn't want to charge in and appear rude.

'How do you know she was a working girl?' he asked. 'We've withheld that.'

'Not from Facebook, you haven't. You know what gossip is like here. It's a small town.'

'Bloody social media. It will be the death of me. You know the score with the details that I can give you, right?' Peter turned serious. We were not at a party now, where a few pints loosened his tongue and his professionalism wobbled. There had been many times previous when he had told me details that were not in the public domain. 'You're not going to use any names, are you?'

'No, this is purely for a fictional story. I just want depth to her past and to make sure I get police procedure right.' That was the truth, but there also a morbid curiosity about the occult connection driving me.

'It's a weird one, Conrad,' he said. She went missing down south two years ago, joined a cult and then decided she didn't want to play that game anymore. There were a few brief calls to her parents and the police, and then she disappeared again. The next time she came onto the radar, she was working the truck stops in North Wales.'

'She definitely joined a cult?' My mind tingled. 'What type of cult?'

'How many types are there?' Peter laughed but there was no mirth in it.

'Hundreds,' I said. 'How long have you got?'

'Apparently, it was satanic. She was into some kind of devil worshipping; whatever that is,' Peter said sarcastically. 'The Met don't think it was anything heavy. She got mixed up with some goths and disappeared for a few months before contacting her parents to ask for some money.'

'So, how did she come to your attention here?' I asked, ignoring his remark about goths. Most people think that it's purely to do with music, but my research had taught me otherwise. There are many groups campaigning to have goth websites monitored by the police because of the influence they were having on their teenagers; many suicides were being linked to their negative effect. I had no idea why she'd left them; I was curious why she'd moved so far north. 'Was she running from something?'

'We don't know much about her. She was picked up for soliciting in Llandudno a few months ago. She gave a false name, but when her prints came back, she was on the system as Pauline Holmes.'

'Did they tie it up with the missing person's report?'

'Yes, they did, but it was too late; they connected it after she'd been released. Uniform released her once she'd been charged, but when the missing person's report flagged up, they tracked her down.'

'Where was she?'

'On the same street corner, they'd arrested her on.'

'That's not very bright. I wonder why she went straight back?'

'Most of them do, Conrad,' he explained. 'Drugs, drink, violent pimps, the reasons go on and on.'

'So, when they found her, did they take her in again?'

'No,' Peter scoffed. 'There's no point. They had a chat with her about the missing person report, but she said she wasn't missing and didn't want to be contacted by her family and that was the end of that. We have to respect her wishes as an adult. The next time we came across Pauline Holmes, she was a murder victim.'

'That's a very sad story. I wonder why she didn't want to be found?' I asked. I didn't understand her rationale. 'She sounds like a mixed-up kid.'

'That's one way of putting it. We're still waiting for forensics to tell us if it's actually the same Pauline Holmes on the missing person report.'

'How come?' I didn't understand why they couldn't just check the fingerprints.

'Working girls use different names all the time, Conrad.' Peter sounded matter of fact again. Sometimes he sounded patronising. 'The prints on file down south match hers, but we have no proof that the original prints actually belong to the Pauline Holmes who is missing.'

'How will you confirm it is her, DNA?'

'Yes.'

'How long will the DNA take?'

'Your guess is as good as mine, mate. She was reported missing to the Met, ended up in Plymouth and then she was found dead on our patch. There are three forces involved now and none of them can invest the time and resources to identify a dead brass.'

'Politics?' I said. 'She might have been on the game but she's still someone's daughter.'

'Yep, afraid so. It slows things down, but we'll get there eventually.' Peter paused and there was an awkward silence. I could tell he was tired and bored of talking to me. So, I changed tack.

'What kind of family was she from?'

'Assuming that she is Pauline Holmes?' Peter sounded patronising again. His voice lowered a few octaves, making him sound like Inspector Morse correcting a young Lewis. 'We don't assume anything.'

Silly me for daring to assume anything, patronising twat, I thought. 'Sorry, yes, assuming that she is Pauline Holmes.' I tried to sound humble and stupid.

'I shouldn't be telling you this but from what we know she was placed into care at a young age and then went through the fostering program until her late teens. She had a colourful record as a teenager.'

'So, the parents that reported her missing were not actually her parents?'

'Foster parents apparently,' Peter yawned. 'Must be embarrassing to lose the child you're fostering, not to mention the financial blow. They get paid decent money to take kids in.'

'That's a bit cynical isn't it?' I laughed.

'This job makes you a cynic, mate,' Peter added. 'Listen, I spoke to my gaffer about you shadowing us on a case and he was keen as long as you stick to the guidelines.'

'Nice one.' It was my turn to yawn. Research as a writer has gained me access to several prisons, hospitals, military bases and police stations. Shadowing a case could only be good, or so I thought at the time. What I didn't know was the superintendent was looking for some information on the cheap. 'Have you got anything in the pipeline?'

'Not yet but I'll be in touch if something comes up okay?' He sounded a little odd when he said that. I didn't think much of it at the time, but now I know why.

'Brilliant, thanks for the help, Peter.'

'No problem, see you soon.'

I remember coming off the telephone a little disappointed. Pauline Holmes was brought up in the care system, dropped out of school and ended up working the streets. It was hardly a groundbreaking character profile for a new book. It was almost the perfect stereotype of a hooker in any town. The bit about a cult was the only unusual part of her profile, but it was the part that interested me, and I had a gut feeling early on that there was more to it than met the eye.

Peter had mentioned that she'd been hanging around with goths, and I searched through dozens of word documents that I'd written for *The Child Taker*. I had page after page of information taken from the news reports which had followed school massacres committed by teenagers in the USA. In every case, the shooters had been influenced by the occult side of the goth culture. I was sure that most of them were nothing more sinister than grumpy, teenage music fans with an attitude and an automatic rifle. However, there was powerful evidence to prove that some of the subversive messages in the music were being translated literally. One group, the Beasts of Satan, were jailed along with some of their roadies for the ritual rape and murder of three teenagers in northern Italy. It was interesting reading, but it was only the tip of a monstrous iceberg that was heading my way.

When I began looking into murders linked with demonic rituals, a very dark world of child abuse, rape and torture opened up. At that point, I wondered how far into that world Pauline Holmes had travelled before she'd decided that she didn't belong there. Anyway, I didn't think that I would hear from Peter for a few weeks, but I was very wrong.

CHAPTER 3

Another Murder

The next day was a normal one, until Peter called just after the late news. I'd been writing all day and was thinking about going to bed when my Samsung buzzed, and Peter's ringtone sounded. I'd set his calls to the theme tune from *The Bill*, which amused me, at least. There was a tingle of excitement as I answered the call.

'Hi, Peter, working late again, I see.'

Peter didn't waste any time with small talk. 'We've found another woman killed in the same area as Pauline Holmes. It's nearly a month to the day since we found Pauline. Do you want to shadow the case, be good for your book?' Peter sounded excited, but there was something else in his voice. It sounded like he wanted to add something but couldn't because others were listening.

'Yes, please, that would be great. What's happened?' He hadn't mentioned any signs of the occult at the crime scenes. I had to restrain myself from asking him straight out. The details may have been withheld for a reason.

'This woman was found in the same woods as the Holmes girl earlier on tonight.' He was annoyingly vague. 'There are similarities.'

'I heard about a murder on the news, but I didn't know it was in the same woods,' I said to him. 'It doesn't seem like a month since Pauline Holmes was killed.' I was lying. I always knew when the moon was full. My father was in the Royal Navy, and he taught me the constellations and the phases of the moon from an early age. I didn't realise why at the time, but the moon always affected my mood. Back then it made me feel excited and strong. Now it makes me feel sick with fear because I know it drives them too. If you look into the O9A websites, you will see that they encourage their nexions to perform their rituals around the full moon.

They say the moon affects women more than men because their bodies contain more water. I don't know if that's true, but if you think the moon's gravity moves the tides, it makes sense that it can affect our brains, right? I know one thing for sure: it affects *them*. The females become far more powerful than the males, and their strength is incredible. So is their propensity for violence and mutilation. The murders I've researched that I think are connected to the Niners are all committed around the time of the moon's peak. My research is irrefutable. Their activity wanes and increases around the lunar cycle. It sounds like I'm writing about werewolves, but they are human; the facts are clear for all to see.

'Well time flies and it's a month since we found her. The Press is out in force, mate. Two bodies in the same area; they're speculating that we're hunting a serial killer already. I can see 'Anglesey Ripper' headlines all over the news tomorrow.'

'I suppose murder sells newspapers.'

'Yes, and it brings out all the nutters too.' Peter laughed. 'We're under pressure on this one and we don't need headlines like that. If you want to tag along, you're more than welcome.'

I sat up and shook my head to clear my mind. The reality of being allowed to watch a real murder investigation had arrived and my heart was pounding. 'Brilliant, thanks mate.' I was struggling for something to say as Peter seemed to be edging around the facts; he was hiding something. I decided to pry. 'So, what happened to the latest victim?'

'From the evidence so far, it looks similar to the Pauline Holmes murder.'

'No wonder the Press are linking it, then.'

'You need to brace yourself. It's not a pretty sight. She's had her throat slashed and there are signs of sexual assault. We can't be sure until the forensics come back, but it looks like she's been raped.'

'Do you know if she a prostitute?'

'We haven't confirmed her identity yet.' Peter became serious again and he wasn't giving any details away. I had the feeling that he was sitting next to another officer. 'I can't say more than that for now. Not on the phone.'

'And your senior officers are aware I'll be there tonight?' I asked. I knew that he'd cleared the idea in principle, but I wanted to be sure. A few days earlier, Peter's superintendent had e-mailed me a confidentiality document, which I returned to him twenty minutes later. I was keen to take the opportunity to follow his team.

'He's okay about it. I mentioned that you were writing a fictional book based on the North Wales Police and the murder squad especially. He said as long as you agree to stick to the confidentiality agreement and he can censor anything connected to the case, and you're constructive – you're welcome.'

'That's great.' I tried to sound grateful, but something didn't feel right. 'Constructive is my middle name.'

'He also thinks that you might be able to help us out along the way,' Peter added, ignoring my joke. Sometimes he was a pompous arsehole. I knew he was beating around the bush somehow. I'd known him long enough to sense that there was an aspect I hadn't been shown yet. 'We'll scratch your back if you scratch ours, so to speak.'

'That sounds ominous. How can I help you?' I asked, trying to add surprise to my voice. I wasn't surprised; I'd sensed something was fishy about it.

'There were some signs cut into the bodies,' Peter said vaguely. I'm sure he thought that I was a mind reader. When he worked for me at McDonald's he'd been a grafter, but he didn't enjoy it. It was the reason he chose a different career. A decade on in our new roles, when we talked about work, I often got the impression that he was trying to prove a point. If I was a psychologist, I'd say that he had a superiority complex, but I'm not a psychologist, so I'll call it 'small man syndrome'. I think it was a power thing, but I didn't mind. It takes all sorts to make a world, right?

'What do you mean, 'signs'?' I asked, pressing for details. I tried not to sound irritated. 'Do you mean there are symbols cut into the victims?'

'Yes, symbols,' he snapped. 'Signs, symbols, what's the difference? It's the same thing.'

'I'm just clarifying what you meant.'

'There are symbols carved into the victims. That's what I said.'

It wasn't what he had said at all, but I decided to leave it. 'Can you describe them or show them to me?'

'The governor thinks it may have something to do with a group in one of your books.' He sounded unsure. 'I'll explain when I see you.'

'Okay.' It sounded simple enough. I'd written ten novels by this time and there were bad guys galore in them. So, I was none the wiser, but I was hoping that it would be linked to the occult. 'Shall I meet you tomorrow?' I asked. It was late and the thought of going out in the rain did not appeal to me. Evie Jones was snoring gently, and I wanted to sleep.

'I'm not sure she'll still be here tomorrow, Conrad. I think it will be wrapped up tonight. They'll transfer her,' Peter said. He lost me completely.

'Who won't be there?' I asked confused. 'Sorry you've lost me.'

'Sorry, I'm way ahead of you here. We have a suspect in custody, but they're taking her to Denbigh Hospital. She's flipped her lid; completely off her trolley.' Denbigh Hospital was once a huge Victorian mental asylum. It was due to close its doors and would end up as a desirable housing project. Parts of it were already closed but they built a new mental health hospital section. It looks inconspicuous until you see the razor wire and high mesh fences around it. The old hospital looked like something out of a vampire movie. It was built from dark sandstone and it had turrets and tall chimneys. I remember the barred windows and the screams of the insane echoing across the grounds. It reminded me of a Hammer Horror set from the seventies. The new facility looked modern in comparison, but you can still hear the inmates – or patients, as they should be called.

'They're going to assess if she's fit to be interviewed. You can meet me there if you like.'

'Okay, I'll be there as soon as I can.'

The asylum was an hour drive from where I lived. I've been in many institutions while researching novels, but never that asylum. The opportunity was too good to miss. I thought about pulling on my jeans and a warm jumper because the wind was still howling, and then I thought better of it and put on a dark blue suit, white shirt and a tie and picked up my laptop bag from the desk. I wanted to look the part of an investigative author. I'm not sure what people expect when they think of an author, but I don't fit the stereotype. Better to look smart at least.

Anyway, back to that night. I dressed conservatively and went through the front door to the side walkway. I could see the waves at Porth-y-Post smashing into the rocks. The wind was howling between Plas Darien and the old Cliff Hotel. Holyhead mountain loomed against the night sky. I ran with my head down so that I wouldn't get wet. The wind was blowing a gale and the rain was almost horizontal. I jumped into the driver's seat and for the first time saw the moon as a complete silver disc. It looked like a lone white eye glaring defiantly down at the world, watching the mayhem below. It was cold and the wind cut through my suit as if it wasn't there. I shut the door of the truck and shivered inside. I was excited about going to the asylum, but I was anxious too. Something was telling me to be careful. I wish I'd listened to that nagging doubt.

The truck played up when it was cold, I think the heater plugs needed changing, but it started on the third attempt. It's a big silver Navara and I loved driving it. I had to sell it because they knew it was mine. It was too easy to spot, and the registration plate would lead them to me easily. I remember the smell of the leather upholstery; there is something about the smell of leather in a car. While I was driving, the rain tried to blind me by hammering on the windscreen in a deluge. It soaked the expressway, and the lightning still flashed somewhere beyond the edge of the Llyn Peninsula, silhouetting Snowdonia.

There wasn't much traffic around at that time of the night, so I reached Denbigh within an hour and I left the truck in a visitor's parking space. The moon was behind the clouds as I got out of the truck, and a tortured scream reached me from inside the asylum. Despite the new bricks and architecturally designed gardens and shrubbery, the place smelled of lunacy.

There were two uniformed security guards in the main reception area. They looked bored and disinterested by my arrival. The presence of police detectives late at night was probably disrupting their television time. Although it was a hospital, it was nothing like the casualty department of Ysbyty Gwynedd. I visited the hospital two weeks earlier, researching the accident and emergency department for a novel. It was madness, packed with sweating nurses, abusive drunks and foreigners shouting, swearing and arguing in any number of languages. The Eastern Europeans were still flooding into the country back then. Brexit hadn't even been thought of. The receptionists were protected by Plasti-glass.

The reception area at the asylum was at the opposite end of the spectrum. It was more akin to a hotel. The lights were dim, and apart from the random screams from the secure wards, it was silent. Peter was waiting near the desk and he walked across the polished tiles and gave me a visitor's badge. I clipped it to my top pocket and straightened it. He looked tired and his jeans were darkened where the rain had dripped from his leather jacket.

'Are you all set?' He was short and had an old man's voice, not suited to his face. He had closely cropped greying hair and a nose that had been broken so many times that it was almost flat against his face. Years of policing the streets of Holyhead and Bangor had taken their toll. Peter was ten years younger than he looked.

'Yes, ready when you are.' I decided not to ask any questions for now and no further information was offered. I think Peter liked it when he was in charge. We headed towards the rear of the reception and pushed through the double doors leading to a corridor. The interview rooms were not far away. The acrid smell of bleach made my eyes water. There was a line of identical green doors, each with a small observation window at head height; an oblong of glass reinforced with wire mesh allowed staff to peer inside. Each door had a letter stencilled on it and F was about halfway along the corridor. Peter knocked once and a uniformed guard opened the door. I thought then how strange it was that they were using private security employees to control mental patients. Peter opened another door and I stepped into a small anteroom. Through a two-way mirror, I saw a girl sitting at a table, which was screwed to the floor. When I saw her, my breath caught in my chest. She was the image of Pauline Holmes.

'Who's that?' I asked, wondering what was going on. I couldn't take my eyes from her. 'Is she your suspect?' I asked incredulously. My excitement caused me to lose control of my volume.

'Keep your voice down.' Peter tapped me on the back and whispered into my ear. 'She was found at the scene. It looks like she did it.'

From our earlier telephone call, I knew they had a suspect, but I was surprised that they'd arrested someone at the scene. The fact that the suspect was such a young woman shocked me too. When I saw her, I couldn't believe it. She looked hardly out of her teens. Two men walked into the interview room and sat down. It was obvious from their dress that one was a medical man, the other a detective. The doctor took a pad and pen out of a white shoulder bag while the other loaded tapes into a machine.

'My name is Dr Brook,' he said to the girl. He hung the bag over the back of the chair. 'I'm a doctor here at the hospital.'

'So, tell me what's going on,' I whispered. I felt like I was about to watch a film that I didn't know the name of. Peter was either too preoccupied to fill me in or he didn't want to. I was beginning to sense that I wasn't welcome. Why invite me here at stupid o'clock in the morning if I was an inconvenience?

'Basically, we need to know how old she is and if she is sane before we can proceed to interview her about the murder,' Peter answered. 'She could be a minor.'

'Hello, Fabienne,' the detective grunted.

'Hello, I'm feeling a little strange; nervous, I mean.'

'There's no need to be nervous. I'm pleased to meet you.'

'I can't say I'm pleased to meet you,' the young girl said to the doctor ignoring the policeman. She shrugged and I noticed for the first time that they'd handcuffed her hands in front of her. The shackles hadn't changed my impression of her. She looked nervous and frightened; not like a killer.

'I'm going to record this interview, it's easier than making notes,' the detective explained as he pressed the record button.

'How come he hasn't introduced himself on the tape? That's the usual procedure, right?' I wanted to know why basic procedure wasn't being followed. I didn't know why, but I was on her side from the first second that I'd set eyes on her. In my mind, the police had the wrong suspect and that was that. She was an innocent girl in the wrong place at the wrong time.

'He's one of our murder team detectives, but this isn't an interview under caution. We just need to know if they can actually interview her on tape first. Then we can offer her a solicitor and do things by the book.'

'Do you mind if we begin?' The doctor asked the detective. He looked hassled, like he didn't want to be there. 'I'm going to ask you some questions. They're quite simple. I need to ascertain your state of mind.'

'Why would you need to do that?' The girl frowned and her lips quivered. She looked close to tears. 'Am I in trouble?'

'Not as far as I know.'

'Do you think I'm mad?'

'I have no preconceived perceptions about you, Fabienne,' the doctor said.

'Then why have I been chained up?' she asked, raising the cuffs as far as the restraints allowed. Her voice was quiet and her tone polite.

'Apparently, you were very distressed at the police station,' he said, smiling thinly. His tone of voice was patronising. 'I believe you bit someone?'

'I did bite someone. I couldn't do anything else. It was self-defence.' She giggled nervously. I could tell that she was close to tears. I felt like hugging her and telling her that everything was okay. 'I was frightened, and he was being rude and aggressive. I thought that they were going to hurt me. So, I bit him.' She shrugged as if she couldn't see the problem. 'Am I going to be charged with assault?'

The doctor shook his head. 'That's not for me to judge.'

'Whatever you need to ask me, let's get it done. I want to go home,' she said. Her accent was akin to the south. It sounded like she said, 'Whateva.' She was wearing a white paper jumpsuit, which I guessed the police had given her. That meant that they'd sent her clothes to forensics for tests. I noticed dark smears on her black skin. She looked so fragile and vulnerable.

'Your name is Fabienne Wilder?' he asked, but she ignored him. He smiled thinly and tried again. 'You have to answer the questions, Fabienne. The quicker we do this, the better for you.'

'Whatever,' she said, nodding her head.

'Is your name Fabienne Wilder?'

'You're a doctor, aren't you?'

'Yes I am.' He looked over the top of his glasses. 'And you're Fabienne Wilder?'

'Are you a medical, measles type of doctor or the loony-spotter type?' she ignored his question again and looked at the floor.

'Both sometimes.'

'But right now, you're a loony type.'

He nodded and shrugged off the question. 'Yes, I suppose I am. This man is a detective and he would like to ask you some questions but first we need to know more about you.'

'Okay.'

'Are you Fabienne Wilder?'

'Yes.'

'How old are you, Fabienne?' he asked. She didn't answer at first. She turned to the mirror and seemed to look directly into my eyes. It chilled me to the core. She smiled at the mirror as if she could see me. It shook me up.

'She can't see us, can she?' I asked Peter.

'No.'

'You know she looks like…' I started to say.

'Pauline Holmes,' Peter said, finishing off my sentence. 'It's her eyes. They could be twins.'

It was her eyes. It was uncanny how much she looked like the murdered prostitute I had read about earlier. She turned to the mirror again and her eyes stared into my soul. Her black skin shimmered with perspiration and there was a hint of a smile on her thick lips. She was stunning, but there was fear in her eyes too. Her face and hands were smeared with something dark. As I stared at her, I realised it was dried blood.

'Fabienne, how old are you?' the doctor asked again, irritably. He looked like the police had called him off his rounds to complete the interview and it was a massive pain in the arse.

'How old am I?' She grinned at the mirror mischievously, ignoring the doctor. Her demeanour changed and the frightened girl was gone for a moment. 'How old do I look?' she said. Her jet-black eyes looked into me again. She didn't take her eyes from the mirror as if she was talking directly to me. I would have put her face at about seventeen. She had smooth, dark skin and gleaming, white teeth. The victim's blood was smeared across her right cheek as if she'd wiped it roughly with the back of her hand.

'It's a simple question. I'm not here to play games with you.'

'Moody bastard,' she snapped. Her face darkened momentarily and then she smiled again. 'How old do I look?' she asked again.

'Has she been charged yet?' I asked Peter.

'Not yet,' he said. 'We need to establish how old she is and her state of mind first. She keeps telling us that Satan made them kill her.'

'Satan made 'them' kill who?'

'We don't know yet. She was rambling when she flipped out.'

'Satan has a lot to answer for,' I said jokingly. I had no idea back then how right I was.

'I think he's in us all. Some people choose not to listen to him.' Peter was fixated on the girl, but he looked at me as he spoke.

'That's very poignant,' I said. 'When did you become a philosopher?'

'You have to be in this job.'

'Occupational hazard, I suppose?'

'It grinds you down sometimes.'

'Have you ever regretted joining the force?' I asked. I could never tell what Peter was thinking because he wore a constant frown. I was trying to break the ice because I felt like an intruder. I thought bigging-up his profession might help to lower the barrier, although I didn't understand why it was raised in the first instance.

'Yes,' he replied, still looking at me. I was surprised. When we met socially, he always raved about how much he loved the job. 'I regretted it the first time I saw a murdered kid.' He wasn't joking. 'His name was Charlie Howard. His stepfather had beaten him to death with a cricket bat because he spilt a glass of coke on his Xbox.'

I felt bad for making light of the situation. Murder is never funny, never amusing, but sometimes we make fun because it scares us. Peter had a three-year-old son, so a case like that would have hit him hard. 'Sorry, I didn't mean to take the piss,' I said.

'No problem. When you do this job, you learn just how evil people can be.' He looked me in the eyes and nodded towards the mirror. 'I'm telling you now that this bitch is evil. Don't be taken in by the little lost girl act.'

'I can't see it,' I disagreed. I've never been able to keep my mouth shut. I speak first and think about the consequences later. 'She looks like a terrified young girl.'

Peter frowned. 'You're looking at a pretty face and nothing more. I have to look at murderers every day and make sure that they're locked up for life. They don't all look like Freddy Krueger. You get a feeling for it, an instinct. We do it for a living.'

'I know you do. You should be proud of what you do, Peter.' I wasn't blowing smoke up his arse. I've always admired people who join the police, fire service, ambulance service, or the forces. They are brave men and women, far braver than me. How do they go home and switch it off in their minds every day? That is bravery. They are life's true heroes, but Peter was driving the point home that he was right, and I was way off, and I couldn't fathom why. I decided to change the subject. 'What are they going to do if she keeps being awkward?' I asked.

'Well, we need to know if she's capable of answering questions. If she doesn't play ball, then they'll section her and wait on the DNA.'

'She seems calm enough.' I looked into her eyes. Despite the fear, they sparkled beneath the lights. 'She doesn't seem bothered about being here.'

'She was bouncing off the walls at the station. The evil bitch bit a lump out of the desk sergeant's face.' Peter shook his head. 'Poor bastard only has a week left until he retires. It took six officers to restrain her; she's stronger than she looks.' Once again, my initial assessment was way off. I couldn't imagine that girl biting anyone. She looked like butter wouldn't melt in her mouth.

'She looks strong and athletically built,' I commented. She did look strong beneath the paper suit, but I couldn't see her biting a police officer.

The doctor was tiring of her reluctance to give a straight answer. He stood up and spoke to her. 'Look, Fabienne. I don't have time for this. I need to ask you some important questions, so I need your cooperation, okay?' He took off his glasses. 'If you don't want to answer them, that's fine, but I haven't got time to waste.'

'Neither have I,' she said.

'Will you answer my questions?'

'What about?' She smiled disarmingly. She seemed to be constantly distracted by the mirror. Her eyes darted towards it every few seconds.

'I need to make sure you're well enough to speak to the police.'

'I'm fine. I'm speaking to you, aren't I?' she said. The timid, young girl returned.

'Yes, but that doesn't mean you're in sound mind.'

'So, you have to find out if I'm sane or insane?' She smiled sadly again.

'We need to know if you're in sound mind to be interviewed,' the doctor replied matter-of-factly. 'And we need to know how old you are, so let's start there.'

'How old do I look?'

'That doesn't matter.' The doctor sighed and rolled his eyes. 'We need to know if you require an adult to accompany you during an interview.'

'How old do I look?' she repeated.

The doctor sat back and decided to indulge her. 'I would say you're late teens.'

'You're miles away. I'm thirty-four,' she said bluntly. She looked at her nails as she spoke. 'I know that I look younger.'

'No chance,' I whispered to Peter. The doctor and the detective exchanged surprised glances.

'She's a barm-pot,' Peter agreed. 'She's never thirty-four.'

'We'll get to your real age in a minute,' the doctor said, looking at the detective. Their faces said that they didn't believe her either.

'So, you don't believe me?'

'I didn't say that.'

'Are you calling me a liar?' she hissed through clenched teeth. Her face changed again, and the contrast was dramatic.

'No.'

'Either be honest with me or I'm saying nothing.'

'Okay.' The doctor sighed. 'You appear to be much younger than you're telling me, that's all.'

'Oh, right, whatever,' she said, and her manacled hands went up to her mouth and touched the smear of blood. Although I realised it was dried blood, I didn't believe she was a killer. It was all over her hands too. She smiled at the mirror again, and I swear she was looking directly into my eyes.

'Fabienne, I want you to relax while you answer my questions, okay?'

'Chillax,' she mumbled.

'What?' the doctor asked. He frowned.

'Chillax,' she repeated, smiling. 'We say "chillax" nowadays.'

'I see. Well, just chillax then.' He cleared his throat nervously and looked at his questionnaire. 'Have you ever had any mental health issues?'

'Oh my God.' She laughed aloud. 'Very subtle, doctor; you don't beat about the bush, do you?'

'We need to know if you're fit enough to be interviewed.'

'Whatever.'

'Have you?'

'Have I what?'

'Had any mental health issues?'

'Loads.' She rolled her eyes to the ceiling and let her tongue dangle from the corner of her lips. 'I'm mad as a box of frogs. Nutty as a fruitcake.'

'Very funny,' the doctor said. 'Have you ever received any professional care?'

'I'm bored already. I want to go home.' She looked at the glass again.

'What day is it, Fabienne?' The doctor decided to take a different route.

'Friday.'

'What month?'

'November.'

'What year were you born?'

She smiled. 'What is this, *Mastermind*?' she asked.

'Just answer the questions and then I can go home to my wife. When were you born?' the doctor repeated.

'Thirty-four years ago,' she said. 'Or thereabouts. I can't be sure as I never saw my birth certificate.' Although she was a lot older than she looked, her mannerisms were childish. She behaved like a ten-year-old. Her demeanour was infantile. There was no way I would have put her at thirty-four.

'Who is the prime minister?'

'Anthony Joshua.' She giggled and put her hands up to her mouth again. There was dried blood on her wrists, too. 'This is so boring.'

'Do you think he is, really?'

'He should be.' She smiled at the mirror again. It was as if she knew I was standing there.

'What's the capital of England?'

'Los Angeles,' she said. She watched the doctor scribble her answer in his notebook and held up her hand, waving it to stop him. 'Was I joking, doctor?'

'I don't know, were you?'

She licked at the dried blood on her hand. 'I was joking. London is the real capital.'

The doctor sat back in the chair and gave her a stern look. She wasn't supposed to be making jokes. She didn't seem to realise the gravity of her situation. 'This is serious, Fabienne,' he said.

'Whatever.' She sighed. She turned to the mirror and looked at me intensely with her jet-black eyes. It unnerved me again. 'Who's in there behind the glass?'

'Where?' the doctor asked uncomfortably.

'Behind the glass.'

'No one.' He looked down as he lied. 'It's a mirror.'

'No, it isn't.' she hissed again. 'It's a two-way mirror, doctor. Don't lie to me. Do I look like a retard?'

'No.'

'Then don't speak to me like one.' Her personality jumped from terrified teenager to outraged adult in milliseconds.

'I apologise, but some patients are uncomfortable with the two-way mirrors. I didn't mean to insult your intelligence.'

'Good.' She seemed to relax into the chair a little. 'Who is watching?'

'It doesn't matter.'

'Is he a doctor?'

'No, I'm the only doctor here.'

'He likes me.' She winked at the mirror as if she could see through it. Her eyes held me with their gaze. She fascinated me and frightened me; how did she know we were there?

'Who likes you, Fabienne?'

'That man behind the glass.'

The doctor looked at the mirror. He wasn't aware I was there. He knew there would be police officers, but not a writer. She smiled at the glass and I felt weak at the knees. It was her eyes.

'Fabienne, forget the mirror please.'

'He's not a policeman.'

'There may be detectives in there waiting to speak to you, Fabienne.'

'There may be, indeed, but he's not one of them.'

'Can we carry on with this please?'

'His name begins with C,' she whispered. She whispered it, but I heard it. So, did Peter. He looked at me wide-eyed. She made the shape of the letter C in the air with her finger.

'Now that is spooky,' he said, turning towards me.

'Whose name begins with C?' The doctor humoured her, but he looked concerned.

'The man behind the glass. He likes me. I can feel it.' She stared at the mirror and the nerves in my spine tingled. The doctor scribbled something on his pad. He thought she was showing signs of some mental trauma.

'Okay, he likes you, Fabienne.' He shrugged off her comments irritably. 'Can you name three cities beginning with the letter L?'

'I've had enough of your game. I want to talk to him.' She pointed to the mirror.

'Fabienne, if you don't answer my questions, they will section you. You will have to stay here indefinitely.' The doctor shrugged his shoulders. He was losing patience with her. The detective looked at his watch, already bored with the exercise.

'London, Liverpool, Leeds.'

'What?'

'You asked for three cities, right?'

'Okay, thank you. What's your favourite food?'

'Are you going to cook for me?' she said coyly.

'No,' he said.

'Lasagne. What's the point of these questions?'

'They help me assess your state of mind. What was the last film you saw?'

She looked up at the ceiling, thinking. There was more dried blood on the underside of her chin, and it streaked down her neck to her chest. She lowered her eyes and looked through the mirror again. I was absolutely sure she was looking through it at me, straight into my eyes but that was impossible; yet she knew the first letter of my name.

'What is your favourite food?' she asked.

'That doesn't matter.' He sighed, tiring of her games.

'What is my favourite food? What is my favourite film? Are you planning a cosy night in for us, doctor?' She touched her lips again.

'Answer the question, Fabienne.' The doctor removed his glasses and rubbed his eyes. He looked tired.

'Would you try to sleep with me on the first date, doctor?' she teased. The doctor shifted uncomfortably in his chair. I was beginning to wonder who was in charge of the interview. 'You would like to, though, wouldn't you?' She pushed her breasts up with her hands and shook them at him. His face reddened, and the detective struggled to hide the smile on his face. 'You would love to bend me over this table and fuck my brains out, wouldn't you?'

'No.' The doctor put his glasses down and looked her in the eye trying to show that he wasn't perturbed by her mischief.

'Why?'

'Why what?' He sighed.

'Why wouldn't you like to?'

'If you're trying to shock me, Fabienne, then you can't.'

'Are you gay?' She chuckled and pointed to the detective. 'Would you rather bend him over the table?'

He ignored the question and carried on. 'Favourite film?'

'Do you want me to answer honestly or give you the answers that I think you want to hear?'

'Whichever suits you.' He shrugged.

'*Hostel*. There's lots of blood in that. Have you seen it?' she asked. 'Is that what you want me to say? I like horror films.'

'No.'

'Do you want me to say that there's lots of blood in that, lots and lots?' She touched the blood on her face and then put her finger in her mouth suggestively.

'What's your favourite book?' The doctor ignored her comment. He wanted to get to the end of the test and go home. His wife hated him working late and she would be frantic.

She looked down at her paper suit. '*The Rats* by James Herbert maybe. Yeah, I like *The Rats*. Have you read it?'

'Which would you rather have, a dog or a cat?'

'It would depend who was cooking it. Dog is greasy. Cats are tough.' She giggled again and licked her lips. The doctor studied her and scribbled some notes again. Her smile turned into a snarl for a second. Her lips curled back from her teeth and momentarily, she looked ugly. Evil. Then the look was gone.

'You don't like animals?'

She shrugged. 'Depends how hungry I am. I ate my pet rabbit when I was eight years old.' She laughed and put her finger to her lips. 'I blamed the dog.'

'Did you?' The doctor raised his eyebrows. He scribbled another note. The detective next to him raised his eyebrows. He couldn't make her out and neither could I. 'Did you eat your rabbit?'

'Yes.' She played with her hair and stared at the mirror.

'How did you kill it?'

'With a hammer.'

'Then what did you do?'

'Are you stupid?' She seemed to change emotionally. She looked away from the mirror and smiled at the doctor. 'Do you really think I ate my rabbit?'

'I don't know.' He studied her. 'Did you?'

'Of course, not.' She giggled again.

'Do you know why you're here?'

'Yes.'

I waited but she didn't expand on her answer, she just sat back and looked at me through the glass. She smiled again as if she could see straight through it. I shuffled my feet nervously.

'Will you tell me why you think you're here?'

'They think I killed a woman in the woods. She had her throat ripped out. There was blood everywhere.'

'And did you kill her?'

'No. She was dead when I found her.' Her voice cracked and a tear rolled down her left cheek. She wiped it away with the back of her hand and her chest heaved as she tried not to break completely.

'What were you doing in the woods?'

'I don't know. I haven't done anything wrong, honestly.' She looked down as she answered, and the tears ran freely now. I wanted her to answer the question and tell us why she was in the woods.

'That's not for me to ascertain, Fabienne. I need to establish your mental state. That's all.'

'I want to talk to him.' She wiped away her tears and pointed to the mirror straight at me. 'He uses his imagination.'

'Who does?'

'The man in there. C. I think he's a writer. Is he?'

'How does she know that, Pete?' I asked. I was convinced that someone had told her that a writer was following the case. It didn't take a brain surgeon to realise something must have been said during her transfer, maybe in an attempt to calm her down.

'I don't know but I'll find out. Someone must have broken our confidence.'

'The last thing I need is a lunatic on my case. She could find out my address in five minutes on Google. Someone is out of order.' I was genuinely concerned.

'Who is a writer?' The doctor looked at the mirror, confused.

'He is.' She pointed again and choked back a sob. 'He writes things. I'm not sure what yet. They hate artists and writers; I think he's a writer and if he is, they'll find him and kill him.'

'Fabienne, you're not making sense.'

'Man behind the mirror. Are you a writer?' She cocked her head like a curious dog and stared at the mirror.

'Okay, Fabienne, forget the man behind the mirror. He is a police officer. What happened tonight?' The doctor was impatient. She watched me through the mirror as he waited for an answer. I shivered as I looked back at her. Those black eyes and the dried blood around her lips will haunt me to my grave. I was fascinated by her; terrified but excited.

'She knows I'm here and she knows my name. She's playing games,' I muttered.

'Okay, I need your attention,' the doctor said. He moved his chair closer to the table. 'You really should take this seriously,' he said to Fabienne, much to the annoyance of the detective, who sat in silence. He couldn't say a word until they'd confirmed her age and sanity.

She shrugged and looked back to the floor. 'I haven't done anything, so get stuffed,' she whispered. 'I mean, it's your problem, not mine. I'll be back at home before you know it. I want to talk to him. He can tell everyone about them. He can tell everyone what they do.' She tried to stand up, but a strap held her to the chair. The guard had threaded it through the manacles and attached it to an anchor point under the chair.

The doctor tried to calm her. 'There are police officers behind the mirror, Fabienne. They're deciding whether to charge you with murder or not.'

'I know there are police officers there and I know he is there, too. You're a liar.'

'Why would I lie to you, Fabienne? I'm here to protect you. I'm here to verify you're well enough and old enough to be interviewed.' The doctor frowned. It was getting late. It was near the end of his shift and he needed to leave on time.

'You can't protect me. I don't want to speak to you anymore.' She turned sideways and smiled at me through her tears. 'You can't protect me either, but you can help me. They'll probably kill you, but we all have to die sometime, right?' She spoke directly to the mirror.

'Someone is going to get their arse kicked,' Peter growled. The fact that she knew I was there was slowing the interview down. She was playing to the audience. Why? I didn't know, but I was convinced one of her guards had told her I would be following the case. Peter opened the door to the corridor and shouted a uniformed officer over. 'Who was on the girl's transfer?'

'Blakey and me, sarge,' the officer frowned. 'Why?'

'Did either of you mention to her that Conrad was shadowing the investigation?'

'Of course not, sarge. You said it was confidential.' The officer looked offended and his face darkened.

'Are you sure?'

'Absolutely sure,' he replied. He sounded like he was telling the truth. I was too busy watching the girl to look at his face.

'Fabienne, can you tell me why you were in the woods tonight?' The doctor stood between her and the mirror. He attempted to hold her full attention.

'Move out of the way.' She tried to look past him. 'I don't want to talk to you.'

'Fabienne,' he tried again, and she flipped.

'Get away from me.' she screamed. Her face turned into a mask of hatred. She pulled her lips back from her teeth and snapped them together repeatedly. The straps strained and held her, but every muscle and sinew in her body was fighting to be free. She howled like a dog and spittle sprayed from her lips and dribbled down her chin. 'Help me!' she screamed through the mirror repeatedly.

'My God, this is freaking me out,' I said to Peter. 'What does she think I can do for her?' As soon as I spoke, she stopped screaming. She wiped the spit from her face, and it smeared the dried blood. Her eyes seemed to focus on me again and she smiled.

'I heard his voice,' she said in a child-like voice. 'I knew you would help me.'

'Who is going to help you?' the doctor asked her. His cheeks reddened with frustration. One minute she seemed to give him all her attention, the next she was fixated on the mirror. The outburst had him rattled.

'The man behind the glass. The writer. He likes me, don't you?' She mouthed the last bit silently. I looked at Peter and shrugged my shoulders. I couldn't think of anything to say. The woman freaked me out.

'I heard what your officer said, but there's no way she can know that I'm here, unless someone told her.'

'I think you've pulled,' Peter joked nervously.

'Just my luck, another bunny-boiler.' I tried to make out that I wasn't perturbed by the fact she knew the first letter of my name and my profession. The fact was, she hadn't guessed. She knew what my name was. That's one of the things they can do but I didn't know that then.

'Can you remember being arrested?'

'Yes. Ask him to come in. I need to talk to him. If they think I'm talking to the police, they'll kill me. They'll kill me anyway, probably.' She looked at the mirror again. This time her eyes pleaded with me. She needed my help I was sure of that, but I didn't know why. I wanted to help her. I needed to help her.

'Where did they arrest you?' The doctor ignored her request to talk to me. He didn't even know I was there.

'Do you think I killed that woman?'

'I want to know if you're well enough to answer the questions that the police officers want to ask you, that's all.' He folded his arms and sighed. He would be in the doghouse when he got home. His wife would be worried sick.

'I didn't kill her,' she said looking at the doctor. 'I didn't kill her, honestly. Please help me.' She looked at me through the mirror again.

'What were you doing in the woods?'

'Why are you repeating yourself?' she shouted. Her ugly face returned.

'To check that your answers are consistent,' he said.

'To check that I'm not lying?' she screamed. The sinews in her neck were sticking out.

'Something like that,' he said. 'But if you've done nothing wrong, Fabienne, you've nothing to worry about.'

'Am I okay then or am I nuts?' she hissed through clenched teeth. 'Make your mind up.'

'You're fine, Fabienne. I think you're upset by what you've seen.'

She calmed down for a moment and grinned at the mirror again. 'Can you do me a favour now, doctor?'

'Depends what you want,' he told her.

'I want to talk to him.' She pointed to the mirror again.

'Are you done, doctor?' the detective asked, 'this is getting weird.' It was obvious to him the woman was a crackpot.

'Yeah, I'm done,' he said. The doctor stood up and smiled at the girl. He packed up his stuff and watched her staring through the glass. She was clearly insane. Her fascination with whoever was behind the mirror puzzled him. In this case, me. 'We are finished here, Fabienne. You're obviously traumatised; I'm going to recommend that you stay here for a while.'

She flipped. Her screams and the hatred in her eyes will stay with me forever. She looked into me and screamed for help repeatedly as the guards dragged her away. She reached out and tried to touch the mirror. I touched it from my side, and for a split second only the glass separated our fingertips. There was a jolt, like a shock from a nine-volt battery.

'What exactly do they think she has done?' I whispered to Peter as I watched her writhe and struggle against the guards. I was shaking inside, and I felt sick as they dragged her out of the interview room. There was a connection between us, and I didn't know why. 'Do you think that she killed the victim?'

Peter frowned. 'It looks like she stabbed the victim in the heart and then slashed her throat. When we found her, she was crouched over her, covered in blood. We haven't found the murder weapon yet, but it won't be long. What we don't want is for her to spring some insanity plea on us. Hence, we needed to know if she was sane. It's the same thing that happened to Pauline Holmes, virtually identical.'

'But what about the rape? I thought you arrested her pimp?' That was how I found the story in the first place.

'Yes, we did. Holmes's pimp is on remand awaiting trial. He denies the murder, and this will help his case, unfortunately.'

'You can't think Fabienne killed two women. She looks so innocent.' I stared through the glass. In my mind she looked back into my eyes, even though I could hear them dragging her down the corridor. She had dried blood around her mouth. They may have found her next to the body, but I thought she was innocent. I wanted her to be innocent. 'Were the injuries similar?'

'From what I've seen, identical,' Peter frowned. He had deep lines across his forehead. He was purposely vague again.

'You mentioned that there were symbols carved into the bodies.' I'd almost forgotten about our earlier conversation. 'Can you describe them?'

Peter lowered his voice. 'This has been withheld from the Press for obvious reasons.' He took out a notepad and flicked open a page where he'd copied the symbols in pen.

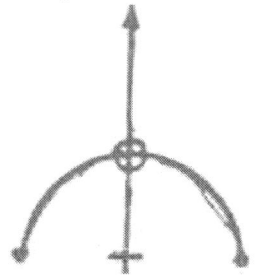

'This was on the Stokes woman.' He pointed to his pad. 'The governor asked me to run them by you.'

'Stokes?' I asked. 'So, you know her name?'

'We found some ID, but it's not enough to verify her identity,' Peter said, fobbing me off. 'Do you recognise this?'

I did, but I was inclined to pretend that I didn't. I wanted to know more about the case though, so I decided that being churlish would be pointless. Peter's expression told me that this was the real reason he'd invited me.

I looked at both symbols. 'This is the symbol used for a ritual sex act. Sometimes it's used as proof to other members that an anonymous victim has been killed or raped as a part of a ritual or sacrifice. It's used as a signature rather than a signpost.'

'What do you mean exactly?' he frowned. I didn't think I could have been much clearer. Like I said, he wasn't too bright.

'If a newspaper reported that a woman had been raped in the town centre and I claimed to other members of my nexion that it was me who had done it, they wouldn't give it any credence unless I'd left this mark,' I explained. 'Do you remember how the IRA used to use a code word before a bomb went off?'

'Yes.'

'This is similar. They didn't want any other faction to claim the credit for their crimes. Well, this is the same thing. It's proof that a satanic order wants the credit for killing this woman.'

'How the bloody hell do you know that?' Peter looked astonished. I knew from the tone in his voice on the telephone that whatever his senior officer had said about my book, Peter put no store in it. He obviously hadn't read it. His senior officer had asked him to use our friendship to gain some insight into the occult. Obviously, Peter didn't want to be beholden to me. Maybe our previous careers had forced a barrier between us.

'From research on the Internet.' I laughed, embarrassed by how impressed he was. 'Seriously, though, this symbol has been found on victims in the US; that's where I've seen it before.'

'So, they were definitely sexually motivated attacks?' Peter stared at his pad.

'No, not necessarily.' I shook my head. He hadn't listened to a word I'd said. Either that or he simply didn't understand. 'Who was this one on?' The second sketch was slightly different.

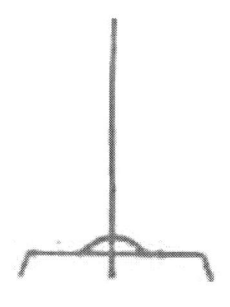

'That was on the Holmes woman.' Peter frowned. 'It looks like they didn't have time to finish it.'

'It's finished all right,' I corrected him. 'That's the inverted cross of satanic justice. Carved into the chest of a victim; it signifies that they're a traitor. It's a very different meaning to the other one.'

'So, they might not be connected?'

'I would be amazed if two victims of a satanic-style murder found in the same woods were not connected.' I didn't understand why he was so keen to dismiss the obvious link between them. The fact was that they'd charged Eddie Duncan with the first murder. Releasing him would leave egg on their faces.

'I'll run it by the governor, but I can't see it making any difference,' he replied, scribbling next to his sketches. 'Now we have the doctor's opinion on her sanity, she can't be interviewed about either murder.'

'I just can't see it. The article about the Holmes girl said that the evidence against her pimp was watertight, but did they know what that symbol meant when they charged him?' I watched the detective in the interview room, fiddling with his notes. He stared at the mirror and never took his eyes from it once. He wasn't smiling though; his eyes looked through the glass in a piercing glare. 'Surely the symbols carved into the victims shed a different light on things. They indicate that both women were killed by occult followers, but for very different reasons. Fabienne was frightened, very frightened.'

'You'd never make a police officer, Conrad. You're too soft. She's the suspect in a very nasty murder case. Save your sympathy for the victim's family.' Peter smiled thinly. 'If you want to shadow me on the case, you can. The forensic team have swabbed her and taken samples. We'll see what they tell us.' I knew he was right, but something about Fabienne intrigued me. I wanted to follow the case, not for the research, but to see her. I wanted to look into her eyes. She'd cast a spell on me. 'Do you still want to follow the investigation?' Peter asked. I knew that he wanted me to say no.

'Yes, please. I would like to do that if you can arrange it.' I wanted to look at the files on the Pauline Holmes case. I wanted to prove to myself that the cult she'd joined slashed her throat, not

Fabienne or her pimp. If there was any evidence that she'd joined a cult, then the marks on her chest meant that she'd been murdered for turning away from them.

'It's already done. I cleared it with the superintendent. He wants as much good publicity as he can muster. He thinks you following a murder case, which was solved overnight, can only be good for the division. And he wants to speak to you about these cults. You're on-board if you want to be.'

'Any chance I can look at the Holmes case files?' I asked. I had no idea of the danger I was walking into.

'I can't see why not. That's in the bag too.'

'Great. When they arrested her pimp, did they find her pimp at the scene?' I asked. I was still looking through the glass into the empty interview room.

'Not quite.' Peter opened the door and waited for me to walk out. 'He was cowering in a bus stop nearby when they arrested him. When they approached him, he punched the glass so hard that he broke the bones in his hand.'

'Did they arrest him straight away?' I asked. He wasn't found next to the body, which told me that her pimp might be a scapegoat just like Fabienne. I wanted to know in my mind that Fabienne didn't kill the prostitute. I wanted to know that she hadn't killed anyone.

'Yes. He was covered in her blood.' Peter opened the door and we walked out of the room. He ground his teeth as he spoke. 'He flipped out in the custody suite. We had to send a tornado team into his cell. He banged his head on the cell door so hard that he knocked himself unconscious. The doctors interviewed him too, but he was sane. He was an aggressive, drug-dealing pimp, but sane. They charged him that night.'

'How can you explain the sexual assault on the Stokes woman if you think Fabienne did it?' I didn't know why I hadn't thought of that earlier.

'There are plenty of sexual assaults carried out by women, Conrad,' Peter tutted. Maybe I was being naive. 'Until we get the forensic report, we're guessing. Don't be blinded by beauty. She's probably insane, and the evidence points to the fact that she's a vicious killer. She was found kneeling over the body with blood all over her face.'

'Okay, I take your point.' I didn't, but I said I did. I did not want to believe it. I couldn't understand why I was so convinced that she was innocent. She was obviously mentally disturbed.

The doctor walked towards us as we were talking, and at the same time the detective came out of the interview room. Both of them looked pissed off. The doctor spoke first: 'Sergeant Strachan, I need a word with you please.'

'Me too,' said the detective. He glared at me as he spoke. I didn't know what his problem was, but I had the feeling he thought it was my fault.

'Who was in the observation room?' The doctor raised his eyebrows in a patronising way. He looked at his watch and pointed to the dial. 'That was a waste of my time.'

'Me and my colleague,' Peter answered. The doctor looked me up and down. I was suddenly glad that I'd opted for the suit.

'We haven't been introduced; you are…' The doctor glared at me.

'Conrad,' I said. I held his gaze and stood my ground. In my mind I had done nothing wrong. 'Conrad Jones.'

The doctor removed his glasses and wiped them on his tunic. He tilted his head and smiled. 'Are you a detective?'

I looked at Peter and he nodded for me to tell the truth. 'No, I'm a writer.'

The doctor raised his voice. 'Who the fuck told her that Conway was in that room?'

'Conrad,' I corrected him.

'What?' he sneered.

'Conrad. My name is Conrad not Conway.' I looked at the detective. He was still glaring at me. 'Conway is a town with a castle.'

'I really don't care whether you're Conrad or J. K. Rowling with a cock. What I do care about is the fact that somebody told my patient you were in the observation room. The entire interview is not worth a flying frig now. She was telling the truth. There was a writer in there, and his name begins with C. This is a joke.'

'What are you saying? We don't know who told her,' Peter retorted. 'We don't know who told her, but obviously someone did.'

'We will have to conduct the entire interview again, without an audience this time.' The doctor held his hands up. There was no other option. 'No wonder she was traumatised, she knew you were in there and I ridiculed her.'

'Great,' the detective mumbled. He turned and walked back into the interview room.

'I want whoever is responsible for this reprimanded.' The doctor pointed his finger at Peter and stabbed the air. He stormed off down the corridor to have his patient brought back down.

'I'll look into it, doctor.' Peter looked at the two constables who escorted Fabienne to the asylum as he spoke. They had their arms folded and they looked annoyed. They didn't look guilty to me, but then neither did Fabienne, so what did I know? Peter was right. I would not make a good police officer. 'You two are in trouble,' Peter growled.

One of the constables stepped forwards and pointed to me. 'Listen, Sergeant, I knew Shakespeare here was tagging along, but the last book I read was at school. I haven't got a clue what his name is.' He sounded sincere enough to me.

'That goes for me too, Sergeant,' the second police constable said. 'I knew he was coming along, but I didn't know his name either.'

Peter looked perplexed. His men sounded like they were being sincere, and he believed them. I shrugged my shoulders as a silent question formed between us. If the officers were telling the truth, how could she have known I was there?

CHAPTER 4

The Fallen Angel

Pauline Holmes was born Julia Kenworthy in the Brixton area of London, notorious for teenage gangs, drugs, guns, and tit-for-tat murders. Julia was beautiful and she was the apple of her father's eye. He was sixteen when she was born; still a child himself. Her mother was fourteen. The teenagers tried hard to bring up their daughter, but the dice were loaded against them. They never had a chance. Her father was on the periphery of the Green Street gang and a rival gang murdered him on his doorstep. Julia was two years of age; fast asleep in her bed upstairs.

Her mother was young and vulnerable. She clung to every man that showed an interest in her and opened her legs to anyone that turned up at the door with a packet of cigarettes and some drugs. She gave birth to five more children in six years and Julia spent her childhood mothering her siblings while her mother tripped out on the settee or entertained men upstairs. When she was ten, the Social Services appeared at the door and whisked the children away into care homes. It was in the care system that the Nine Angels first spotted her. They use institutions to spot both their victims and potential members, while they're young and easily influenced. The care system homes are like battery farms for the feeders.

Julia was separated from her brothers and sisters and she didn't gel with any of her foster parents. Instead of going to school, she spent her days shoplifting in order to buy booze and weed. They changed her real name several times to give her a fresh start and there was some debate as to whether Holmes was her name at all. The last set of parents she had reported her missing and the police investigation discovered that she'd joined a group on the south coast; because she was an adult, they left it at that. She had a history of running away and eventually, because of her age, they stopped looking for her.

The Niners baited the trap with the offer of her own room in a big house near the seaside. She'd never had her own room growing up and they let her pick her own bedding and furnishings. They were charming at first. Pauline enjoyed her time with her new family at first. They spoilt her, bought her clothes and make-up and she had her own music system. As time went by, the sinister side of the group revealed itself. She was encouraged to join in their ceremonies. They seemed odd but not too bad. There was some chanting and a few strange rituals, but after a few months they explained that her initiation was due.

Then it became bad. As her new family stripped her and tied her up, she realised that all the presents and kindness came at a price. The price was her body and soul. Pauline lived with the abuse and pretended to enjoy their ceremonies until the night she watched them kill a man in cold blood. He was an ex-member accused of blabbing in a local pub about the group sex sessions he'd had with other members. They tortured him for hours, burnt him with a soldering iron and finally murdered him. He was found with his lips sewn together as a warning.

Pauline fled and contacted her foster parents and the police. Her parents were wary of her coming home and she didn't trust the police. There were police officers in the nexion she joined. She couldn't trust them.

The only option she had was to head north and start again. Life on the streets of a big city like Manchester is no fun and she headed to the coast of North Wales. An older girl, Susie, who had a bedsit near Llandudno station, befriended her, and within a month she was turning tricks to pay the rent. She'd been having sex with the cult members; having sex with strangers for money couldn't be any worse. Susie and Pauline looked after each other for a while, but her friend went with a client one night and never returned. The police carried out a cursory investigation, which turned up nothing, and Pauline never found out what happened to her. She struggled to survive on her own until she met Eddie. Eddie Duncan was black like her and he was a pimp. He took care of her and offered her protection. In return, she slept with him whenever he wanted her, and he took a cut of her earnings. It was the closest she would get to a real relationship with a man. What she didn't know was that the Niners had tracked her. The time to pay for her betrayal had come.

On the night she died, Eddie took Pauline to the truck stop near the rear of the station and dropped her on the corner where she worked. He parked his Subaru down an alleyway and checked on his other girls before returning to look for Pauline. When he reached the corner, she was gone. Eddie guessed that she'd gone with a client. He was correct, but it would be the last client that she ever serviced. As Eddie drove by, Pauline was across a dual carriageway in a small park frequented by addicts and prostitutes. The park was dark that night, so dark you wouldn't believe it. The only light was cast momentarily by the moon, as it was shrouded with thick clouds.

Pauline walked in silence with her client. Some of them were chatty, but most of them were quiet. This man seemed preoccupied. He was looking over his shoulder constantly and he kept loosening his tie. His suit looked expensive and his cologne was subtle. It wasn't her favourite aftershave, but at least he didn't stink of sweat. Some of her clients made her gag. Despite the air of normality, there was something strange about this man.

She was uncomfortable. She'd never liked the dark. She couldn't see the sky, not even a glimpse of a star in the blackness. She couldn't see the moon either, but she knew it was up there somewhere. Her client didn't quibble at the price she'd quoted so there was no reason to worry, but something niggled at her mind. He wanted full sex and Pauline took the forty pounds from him when they reached the park.

'Are you here on business?' she asked as they stepped out of the glow from the street lights.

'How far is the place we're going to?' he grunted. His voice was tinged with a southern accent, though he sounded well-educated.

'Just through the trees here, it's not far.'

'Do you work with anyone else?' he asked. The question seemed unusual.

'How do you mean?' Pauline asked as she weaved a path through the undergrowth. 'Through here.' She guided him to a clearing in a rhododendron bush. A thick oak tree towered above them.

'I just wondered if you worked with anyone else, that's all.' He glanced around nervously. 'I know some of you pair up. You know what I mean; to look after each other.'

'Don't worry, we won't be disturbed,' Pauline reassured him. Nervous clients sometimes struggled to get an erection. She didn't want to waste any time trying to get him hard. 'So, are you up here on business? You don't sound like you're from around here.'

Pauline pressed her back against a tree and pulled up her miniskirt. 'We can do it here. Put this on the end of it.' Her client undid his trousers and pulled his boxer shorts down. His skin looked pale. He fumbled around with the condom and Pauline sighed while she waited for him. There was a scuffing sound somewhere in the bushes, but she couldn't see anything. She guessed it was either a pervert sneaking a look or an animal. 'You've paid for straight sex, okay, so no funny business. I don't do anal stuff and I'm not going to touch yours either, so don't ask.' Pauline went through the usual spiel.

The client ignored her. He pushed up against her, squashing her against the tree. His breath was rank, and it evoked bad memories. She took a deep breath and turned her head away from his face. Some clients wanted to kiss her while they did it, but Pauline didn't do that. It was far too intimate. He bent his knees and roughly forced himself into her. Even though it was dark she noticed the expression on his face. His mouth was twisted into a sneer. He began ramming his hard penis into her. Every thrust crushed the air from her lungs.

'Take it easy. You're hurting me,' Pauline gasped between thrusts. She tried to push him away, but he was too strong. His grip on her was frightening.

'Shut up, you slut.' Her client continued to thrust. He put his left hand over her mouth and squeezed, biting her neck hard. 'Do you like that, eh? Do you like it rough?'

Pauline couldn't breathe through her mouth and she sucked air in through her nostrils. It wasn't the first time a client wanted rough sex. It happened every day. She decided to let him finish. He wouldn't last long at that rate. Pauline tried to wriggle free, but it was pointless. She decided to let him get on with it. The cult members loved her distress when they used her for their pleasure. When she ran from them, she vowed that no one would ever abuse her body in that way again.

She heard another rustling sound in the bushes as her mind drifted away from her body. Pauline had learnt to ignore what was happening to her body by travelling to a bright place in her mind. It was her coping method. Her clients rarely took long to satiate their needs.

The rustling became louder. She couldn't move her head to look towards the noise. She hoped it was a mugger and that her client was the target. Watching him being attacked would make her night, but no such luck came forth. The man continued to pump her. She could feel his saliva dribbling down her neck as he nipped her skin with his teeth. He whispered obscenities in her ear as he used her. Most of it was incoherent, but some of it sounded vaguely familiar. His voice was a rasping whisper, but she picked out some of the words. 'You love it don't you, you slut? You love it rough. You've been fucked like this before in front of her. You've been fucked in front of Baphomet.'

The name Baphomet sent a jolt of fear through her. He was a Niner. She began to struggle violently. There was another shuffling sound, closer this time. She thought that it could be a rat rustling through the undergrowth, but she prayed for it to be another human, anyone who could help her. Suddenly a shape emerged from the darkness of the bushes. Pauline was frightened at first but then she realised it was a woman. She struggled against him, but he was too strong. Pauline tried to scream but the hand over her mouth reduced it to a gurgling noise. A blonde woman came into view over his shoulder. Pauline relaxed a little and wondered if she'd misheard his rambling abuse and panicked unnecessarily. The woman didn't look surprised to see them fucking against the tree, and Pauline thought she was probably another hooker on her way back to the arches or a crackhead looking for a hit until she realised that she wasn't passing by; she was staring at them. The punter didn't stop thrusting, in fact he became more frantic. Pauline was pinned to the tree. She couldn't believe how strong he was.

'Go on, do her now,' he gasped. Pauline tried to move but she was helpless. His hand tightened over her mouth and the air hissed from her nostrils. 'Do it now.'

Pauline was confused. He was talking to the blonde woman. He moved his body away from her slightly as his excitement grew, but Pauline still couldn't break free. The clouds shifted and she caught a glimpse of the woman. She was beautiful but her eyes were as black as the pit of hell. They seemed to hypnotize her, and she stopped struggling. The woman tilted her head slightly and she smiled as a mother would at her newborn baby. Then her smile turned into an evil sneer.

'Did you think we would let you walk away?' She tilted her head to the side again and closed in on Pauline. She caught a glimpse of steel in the moonlight and there was a flash of light as the woman pounced. The man groaned and climaxed as the woman thrust the knife into Pauline's chest. Pauline tried to scream but she couldn't. She felt the coldness of the blade inside her and the warmth of her blood as it poured down her torso. The woman thrust the blade into her chest so hard that she cracked her ribs and shattered her sternum. The man pushed her head backwards and smashed it into the tree. He lifted her off the floor. Pauline's feet danced in the air as the woman ripped out her throat from ear to ear with the knife. Blood sprayed her killers as her life expired and the world became nothing but blackness. They licked at her life blood and then kissed each other deeply as the clouds covered the moon once more.

Half an hour later, a concerned Eddie stumbled across her body. He knelt down and touched her cheek with his fingers. She was already cold to touch. Her head was hanging by a few sinews. Only the spinal cord held it to the body. Eddie was stunned. Pauline was special. They'd hit it off straight away, and he planned to take her off the streets and settle down to have a family with her. He held her dead body close, her head dangling against his thigh. A junkie staggered through the trees as he cradled Pauline's body in his arms. The clouds parted and the gruesome scene was illuminated by the moon. Eddie panicked and ran like a greyhound to the main road and called the police. As he ran, he heard a woman laughing in the bushes behind him; he followed the sound of laughter, but there was no one to be seen. He was angry and distraught. Before he knew what was happening, he was on the main road near a bus stop. Grief and shock gripped him, and he fell to his knees.

When the police saw him, he knew what they would think. He was her pimp. He was soaked in her blood and a witness had seen him holding her. As they approached, he lost the plot and punched the bus stop so hard that he cracked three bones in his hand. It was four days later when he calmed down. He began to deny murdering Pauline Holmes, but by that time no one was listening.

CHAPTER 5

My First Warning

When I left the asylum that morning, it was gone two o'clock. I was tired and confused. It was late and the interview with Fabienne Wilder was replaying in my mind. I needed some food and a drink. I drove down the expressway and stopped at the McDonald's in Abergele. It's open twenty-four hours a day and it was on the way home. The car park was looking scruffy that night, littered with fast food containers and drinks cartons. The street lights reflected in puddles of dirty water left behind by the storm.

I decided to use the toilet inside. As I walked towards the restaurant with my head down to deflect the wind, something grabbed my leg and I jumped. I reached down to see what held me and my hands met wet paper. It was a newspaper blown across the car park by the wind. I shivered and pulled away the scraps of paper from my clothes, crumpling them up into soggy lumps and throwing them to the side. I didn't know why I was so jumpy.

With my heart beating like a drum, I went inside and ordered a quarter-pounder with cheese. My burger was spot on. Unfortunately, the fries were crap, but rather than complain I chucked them away. I decided to take my latte with me and drink it on the way home.

There were two vehicles in the car park, and I know from my days with the company that they were in the bays used by the staff. As I walked back to my truck, I could hear a slurping noise, like the sound of an animal drinking from a bowl. I realised it was the slurping sound you get when you reach the bottom of your milkshake. I turned towards the noise and looked into the darkness, but my eyes couldn't penetrate it. The thought of somebody watching me from the darkness bothered me. Of course, back then I wasn't to know exactly what I had to fear.

'Leave it alone,' a voice came on the wind. My eyes were adjusting, but I still couldn't make anything out. The slurping noise came again. The owner of the voice coughed from deep in their throat as if they were having trouble breathing. It sounded male, but in hindsight I can't be sure. I can't be sure of anything anymore. I didn't know if they were talking to me, so I ignored the comment. There could have been people there talking between themselves, hidden by the night, but as I climbed into the truck the voice repeated itself, louder this time. 'Leave it alone or you will be sorry.'

'Are you talking to me?' I felt silly talking to shadows at the back of the restaurant. 'Hello?' I called out, but the wind took my words away. There was no reply.

I was convinced that they were talking to someone else. They couldn't mean me, could they? What could I leave alone? My cheeseburger? My latte? I started the truck and pushed it into gear. As I reversed, the headlights illuminated the area where the voice had come from. It was a deserted section of the car park where the street lights couldn't reach. There was nobody there. I pushed a Billy Idol disc into the slot and 'Sweet Sixteen' started playing. I love that track. I rarely listen to music anymore as I need to be able to hear them coming. I want to have the chance to get away. I won't give up just like that.

Anyway, as I drove away, I munched my burger and sipped the milky coffee. The roads were quiet as I crossed the bridge onto the island. Suddenly, headlights appeared in my mirror. They were on full beam and they dazzled me. I took a bite of my burger and swore under my breath, 'What an idiot, turn your main beam off.' I thought it was a car full of boy racers on their way home from a night out in town, buzzing on cocaine and testosterone, but the headlights flashed and then a blue light whirled on the roof. It was a police car.

'Great, just what I need right now,' I moaned to myself as I pulled over. It was late and they probably thought I was a drunk driver.

Normally I would have got out and greeted the them, or at least wound my window down, but I was tired and hungry. I took another bite of my burger and munched it greedily while I waited for the officer to knock on my window. I could see him climbing out of his car and closing his door. Though I had no reason to be afraid then, I had a funny feeling something was amiss. The officer neared the truck, and I stuffed the last of my supper into my mouth and washed it down with a mouthful of coffee before opening the window.

'Where are you going?' the officer grunted. He didn't look me in the eye. He glanced up and down the road. There wasn't a soul in sight.

'Home,' I said. 'I live in Trearddur Bay.' I smiled. I thought if I was polite, he would realise I was sober and let me on my way. I had no idea what was going on. 'I've not been drinking, officer.'

'Where have you been?' He looked at me and put both hands on my window. He leant too close to the truck. I could sense aggression coming my way. His breath smelled of rotting food and I recoiled.

'What's the problem, officer?' I asked politely. I leant back out of range of his fetid breath.

'I asked you where you've been.'

'And I chose not to tell you because it's none of your business.' I didn't like this guy one bit and I can't stand bullies. He got my back up immediately, and as I can't keep my big mouth shut, I decided to stand my ground. To be honest, it wouldn't have made any difference. 'I'm on my way home and I haven't been drinking; that's all you need to know.'

'Smart-arse, are we?'

'Not really, I'm just tired. What's the problem?'

'You,' he said flatly. 'You're the problem.' He didn't smile. He didn't frown. His face remained deadpan. He licked his lips as if he was deciding what to do. I was a little shocked to say the least. If he was Joe Public, I would have knocked him on his arse, but he was a police officer. I took a deep breath before replying.

'Okay, I apologise if I was vague earlier. I've been to Denbigh Hospital with Sergeant Peter Strachan from the murder squad. Then I called for a cheeseburger on the way home. Do you know Peter?' I thought dropping in Peter's name might help. I didn't look at him because I was fuming inside. I was in grave danger of saying or doing something I would regret. I have a short fuse when people are rude or aggressive. The red mist descends, and it has landed me in big trouble all my life. I'm older now, but I still have to check myself before I shoot my mouth off.

The officer looked at me and shook his head slowly. 'Sergeant Strachan is an idiot and he doesn't realise how much shit he is in. Do you know what you're getting involved in?'

'Look, if you have a problem with Peter that's your business. It's just work to me, nothing more,' I explained. I didn't want to get involved in some kind of feud. I wondered what rank the officer was. I looked at his shoulder, but his numbers were missing; he had removed them. That meant he was off duty – or hiding his identity. That was the first time I realised that I was getting into something I didn't understand. He had no right to pull me over if he was off duty.

'Listen to me and listen well because your life will depend on it,' he said in the same monotone voice. I was going to speak but thought better of it. There was a hammer under my driver's seat, and I twisted slightly so that I could reach it if I needed to. This bloke was dodgy. If there was trouble, I would be ready. 'Leave the investigation alone. We will not warn you again.'

'Which investigation?' I shrugged. In my mind I was thinking, *how dare you threaten me.* I pretended not to know what he was talking about.

'Pauline Holmes.' He leant forwards, daring me to do something. On the other hand, was he trying to frighten me? He stared at me as if it was a challenge. He was trying to intimidate me.

'I was invited to watch an interview with a woman called Fabienne Wilder, not Pauline Holmes. What is your problem?' I was losing it. I should have said okay, fine, whatever and driven off, but I was curious as to why this arsehole was threatening me. What was he playing at? What was he talking about Pauline Holmes for, and why would he tell a writer to back off? I was following an investigation, not picking holes in police procedure.

'You and I both know they're connected. Drop it or you will regret it,' he said. Then he made a gurgling sound at the back of his throat and spat in my face. He turned and quickly walked away. I was so appalled that I literally couldn't move out of my seat. I laughed aloud and banged on the steering wheel. I wiped the sticky liquid away with a napkin from the restaurant and looked at it instinctively. It was mucus coloured red with blood. The smell made me feel sick; it was like rotting meat. I wretched and nearly brought my burger back up. As his car sped past, he looked me in the eye, and for a second his face turned into a hideous mask of hate. His mouth twisted into a snarl. I blinked and the car turned left and disappeared from my view. I didn't have a clue what it was all about, but I would find out soon enough.

CHAPTER 6

The Next Day

The next day, when I opened my eyes, sweat soaked my skin from head to toe. The Staffie was lying next to me, licking my face affectionately. She made a point of sniffing the skin where the police officer spat. I could still smell the stench of decay despite washing. He had serious halitosis. It didn't matter how many times I washed my face I couldn't get rid of it. I was shaking involuntarily, and my eyes felt gritty and sore. I felt like I hadn't slept properly. I had tangled the quilt up and the pillows were scattered on the floor. My mouth was dry, and swallowing was an effort. I threw the quilt off and swung my legs over the edge of the bed. I felt like I had a hangover as I wobbled down the hallway to the kitchen. The thick beige carpet felt nice under my feet and contrasted with the cold laminate on the bedroom floor. The walls were matt white and the flat had a bright, airy feel to it. I took a few minutes to look at the sea; it was dark and moody today, but the mountains were crystal clear. I loved living there.

 I took a carton of semi-skimmed milk from the fridge and gulped it thirstily. My partner had already gone to work and the Staffie was weaving between my legs as I walked. She wanted to go for a walk. Every day is the same when you have a dog: wake up, walk, food and dognap. Then the entire process begins again in the afternoon. Evie Jones is a demanding dog; a real pain in the arse at times, but I love her. I didn't know then how important she would be in my life. She sensed a dog walking by the flat and hurtled to the window at a hundred miles an hour. I could hear her barking and snarling her way along the settee every time a dog walks past the flat, Evie Jones turns into the exorcist and hurls herself at the window. It's comical really. Some of the regular dog walkers cross the road rather than passing the flat. She is nuts, no doubt about it.

I filled a pint glass with milk and tipped some into her bowl. It mixed with the water that was already there. I leant against the cupboards and closed my eyes to clear my head. Evie bounced back through the door with a clatter, wagging her tail to let me know that the danger had passed. The dog and its owner had moved on. She sniffed the water bowl and looked at me as if to say, *why did you just fuck my water up with that stuff?* I laughed and walked back to the bedroom, trying desperately not to trip over her. I explained to her that I needed to go to the toilet and brush my teeth before we set off on the first walk of the day. She seemed to understand and jumped up on the bed, waiting for me to get ready. The mirror in the bathroom told me I didn't look any younger. The wrinkles were getting deeper and spreading across my face. I moved my head from side to side, half expecting to see marks on the skin where the policeman spat at me, but there was nothing there. I rubbed my hand across my chin, feeling the stubble, which is speckled with more grey every day. I have to shave my head daily. I tell people that I choose to shave it. I say it's cosmetic, not genetic. I can kid myself, right?

I brushed my teeth and used the toilet, reading a few pages of this week's toilet book. I always have a book next to the loo; I think it's a bloke thing. I went back into the bedroom and took another mouthful of milk. The Staffie jumped off the bed and made a fuss. I think she sensed I was rattled. That was weird; straight from a horror movie. I was shaken up by the events of the past twenty-four hours. I thought back to the previous night and tried to make sense of it all.

Fabienne Wilder had made an impact on me that I couldn't explain. She was a conundrum. The interview with the doctor and the way she behaved were bizarre. The blood on her face and hands proved that she'd been present at the scene of a brutal murder, but I couldn't accept that she was the killer. It just didn't fit. There were two victims bearing the signature of satanic worshippers, yet the police didn't seem to be focusing on that fact. Fabienne's behaviour was bizarre. Was she putting it all on in an attempt to demonstrate that she was insane and therefore not responsible for her actions, or was she just an innocent passer-by trying to help? The whole thing was surreal. The way she pretended that she could see through the mirror threw the doctor and the detective off balance. Was that her intention all along? Did she overhear someone discussing the fact that a writer was shadowing the investigation and then use that information to twist the interview on its head? Was she innocent or was she a clever, manipulative psychopath? My mind was racing. In the cold light of day, the alternatives were simple: either someone inadvertently discussed my presence in front of her or she was psychic, and she sensed that I was there. The latter didn't wash with me, which meant that she was acting. If she was innocent, why would she concoct this strange persona? If Fabienne Wilder was a vicious murderer, then she deserved an Oscar for her performance so far. The interview was strange enough, but the aggressive behaviour of the police officer on the way home was off the chart. What was that all about? He pulled me over, threatened me and spat in my face. The look of hatred on his face as he drove away made him look insane, like Fabienne, almost animal-like. Why would a serving police officer behave in such a fashion?

    I was tired and my mind was playing tricks on me, or so I thought. I needed to speak to Peter. I didn't want to drop anybody in it, but that police officer was out of order and I intended to seek Peter's advice before I made a complaint. In hindsight, I should have picked up the telephone as soon as I arrived home and lodged a formal complaint. I dressed, put on Evie's harness and set off to walk her. The front lawn is communal and split by a stone path which leads to the front gate. The grass was looking long and untidy and rotting leaves swirled on the breeze. I hate the garden in the winter months. It looks so scruffy when the leaves fall.

    The road to the beach lined with cherry blossom trees, their flowers and leaves long since gone. The bare branches made the trees look dead. The storm from the night before had passed by, but there was still a strong breeze blowing. I looked forward to our walk. The fresh air would be good for me. I tried to clear my head, but my mind was buzzing with thoughts of Fabienne Wilder and the murders. I wanted to call Peter, but I knew he would be just waking up and he had said he would call me on his way into work. Evie was pulling like a steam train and I had to keep tugging her back. Staffies aren't big dogs but they're very strong. If Evie wants to go left, we go left. We walked the five hundred yards along the peaceful coast road. The waves were crashing onto the rocks below Criag-y-mor and splashing up onto the road. Detached houses built in the forties flank the road. The dark slate roofs looked shiny and wet. The cars parked next to the kerbs were newish family saloons with the odd Porsches and Ferrari throw in. Rich tourists were snapping up property around the Bay.

As we cut through a sheep gate onto the grass, I allowed Evie Jones to run the full length of the extendable lead, which she did at breakneck speed. She galloped in a huge circle, scouring the sand and greens for other dogs to kill. As she frolicked, I checked my watch and decided to give it half an hour before we turned back for home, when a voice interrupted my thoughts.

'Pick that up, please,' the voice said. It was a female voice. I had no idea who she was talking to, so I looked around. There was nobody else nearby. 'I'm talking to you,' she said, pointing at me. She was mid-twenties and dressed in forest-green trousers and a matching fleece jacket. The gold lettering on her jacket told me she was a beach warden. Her face told me she was pissed off with me about something.

I pulled the Staffie in on a tight lead as she had tensed up and was about to kick off. I saw her launch an attack on a young bloke one day. It was completely out of the blue, and if she'd not been on the lead, she would have hurt him. He was wearing a dark shell suit with the pants tucked into his socks. She went bonkers at him, which makes me think her previous owner, who abused her, wore similar clothing. Normally she is fine with people, but she didn't like this woman. Her ears were up and she puffed her chest out to full capacity.

'I'm sorry?' I said. I wasn't sure what she wanted. 'What's the matter?'

'I said, pick that up.' She was pointing towards a steaming pile of sloppy dog excrement. It looked like a small dinosaur had deposited it. Evie and I were thirty yards away from her and she was closer to the mess than us.

'I think you've made a mistake. My dog didn't do that.' I turned and walked away from her. The thought of picking up dog mess at the best of times turns my stomach, and to be honest, when no one is looking, I pretend she hasn't done it and leave it for the insects to eat. This particular deposit would need a spade, not a poo bag. Anyway, my Staffie was not guilty and there was no way I was picking it up.

'If you refuse to clear up after your dog, you will be fined fifty pounds on the spot.' She snarled the words, aggressively marching towards us. 'It's up to you to pick it up or pay a fine.'

'My dog didn't make that mess.' I continued to walk away.

'I saw your dog do this shit.' She pointed at the steaming pile.

'You're mistaken.' I turned to face her. She was five yards away now and I could see the contempt on her face. 'She hasn't shit anywhere yet, lady.'

'I saw it with my own eyes.'

'You're a liar,' I replied. I had heard enough. I cannot tolerate liars. 'I don't know what your problem is, but she didn't do that.'

'Are you threatening me?' she shouted at me. Other dog walkers heard, and they stopped to see what was going on. I looked around. There were half a dozen people watching a six-feet-tall skinhead with tattoos and a dangerous dog squaring up to a petite, female warden. There was only one thing they would be thinking. I'm a thug refusing to pick up my dog mess, a warden has collared me and now I'm threatening her. Great – explain that one to the judge, Conrad. 'Help, please, call the police,' she shouted to the onlookers. 'This man is threatening me.'

I was baffled and deciding what to do when the warden's scowl turned into a snarl. A low-pitched growl came from her throat. The Staffie freaked, and when she goes, she looks like a rabid monster. Within seconds she was up on two legs, foaming at the mouth and straining at the lead. She was barking and growling in frustration because she couldn't reach the warden. From a distance we must have looked a right pair. If she could have reached her, she would have tried to rip her to shreds. The warden took her camera phone from her pocket and began snapping pictures of the Staffie and me. Evie was on two legs, attacking her. Explain that photograph, Mr Jones; your dog is a dangerous animal.

'That dog needs putting down,' she chuckled. 'I'm reporting you for having a dangerous dog.'

'You're a nutjob,' I replied. It was the politest answer that I could come up with. I yanked Evie a few yards in the right direction and decided to retreat.

'I'm going to report you.' She carried on taking pictures.

'Do whatever you like, you nutter. She didn't make that mess and I'm not picking it up. It's your fault that she's flipped, stupid cow.' I was walking my dog and minding my own business. This woman had created a major drama from nothing. Some of the other dog walkers had changed direction to watch what was going on, and a chubby female jogger stopped running and reached for her mobile phone. It was obvious from their expressions that I was an undesirable troublemaker, bullying a defenceless woman.

An elderly man with a white Yorkshire terrier approached. 'I've called the police, luv, are you okay?' His back was stooped by age and his flat cap was pulled low just above his eyebrows. He poked his walking stick towards me as he spoke. 'I've witnessed that, young man,' he added. 'You should be ashamed of yourself.'

Now, you know that Evie hates other dogs, but white dogs are her total nightmare. Small, white, fluffy dogs send to her a new level of rabidity. She was spinning around on two legs, snarling like the exorcist. I was baffled by the woman's behaviour. I knew that I was flogging a dead horse trying to explain myself to any would-be witnesses. I looked around; people outside the Black Seal were watching. Three men were standing on the lifeboat station gantry, looking at what was going on. I knew how it would look to them. One of them, Barry lobster as he was known, waved a hand at me but shook his head as if to say, walk away. He was right; I just needed to get Evie home safely. I decided that I would come back to the beach later when she was settled and have things out with the warden, in case she did report me to the police. I grabbed Evie Jones and made a sharp exit from the beach. She was on her phone as we left. I jogged to the entrance of the Trearddur Bay hotel before slowing to a walk.

Evie was distressed and circled me all the way home; it's a protective gesture, apparently. We stuck to the pavement and didn't stop, not even for her to sniff. It's a ten-minute walk from the beach to my flat, and as we turned into the communal car park, the first police car arrived.

CHAPTER 7

My Second Warning

I took the Staffie up the stairs to the front door and hurriedly unlocked it, which is more difficult than it sounds. There is a lock on the outer door and then a small porch area. Getting Evie Jones between the two doors when she's on one can be a struggle. I closed the first door and unlocked the second before pushing her into the hallway. I wanted to get her safely inside before I faced the police. Once behind a locked door, it would take a court order to remove her. I had a feeling that there was going to be a heated argument at best. If things got irate, she would not do herself or me any favours, and if a policeman got bitten then it would be curtains for her. It wasn't her fault she was unduly protective, and I had to protect her.

I got her into the vestibule and locked the main door. She was bouncing off the back of the door, snarling like a grizzly bear as the policeman opened his car door. She could sense my concern. I went back downstairs onto the front path. I turned to face the police car, which had parked up in a lay-by at the front of the building. The building is set back from the coast road and the police car was at the junction of one of the access roads. The police officer was talking on his radio and looking at me through his window. I waved and walked towards the front gate. He waved back and half smiled, which gave me some hope that this whole thing could be put down as a misunderstanding. It was hardly a police matter in my opinion.

That was until a second police car arrived and my favourite police officer from the previous night pulled up to the kerb next to the first. My heart sank when I saw him. I knew I was in trouble and there wasn't much I could do about it. For some reason he had a problem with me and now he had an excuse to throw his weight around. Things became worse still when I looked into his car. Next to him in the passenger seat was the beach warden. The stupid bitch was pointing at me through the window and laughing. Her nose was bleeding, and she stemmed the blood with a paper tissue. That bothered me immensely.

'Have you just been to the beach?' the first police officer asked politely as he climbed out of his patrol car. He seemed confused. They say policemen get younger as we get older and this guy looked wet behind the ears. His short dark hair was spiked up with gel.

'Yes,' I answered. I walked to the gate and closed it between us. It was a psychological barrier more than a physical one, and I was anticipating conflict. 'I've just walked the dog.'

'What's your name please, sir?' he asked, taking his notebook from his top pocket. The officer was in his early twenties, I guessed, and his body armour covered a white short-sleeved shirt, open at the neck.

'My name is Conrad Jones,' I replied. I had my eye on the other patrol car as I spoke. I wanted to get my side of the story over before they did. 'Look, I can explain all this. That beach warden accused me of not picking up my dog waste, but my dog didn't make the mess. The warden was mistaken, and she frightened my dog. She's a rescue dog and she's a bit highly strung because she was mistreated. That's why she kicked off.'

'I'm not here about your dog, Mr Jones.' He frowned. 'We've had a report of an assault on one of the council workers.'

'Assault? Are you joking?'

'Do I look like I'm joking?' He eyed me sternly and took out his pen. 'Can you tell me exactly what happened on the beach please?' He looked over his shoulder as the other police officer got out of his vehicle. As he approached, he looked at me with the same contemptuous expression as the night before. He didn't like me one bit and that's unnerving. 'I was walking the dog when the warden accused me of not picking up dog excrement. My dog didn't make the mess; she was mistaken,' I began to explain as the bad officer and the warden approached. 'The next thing, she was raising her voice and waving her hands around and Evie tried to protect me. She didn't bite anybody, and she didn't shit anywhere.'

'That's him. He threatened to smash my face in and then he elbowed me in the face as he walked past,' she lied. The tissue was spotted with blood. Her nose was bleeding – there was no argument there – but it was nothing to do with me or Evie Jones. I couldn't believe that this was happening to me. I looked to the skies for inspiration. What was wrong with the woman? The look on bad officer's face answered my question. He was smirking from ear to ear until the first officer looked at him and he feigned a look of disdain. They were setting me up. I felt like I was being paranoid, but what else could it be? Why would they be doing this? Why would they lie? 'I want to press charges against him, officer, and I want to report his dog as a dangerous animal. It attacked me and it needs to be put down.' I looked at her forearm and couldn't comprehend what I was seeing.

'Can you tell me your side of the story, please, Mr Jones.' The first officer was calm and went about his job in a professional manner. I was glad he was there. I took a deep breath to calm myself down; the warden was making my blood boil. Threatening to have my dog put down in front of police officers was provocative to say the least. I didn't like the woman but that didn't mean I wanted to smash her face in, like she said. The thought would never have crossed my mind. Being accused of something as deplorable as elbowing a lady in the face when you're innocent is very difficult to comprehend. At that point, I was confused and angry, but haven't we all felt like that? Feeling aggrieved and backed into a corner by a liar would incense anyone. I gathered my thoughts before I replied.

'She was mistaken about my dog fouling on the beach. I refused to pick up the mess and she threatened me with a fine. I refused again and then she lost the plot,' I explained. 'I did not make any threats at all and I certainly didn't elbow her in the face.' The car park was quite busy, and drivers were slowing down to get a look at what the two police cars were doing at the building. A taxi honked its horn loudly and one of my friends from my local pub put his thumb up as he drove by. This would be a topic of conversation at the bar for days to come. Don't tell a taxi driver anything that you want to remain a secret.

'I want him arrested. He broke my nose and he has a dangerous dog, too,' she shouted from fifteen yards or so away. 'It wasn't muzzled, and it attacked me. I want to press charges.' She lifted her left arm up and pointed to a rip in her sleeve. She held a gauze pad to her arm. There was blood on the dressing. Now that upped the ante. Not only did she have an injury allegedly caused by me, she also had a wound that she was saying was from my dog. Evie would be destroyed and there would be nothing I could do about it.

I couldn't believe it. She had blood flowing from her nose and a wound on her arm. Her sleeve was ripped, and the skin was broken. I felt sick inside. I was gobsmacked. I was terrified. Evie Jones did not get close enough to bite her; she was a liar. The woman was trying to get my dog destroyed.

'That lady is making this up. I know how this looks but she's a liar. The dog didn't touch her and neither did I,' I said as calmly as I could. It was taking all my self-control not to panic. How could I make her tell them the truth? I was helpless.

'You can clearly see she is injured. How do you explain the injuries, Mr Jones?' The first officer shrugged his shoulders. 'This doesn't look good at the moment. I think we should go to the station and sort this out, okay?' He was fair enough. 'I don't want to arrest you at this point, but if you refuse to come in, I'll have to.'

The taxi beeped loudly as it past again; louder this time. Big Gordon had obviously driven around the roundabout to get another look. Under different circumstances, I would have laughed and flicked the fingers at him, but right then I was panicking. I was being accused of something that I clearly had nothing to do with, but I was there, my dog was there, witnesses saw her kicking off and the warden had pictures of us both at the scene. How the hell could I explain the woman's injuries? I actually had to question myself silently as to whether we could have been responsible. Had I lost my temper and lashed out? Not a chance. This wasn't a mistake; she was setting me.

The woman had wound both me and Evie Jones up, but not to the point where I'd become violent. This was pure fantasy, made up to drop me in it but I couldn't fathom why; not for one minute.

'I have no problem coming to the station,' I replied. 'I haven't done anything and neither has my dog.'

'If you haven't done anything wrong, then you don't have anything to worry about,' the first officer said calmly. 'I'm going to call this into the custody sergeant and tell him that you're coming in voluntarily. When we get there, we can sort things out okay?'

'Fine,' I replied resignedly. What else could I do at that point? The first officer walked the ten yards across the lay-by to his car and reached inside for his radio. As soon as he turned his back, bad cop marched towards me. He was glaring at me as if I'd just eaten his children.

As he neared the gate, he shouted at me, 'Step back from the gate.' He reached for his baton and placed his right hand over the CS gas spray attached to his utility belt. 'I said calm down and step backwards.'

'What is your problem?' I asked. This was a set-up and I was convinced he was at the root of it. The traffic on the coast road had slowed to a virtual standstill now. He had his number on his shoulder today; he was Constable 6540. 'I see you've got your numbers on today. That's good because I'll need them when I make a formal complaint about you spitting in my face.' The first officer could see something was amiss and he shouted over from the car.

'What's the matter?'

'He's threatening the victim,' 6540 replied, over his shoulder. The other officer looked confused. 'I'm arresting him for assault and threatening behaviour. Step back from the gate now, this is your last warning.'

'Officer,' I shouted, 'this officer is threatening me again. What is your name, please?' I asked loudly. He appeared to be normal, whatever normal is, and he looked at 6540 with a concerned expression. My accusation didn't seem to surprise him one bit.

'Constable Wright.' He was eyeing me suspiciously now. What else could he think? The warden was making accusations; she was injured and at face value, the suspect was a tattooed skinhead with a Staffie. I was guilty before I'd opened my mouth. He shook his head as he spoke on the radio. 'Both of you just calm down and wait a minute.'

'This is your last warning,' 6540 shouted at me. I saw the warden grinning like an idiot as he stepped closer to the gate. Some of the vehicles had stopped and the drivers were climbing out of their cars. In the corner of my eye, I noticed Big Gordon approaching from the left, his taxi abandoned on the pavement. His presence offered me some support. He's twenty-odd stone and he's a good friend. Policemen or not, he would jump in if there was any chance of me being roughed up.

Officer Wright shook his head as he walked back towards us. 'Just calm it down, Knowles, there is no need for this.' He called for another car to attend. 'Mr Jones has agreed to come in of his own accord. Back off and calm down.'

'Shut up, Wright,' Knowles growled. They exchanged angry glances. I had a hunch that there was no love lost between them.

'This officer pulled me over last night, threatened me and then spat in my face,' I said as he neared.

'When?' Wright looked incredulous.

'Last night at the top of Long Lane.'

'Did you report it?'

'No,' I answered, embarrassed. I should have called the station immediately. Now it sounded like sour grapes. 'I was going to ask my friend Peter Strachan for his advice. Do you know him?'

'Yes, I know Peter.' Wright looked at Knowles. 'Did you pull him over last night?'

'Don't be stupid.' Knowles never took his eyes from me as he spoke. 'He's making it up because he's going to be arrested.'

'We'll sort it all out at the station.'

'I can see how this looks, but he's setting me up,' I shrugged and realised how ridiculous I must have sounded. 'I don't know why she's lying, but she is. I never touched her and neither did Evie. I want to make a formal complaint against Officer Knowles.' I took out my Samsung and took a photograph of Constable 6540 and his friend the warden. The tables were turned, and they didn't like it much.

'Put that camera away now.' He did not like that at all.

'I'm in my own car park and you've threatened me. I'll do what I like.'

'We'll see about that,' he growled.

'I don't know what your game is, but you and your little friend there are out of order.' The presence of the other police officer gave me some confidence, so it felt good to give him some grief.

'Calm it down, both of you.' Constable Wright took the radio from his utility vest and called into the control room again.

'7432.'

'Go ahead.'

'I'm going to call in your complaint and then I think we should all go back to the station to sort this out,' he said to me. He turned and walked back to his car to call it in with some privacy. Obviously, a member of the public had accused the other officer of a serious offence. He didn't seem to have any affinity to Knowles. 'I'm warning you for the last time, step back from the gate,' Knowles said quietly.

'Not a chance,' I replied and leant against it, barring his way. There was no way he was coming through that gate. The other officer could enter my garden, no problem, but not him.

'Step back now.' he ordered in a loud voice. The warden was still grinning.

'No chance.'

'Calm down!' he shouted at the top of his voice for effect. It made me jump. I was perfectly calm. He wanted onlookers to think that I wasn't. He shouted at the top of his voice again. He wanted it to look as if I was being aggressive, but I wasn't. 'I said calm down.' He took his pepper spray off his belt and held it at arm's length, pointing it at my face. Officer Wright climbed out of his car and shouted something, but I didn't hear it. I was shocked by Knowles's behaviour.

'Get down on the floor. Get down on the floor.' he screamed at me as he neared the gate.

I've seen what that spray can do to a man and I didn't fancy a face full of it. I stepped back away from the gate and he pushed it open. I held up my hands instinctively. He kept coming forwards. Everything became slow motion in my mind. The warden was sneering and glaring at me with a look of sheer hatred on her face. Officer Wright was running towards us and shouting into his radio for backup, and then Constable 6540 sprayed me in the face with the chemical.

The stinging sensation was so bad my eyes felt like they had acid in them. My airways constricted and I couldn't catch my breath, and the skin on my hands and face was on fire. Debilitated is not the word. I was out of the game completely. I was rolling around my lawn, coughing and spluttering when the officer dropped his knee onto the back of my skull. I heard Big Gordon shouting, his voice mingled with Officer Wright's, and the first kick in the head landed. White light flashed through my brain and I felt like I was going to choke to death. The second kick sent me to a world of darkness and pain.

CHAPTER 8

In the Cells

The journey to Ysbyty Gwynedd hospital was a blur. I was handcuffed to a policeman and my wrist was twisted at an awkward angle. The paramedic rinsed my eyes and skin with something, but the burning sensation didn't wane. My eyes streamed and, my throat felt like I had swallowed glass; my head felt like it would explode. I couldn't help but wonder what I had done to deserve this. Was the police officer mad, or was I? I know I'm not everyone's cup of tea and can wind people up sometimes, but I genuinely didn't believe I had done anything wrong. I knew categorically I hadn't done anything wrong. Something else was going on. I could only feel grateful that Officer Wright had attended the scene or things could have been even worse.

At the hospital they cleaned my eyes again and bathed my hands and face. They checked me for signs of concussion and X-rayed my skull before giving me the green light to be handed over to the police. They cuffed me and put me into the back of a patrol car and drove me to the cells. Brilliant – kicked senseless and handcuffed for my troubles. The highlight of my day thus far was chatting to one of my escorts about my books. He'd read all of them during a two-week holiday in Turkey. Interestingly, he let slip that Knowles had been investigated before. He also told me that the warden's injured arm had raised a few eyebrows at the hospital. The doctor informed the police that the wound had been caused by a thin sharp blade, like a Stanley knife, and was definitely not caused by a dog. That information made me feel relieved that Evie Jones was off the hook, but it was almost incomprehensible that the woman had gone to so much trouble to set me up.

They processed me as any other criminal would be. They took my belongings from my pockets and the chain from my neck and bagged them with my wallet and mobile. The desk sergeant asked me to remove my belt and shoes and then they put me in a urine-stinking cell. There was a stainless-steel toilet in one corner and a thin rubber mattress in the other. There was graffiti on the tiles near a narrow window high on the wall. Apparently, 'Paul Howarth takes it up the arse.' The cell door was painted navy blue, and as it slammed closed it seemed to be fifty feet thick. I sat down and tried to make sense of it all. If I'm honest, I was so frustrated that I felt like crying. I don't remember falling asleep, but I must have done because the next thing I remember was waking up with my neck at a painful angle against the wall.

The police were looking into the incidents and keeping me locked up while they talked to officers Wright and Knowles. I had seen plenty of police cells before, but I could always walk out of them when the job was finished and being locked in one is no fun at all. I had an idea of how innocent men who are convicted of crimes they didn't commit must feel: completely helpless. I remember a friend, a prison officer, taking me into the punishment block of the prison where he worked. I can't name it as I shouldn't have been there. They showed me the strip cell, which was for prisoners who had lost the plot. As I stepped in to look at it, they closed the cell door and locked me in. It was funny for five minutes, then it wasn't funny anymore. This time around it wasn't a jest; this was the real deal. I was locked up for something I hadn't done, and the system had started its process; once the process has started, there's nothing you do except wait and trust that justice will prevail.

That afternoon and night dragged by. I was half sleeping and half awake. The sound of drunks yelling and kicking their cell doors added to the madness of it all. They held me in a police cell against my will, but what can you do if a police officer lies? The truth is, nothing. They can frame you and throw away the key. The warden was a responsible member of the community making allegations of assault against Evie Jones and me, and Officer Knowles was accusing me of attacking him. Who would they believe? As I contemplated trying to explain myself to a judge, I heard footsteps approaching and the metallic grind of the lock opening.

Sergeant Peter Strachan put his head around the door. I was pleased to see him, to say the least.

'What have you been up to?' He smiled, but there was concern in his eyes.

'I think I pissed someone off,' I replied. My throat was still sore and talking was difficult. Peter handed me a cup of weak tea and a bag, which contained my belongings. I gulped the tepid liquid down. 'I didn't do anything, Peter. I honestly don't have a clue what's going on.'

'Officer Wright and your big friend, the taxi driver, have backed up your story.' Peter smiled.

'Thank heavens for that,' I said.

'What can you remember?'

'Not much to be honest.' I sipped the tea noisily. The liquid eased my throat a little. 'There was a bit of a row at the beach with some jobsworth warden who accused me of not picking up dog shit, and the entire thing got out of hand. When I got home, your lot arrived. Officer Wright was sound, but Officer Knowles kicked off for no reason and tried to make it look like I was being aggressive. I wasn't. He's a nutter. I can't believe he's a police officer. Did they tell you what he did the night before?'

'It's the talk of the station at the moment. They've suspended him from duty. It took three officers to pull your mate Gordon off him.' He laughed. 'Tell me what happened when he pulled you over.' Peter sat down on the mattress next to me, a look of concern on his face.

'I was on the way home from the hospital and Knowles pulled me over for no reason.'

'When, after we met at Denbigh?'

'Yes.' I drained the tea and looked around for somewhere to put the empty cup. Cells are short on coffee tables, so I opted for the floor. 'I was hungry when I left so I went for a burger and coffee.'

'Where did he follow you from?'

'I can't be sure. As I crossed the bridge, he pulled me over. He asked me where I'd been and he had a real nasty attitude on him, but after a bit of arsing around I told him I'd been at Denbigh Hospital with you. He had a real bad attitude. He said you were an idiot and that you didn't realise how much shit you were in. What did he mean by that?'

'I have no idea. I hardly know the man, Conrad,' Peter frowned, but he didn't look confused. There was something else which flickered in his eyes. Maybe it was fear, maybe it was anger; I'll never know. 'What else did he say?'

'He told me to leave the investigation alone or I would regret it. He told me my life depended on it.' I swallowed hard and watched the expression on his face. He wasn't giving much away. 'What does that mean?'

'Not a clue. Sounds a bit dramatic,' Peter scoffed. 'Did he mention Fabienne Wilder?' His eyes focused on mine, reading my response. It was my turn to be confused this time.

'No. He didn't mention Fabienne but, he did mention the other girl,' I said. 'Pauline Holmes. He said that we both knew they were connected and that we should leave it alone. Whatever that meant.'

'Then what?' he asked.

'Then he spat in my face, ran back to his car, and drove away,' I shrugged. It was all getting on top of me. I wanted to go home. 'The next thing is the beach warden kicked off and Officer Knowles was at my gate with his pepper spray and I ended up in here via Ysbyty Gwynedd.'

'I don't know what's going on, but there have been some very strange things happening since the Holmes murder and most of them involve Knowles.' Peter shook his head and frowned. 'We won't mess around with bad coppers, Conrad. He'll be sorted out; you mark my words.'

'I'm glad to hear that. He's the type who gives the force a bad name; as for what's been going on, 'strange' is not a good enough description for the last twenty-four hours. I feel like I've woke up in the twilight zone.'

'Yeah, well, the Wilder girl seems to be rattling a few cages upstairs. The top brass want her charged and moved,' he said. 'To be honest, the doctor still can't give us straight answer about Fabienne's state of mind; he can't tell if she's giving him the run around or if she's away with the fairies. It isn't going well.'

'I thought you said it was open and shut.' I coughed; my throat burning. I needed another drink.

'Yeah, didn't I just? We got the report back from forensics and it was the victim's blood on her face and hands, no doubt about it. We have positively identified the victim. She was Caroline Stokes. She was a twenty-year-old hooker from Wrexham.' Peter shrugged. 'The problem we have is there was no blood on Fabienne's clothes, which backs up her version of events that she found the victim and tried to help. Whoever killed Stokes would have been covered in blood.'

'What has Fabienne Wilder said since we left?' I threaded my belt through my jeans and fastened it. I feel vulnerable without a belt, as if my pants would fall down. Putting my keys and phone in my pockets almost made me feel human again. I was gagging for a shower and some proper sleep.

'Well, she keeps asking to talk to you, which is complicating things. My governor has gone apeshit that she was told you'd be there. She's ranting about a group called the 'Order of Nine Angels'. She's rattling on about one of your books which mentions them.' Peter looked into my eyes as he said their name. 'that's what the governor wanted your help with. You've written about them, haven't you?'

'Yes. Many times. I call them Niners.' I think Peter already knew the answer to that question. He was as subtle as a brick. 'I used a similar cult in my second book, but I changed their name. And then I alluded to them in *The Child Taker*.' Peter looked confused; the significance of the name change was lost on him. 'Since then, they're in several more.'

'She says they killed the Stokes woman to convert one of them into a feeder, whatever that is. We haven't got a clue what she's talking about and she won't elaborate.'

'You have to understand that there are different levels of crazy among the Niners. Some are just along for the ride and stay on the periphery, but others go in much deeper,' I said, wondering if he would believe a word I said about them. It's a difficult concept to grasp. 'To become a feeder, they have to feed on a victim's blood at the time of death.'

'Like a vampire?' Peter said, eyebrows raised in surprise.

'Yes. Cannibalism is recorded as far back as written records go. The truth is, it probably goes back way further.' He stared at me blankly; his detective's poker face showing no reaction. 'What exactly did she say about the Nine Angels?' I asked. I was uncomfortable talking about it in a police cell for obvious reasons; not everyone in uniform could be trusted.

'She said that they killed Caroline Stokes. They were trying to initiate one of their members because she has the ability to see things.'

'Sees things?' I repeated. I had read about seers among O9A. They were gifted with an increased sense of perception. Not psychic; that would be silly, but perceptive. Very perceptive.

'Yep. What she sees is beyond me. She's babbling most of the time. We've had a toxin screen done and she's clean. There are no drugs in her system. She's obviously mad as a hatter, but she's drug free. I don't get this angels and angles crap. Let's pretend I'm an idiot,' he said. 'Give me the idiots guide to what they're all about.'

'I've researched the Nine 'Angles' more than Nine Angels, but they're all from the same mould. There are literally dozens of similar cults but they're the real deal.' I walked out of the cell and pulled on my boots. They were outside the door as if I had left them there to keep the cell floor clean before I went to bed. As I glanced around, there were half a dozen pairs of men's shoes and a pair of red stilettos neatly placed next to the cell doors. It looked like it had been a busy night for the custody sergeant.

'You have looked into both, though?' Peter frowned. 'So, what's the difference?' He was a nice bloke, trying to understand a nonsensical concept. I'm no mastermind, but my writing requires all kinds of research into all kinds of things. I'm lucky because my mind retains information; if I read something that I'm interested in, I can remember it word for word. I remembered the 'Nine Angles' well from researching my second novel, but their information was dated. The newer sites and more recent postings were related to the Nine Angels. I researched them in-depth.

'Well, there are two distinct groups.' I finished sorting my belongings out as I answered. Peter wanted answers, but I wanted to taste fresh air again. 'Can we get out of here now and talk on the way?'

'Let's walk to the custody desk and get you released.' Peter patted me on the back. I flinched. There were obviously bruises there. 'We can talk in the car.'

Peter led the way through from the cells to the custody suite. There were curious looks here and there from his fellow officers, or maybe I was being paranoid. I think I had every reason to be.

'Look, I'll tell you what, we've just got a warrant to go around and check out her place,' Peter said, lowering his voice. 'Why don't you come?'

'I'm very tired and sore. Do they want to take a statement from me before I leave?' I asked. I couldn't face a detailed interview. I was knackered, but I was at the mercy of the police force. They would be waiting to see if their officer was guilty of a serious assault; I was hoping that interviewing me at that point was premature.

'No, the warden has dropped her allegations. The wound on her arm wasn't caused by a dog. She's been interviewed for wasting police time,' Peter said quietly. 'The governor wants to gather all the information first. I think there's more going on here than we know about.' He didn't expand. 'Do you want to come to Fabienne's flat or are you too tired?'

'I'm interested enough to wait a few more hours for my bed,' I agreed eagerly. Too eagerly maybe, but the girl intrigued me, and I wanted to see inside her mind. I thought that a visit to her home might provide some sort of insight into who she was.

The custody sergeant was a portly man in his fifties, probably serving the last few years of his career behind the safety of a Perspex screen. He ignored us just long enough to let us know who was in charge.

'You're being released without charge, pending further investigation, Mr Jones,' he said chirpily. 'If you sign that you've had all your belongings back, Sergeant Strachan can show you the way out.'

'I would normally say thank you, but under the circumstances it doesn't seem to be appropriate,' I replied, equally as chirpily. 'But you can't tar everyone with the same brush, so thank you anyway.' I signed the form without reading it and handed it to him with a half-smile. The custody sergeant eyed me coolly and went back to his computer screen without another word. Peter grabbed my elbow and ushered me towards the door before I could do any more damage.

We left the cellblock and the fresh air smelled good. Although the station is situated in Caernarfon, the air was as good as it is in the heart of Snowdonia, although the cloying scent of urine lingered in my nostrils for a while. We climbed into Peter's silver Citroën and headed out of the compound. It was a sporty hatchback, which looked like most of the other sporty hatchbacks on the road apart from the Citroën logo on the bonnet.

'The SOCO team have been in her flat all morning. I hope they'll be finished by now and we can have a snoop around,' he said as we pulled into the traffic. A bus was pulling out of the station as we drove by. The line of black cabs outside was shortening slowly as passengers emerged with their suitcases. Life was trundling along normally for most people; it was my world which had spiralled into the bizarre.

'Do you mind if I pick your brains about these Satan worshippers on the way?' Peter asked, keeping his eyes on the road ahead. I didn't know as much about them then as I do now, but I knew a lot more than Peter and his colleagues. Had I known what I know now, I would have run a mile.

'I can tell you what I learnt from my research, although there are far more knowledgeable people out there than me and a rack of books on the subject.' I shrugged. 'I can tell you what I do know: these groups are widespread but fractured. There are dozens of groups who publish information online about their culture and beliefs, and you can take it for granted that there are dozens more individuals and small groups that aren't using the Internet. They're the dangerous ones.'

'How so?' Peter tried to look interested, but I could tell that he wasn't grasping the subject. His superior had told him to ask me a few questions about it, but I could tell that Peter had already made up his mind about the girl.

'Their axiom is 'Do as thou wilt', which basically means do what you want. They encourage indulgence as opposed to abstinence, to cut a long story short; their goal is chaos and anarchy beyond the normal boundaries of society.'

'Sounds like a punk rock band from the seventies,' Peter scoffed.

'You're not far off the mark there with some of these people.' I laughed because I knew what I was talking about. Peter threw me a puzzled glance. 'Look, there are as many anti-satanic websites as there are pro-satanic. I remember one that I looked at will always stick in my mind, *godhatesgoths.com*.' I waited for Peter's expression to change but it didn't. 'You know what goths are, right?'

'God hates goths? Are you taking the piss?' he snorted.

'No, far from it.' I sighed. 'Google it when you get home. There are groups of Christian families campaigning against music that some believe has motivated teenagers to practice the occult and kill themselves and others. They attribute some of the recent school massacres to the messages in the music.'

'Bollocks,' Peter said. 'That's just stupid people trying to put the blame at someone else's doorstep.'

'Maybe it is, maybe it isn't. We can't ask most of the shooters because they kill themselves in the act. What we do know is most of them are disenfranchised from society. They don't fit in; They're not popular. People say they've bought into the concept of chaos and maybe they have a point.'

'Enlighten me,' Peter mumbled.

'Okay. I'll try. Do you remember the Columbine massacre?' I looked at him and he nodded. 'Most goth websites hail the perpetrators of the massacre as heroes. It's a fact that they both dabbled in the occult.'

'You can't blame a massacre on that,' Peter said, shaking his head.

'I'm not blaming anyone for anything. It's all theory and speculation; all I'm telling you are the facts. There was a similar shooting at a place called Red Lake High School, carried out by a kid called Jeffrey Weise, which claimed ten victims and seven wounded.' Peter was about to interrupt, but I held up my hand and carried on, 'Let me finish or you won't get the point.'

'I'm not stupid,' he snapped, glancing sideways.

'I know, but if you look at this in isolation it means nothing. You have to follow the patterns. Please bear with me.'

'Sorry, I didn't mean to snap.'

'I know it's hard to believe, but keep an open mind,' I said calmly. He nodded that he would try, although his face said a different thing. 'There was a case at another school, Dawson College, which fortunately claimed only two victims, but nineteen were critically injured. Both of these 'goth' school shootings have one thing in common. All of the killers claimed the two shooters involved in the Columbine massacre, Eric Harris and Dylan Klebold, were their 'heroes', and they were both fascinated by the occult. The occult influence is undeniable.'

'It's a coincidence, that's all it is. Like I said before, people trying to blame other people,' Peter grunted. 'What has that got to do with anything here?'

'I like coincidences,' I replied to the challenge. Debating things that I know a lot about is one of my favourite pastimes. 'Did you know that the 19th of April is one of the most important dates in the satanic calendar?'

'Funnily enough, I didn't know they had a calendar,' Peter said.

'They do.' I tried to keep him with me. 'They have holy days just as the Christian calendar does. From the 19th of April a thirteen-day festival called the 'Blood Sacrifice to the Beast' begins, culminating on the 1st of May.'

'How do you know all this stuff?' he asked. He was laughing, but there was little humour in his laugh.

'Remember those dates,' I pointed my finger at him. 'Many believe that Adolf Hitler was sent by the devil, and on the 19th of April 1943, Nazi storm-troopers incinerated the last few Jewish freedom-fighters in Warsaw.'

'Oh, come on.' Peter groaned. 'Now you're pushing it.'

I ignored his complaint and carried on.

'Precisely fifty years later to the day, the siege at Waco ended with eighty-three dead. In occult gematria, the number five is the number for death.' Peter was going to speak again, but my raised hand stopped him once more. '19th of April 1995, precisely twenty-four months to the day after Waco, a huge bomb devastated the Murrah Federal Building in Oklahoma City.'

'Like I said, coincidence.'

'24th of April 1998, a goth shooter struck in Pennsylvania.'

'Coincidence.'

'20th of April 1999, avowed Satanists struck in Columbine, fifteen dead and fourteen wounded.'

'It's all bollocks.' Peter shook his head.

'26th of April 2002, a shooter struck in a German high school.' I was counting the coincidences off on my fingers as Peter's face reddened. '29th of April 2002, a shooter struck in Bosnia. All the shooters were into goth culture. They were into the music and the satanic side of it. Can all those dates be coincidence, or did they pick those dates for a reason?'

'Fuck knows,' Peter mumbled. 'So, are the Nine Angles goths?'

'I'm not saying that every black-haired teenager in a trench coat is a devil worshipper. I'm saying that their music and culture obviously influences young minds.'

'But are they connected?' he asked frustrated.

'Who knows, Peter? I don't.' I raised my hands in the air. 'I'm trying to explain to you that these groups are fractured, but there are thousands of them.' I breathed in deeply and calmed myself. 'The first group to openly admit to following the left-hand path surfaced in the sixties.' I was using jargon, so I explained myself. 'The followers of the left-hand path worship the devil as opposed to God.'

Peter nodded that he was following. 'Like I said, I'm not thick.'

I ignored his snipe. 'It was founded by a guy called Anton LaVey. He wrote *The Satanic Bible* and most of their other teachings before he died in the late nineties. They evolved into the Church of Satan under his daughter's leadership, but many of his disciples split and founded other groups. You can buy a membership card into the Church of Satan online for two hundred dollars, which tells me that they're harmless enough. They're making money from idiots. It's the splinter groups that are far more dangerous than them. They're the true believers'

'You mentioned that some of them are neo-Nazi?'

'Some of them are. Just look at the goth bands and listen to their lyrics,' I nodded, and searched for my smokes. I thought that Peter was barking up the wrong tree, but I humoured him with an explanation. 'A guy called David Myatt was linked to one of the splinter groups who broke from the Church of Satan and he was also heavily involved with some of the more violent British right-wing groups.'

'What, like the BNP?' He looked pleased with himself that he was following.

'Way before their time, mate.'

'Carry on about the fascist side to them.' Peter seemed keen to go into the fascist theme probably because it was something tangible that he encountered every day at work. It was more believable and easier to grasp than Satan-worshipping.

'Well, when I looked into them there were a few websites that stood out. When you read the first few pages, it's all about causing chaos and mayhem by using the dark arts, but then the next few pages are praising Hitler and his extermination of the Jews. I'm not sure where the two things marry, but several of the sites I looked at had a similar ethos.'

'I don't get it,' Peter said, shaking his head, 'are we talking Nazi-loving skinheads – no offence.'

'None taken,' I smiled. 'I know it sounds odd, but the two seem to gel. Evil breeds evil and a lot of the iconology used is based on Nazi regalia. You have to remember that the Nazis were convinced that they were the superior race. The people who choose the sinister way believe that their way is better than the civilised norm that we accept. They call us the 'mundane', which is derogatory, right?'

'I guess so.' Peter nodded. 'So, what did you change the name to in your book?'

'The Eighteenth Brigade,' I tried to explain it simply: 'There are some hardcore fascist groups who use the number '18' as a euphemism for the name Adolf Hitler. The one translates into the letter A and the eight becomes H, the first and eighth letters of the alphabet.'

'Oh, I get it.' He nodded. 'I've heard of 'Combat 18'. Now I know where they get the '18' from.' He laughed.

'Have you heard of 'Column 88'?' I used another high-profile group with a strong presence on the Internet.

'Yes.' Peter glanced at me. 'They're on our lists of right-wing extremists.'

'The same thing applies with them, '88' translates into 'HH': 'Heil Hitler', and Myatt was connected with both of those groups and the Order of Nine 'Angles'.'

'Interesting,' Peter said, 'but what do they all want?'

'What do you mean?' I asked, confused.

'What are they trying to achieve?'

'That's like asking *why are we here* or *what is the meaning of life?* My understanding of it is that it's similar to most conventional religions in essence; the more they believe and live by the sinister code the more will be revealed to them by the evil forces in the cosmos.'

'Gobbledegook,' Peter said.

'What, religion as a whole or just their religion?'

'All of it.'

'You got married in church, didn't you?'

'Yes. What's that got to do with it?'

'You went to place of worship to conduct an antiquated religious ceremony in front of an altar. What difference does it make whose name was above the door?' Peter's face was a picture of confusion. 'All religions look to a divine power, theirs is evil.'

Peter gave me a sideways glance. He obviously thought that I was talking gobbledygook.

'Come on, Conrad – divine power?' He laughed. 'Aren't we talking about a bunch of crackpots who want to join a club with a difference?'

I agreed with him to a degree. Some of them would be lowlife losers who wanted to belong to something, but there were genuine believers out there too. I decided to play devil's advocate, excuse the pun.

'Do you mind if I smoke?' I'd not had a cigarette for hours. He shook his head, but he didn't look totally happy with my request. I lit a menthol with my Zippo. 'Why would anyone believe in a deity who created our planet in seven days when we know that our solar system was formed by a huge explosion?' I lowered my window and exhaled the cigarette smoke. 'Do you honestly believe that Jesus was the son of God, who fed the five thousand with a few loaves and fish, walked on water, died on a cross and then came back to life?'

'Not completely,' Peter conceded. 'I know that the Bible is exaggerated.'

'Exaggerated.' It was my turn to give him a sideways glance. 'We know for a fact that the Bible was compiled by the Emperor Constantine, who decided which bits of documented scripture to include and which ones to bury in pots near the Dead Sea. In my opinion the Bible was created to control the Christian population.' I paused and pulled on my cigarette deeply. 'They were causing unrest for a crumbling Roman Empire and they needed a way of bringing them into line. It's a rule book of how to be civilised, and nothing more.'

'You don't believe in God, then?' he said sarcastically.

'I don't believe in a compilation of scriptures written by fuck knows who.' It was my turn to be sarcastic. 'No one knows who wrote Genesis, Exodus, Leviticus, Numbers or Deuteronomy, but it's assumed that they were written by Moses. Since Deuteronomy records his death, it seems like bullshit to me that he wrote any of it. It's a compilation of works by scholars dating back nearly a thousand years before Christ, and it's full of contradictions, yet millions take its teachings literally.'

'You think it's all a big con?' he asked.

'The Dead Sea Scrolls have been in the Vatican for decades and they still won't tell us what's in them. Why do you think that is?' I was waffling on. 'Religion makes my piss boil. We know it's manufactured, yet it's the root cause of so much pain and destruction, and always has been.' I took a deep drag and inhaled the minty smoke. 'I'll tell you why the Catholics won't release their translations, it's because it will shatter their grip on the millions who pay to keep the Catholic Church in business. It's all bollocks in my opinion, but what we have to accept is the fact that millions do truly believe in God, Buddha, Allah, and, in this case, the devil.' Lecture finished, I flicked my stump through the window and closed it. There was an uncomfortable silence for a few minutes as Peter digested what I'd said. 'What we think doesn't matter. The fact is that people believe in whatever they believe in and we can't argue with them because no one knows what the truth is. They can't all be right.'

'You wouldn't get on with my Sunday school teacher,' he joked. 'Fancy disrespecting Jesus and the Catholics; that's shocking.'

'I'm not disrespecting Jesus.' I laughed. 'I have no doubt in my mind that he existed and that he was a charismatic prophet with values to share, but I don't believe he was the son of God. I believe he was human. The point is that it doesn't matter what I believe. It's what *they* believe that's important. That's what makes them do the things they do.'

'We're nearly there.' Peter indicated left and slid out of the traffic. 'I need to explain all this to my governor, and he has his feet firmly on this planet, so I need to translate what you've told me into plain and simple English.' We pulled off the A55 and travelled a short distance to a converted farm, which developers had transformed into a block of apartments. They overlooked the breakwater and Soldiers Point.

'So, in the nineties there were a lot of fascists that worshipped Satan and allegedly they evolved into the group which Fabienne Wilder is talking about?' He looked at me for confirmation. I nodded and he carried on. 'According to your research, their sites are plastered with swastikas and racist ranting mixed in with the occultist stuff, but then on the other hand there are the real hardcore devil worshippers, too. Is that it in a nutshell?'

'Basically,' I said, nodding. 'Look, this occultist stuff goes back to ancient Egypt and Babylon. It's intertwined throughout history. The Templars used images of the Goat of Mendes in their chapels and the Freemasons teach that Lucifer is the light-bearer, but that doesn't mean that they worship Satan. If you look into it, occultism is older than Christianity.'

'Who says that the Masons are devil worshippers?' Peter asked chirpily.

'Conspiracy theorists will tell you that the Masons are satanic, but if you look into their history, the evidence contradicts that.'

'Good, the governor is a Mason.'

'My dad was a Lodge Master, so I'm pretty sure about that.' I smiled, but the memory of my father tugged at my heart. 'The Niners' are the real thing. Their shit is really off the chart.'

'Fascist devil worshippers?' He shook his head. 'Sounds like bollocks to me.'

'It is bollocks to us. Google it.' I laughed. 'It will take you two minutes to find them.'

'Is the superintendent going to go for that?' Peter frowned again and looked at me in disbelief. 'Sounds like a weird combination.'

'It's true, though,' I explained. 'Tell him to search for them. It will take him thirty seconds to find a page full of them. There are dozens of groups with the same agenda. They're racist, homophobic Satanists, but don't make the mistake of thinking they're thick Nazi thugs stomping around in Dr Marten's boots; far from it. From what I can remember, they boasted some powerful business leaders and politicians as members.'

'And then they became the Niners?'

'They originally called themselves Ophite Cultus Satanas, I think, but then that group either disbanded or went underground because of the attention they were attracting.' I could tell that the name confused Peter. 'Or maybe no one could remember the name,' I joked.

'The Nine Angels and Angles are much more current. They were established in the nineties. They have clandestine groups known as traditional nexions or sinister tribes. Their lingo is quite distinctive, but it struck me how consistent it was.' I shivered as I explained the group to Peter. Something walked over my grave. Peter pulled the Citroën to a halt in an empty parking bay marked 'visitors'. The main entrance door to the apartment block was wedged open and guarded by a uniformed officer. It was, in essence, a huge converted engine shed, and it had retained its historical features while being transformed into a desirable apartment block.

'What do you mean, 'consistent'?'

'The sites which are well developed with tons of information on them all use the same terminology.' I reached for another cigarette as I tried to explain. 'The language they use in their teachings is consistent across the different groups, which tells me that their information comes from the same original source. Does that make sense?'

'Yes.' Peter nodded. 'So, what are they up to then? How do we relate all this to what Fabienne Wilder is saying?'

'That's a question I can't answer.' I shook my head and lit up. Instead of opening the window I opened the door and twisted my body to swing my legs out of the car. 'I remember there were rumours of sexual deviancy, rape and murder during their gatherings. There's a hierarchy within the group and there were helpers, sympathetic to their ideals. They had loose members, or colleagues, who participated in their ceremonies and then there was the upper tier, about which there was little information available for obvious reasons. But I picked all this up from Internet chat linked to the sites. It could be just hearsay.'

'Fabienne mentioned feeders?' he asked. 'You explained that to me, but the boss isn't going to buy that.'

'You're missing the point,' I said.

'Which is what?'

'Your senior officers are reasonable men and women. Will they believe that feeding on the blood of a dying victim will enhance the killer with power and bring them closer to their God?'

'Of course not.'

'Yet Christians take the blood of Christ at communion.' I watched the cogs turning in his mind. 'Explain what it means. Whether they believe it or not is irrelevant. All they need to do is accept that the Niners do.'

'Have you come across any evidence of these groups locally?'

'No, not really. Look, these groups are like ghosts; there are only whispers that they ever existed. Fabienne could be telling the truth that she's innocent or maybe she is involved in some kind of devil worship. Then again, she could be bonkers, right?'

'You said they're racist.'

'They are when it suits them. If they think that someone could be of use to them, then who knows where their prejudice stops and starts.' We walked by other cars as we talked. I noticed that there were some top-of-the-range BMWs parked outside the apartments. The development was fairly new, and they looked expensive. As we reached the foyer, I noticed the ceiling was vaulted and tiled with white squares. 'What happens to Fabienne now?'

'We need to decide if she's crazy or telling the truth.' Peter spoke to the officer at the entrance and then waved me in. 'SOCO have finished; we can take a look.'

Fabienne's apartment was on the ground floor, thirty yards down the corridor from where we were standing. The floors were carpeted with beige cord and the walls were painted in neutral colours, whites and beiges. Peter pushed open the apartment door and we stepped into a hallway which revealed nothing about the person who inhabited it. Peter scanned the hall. 'Looks normal.'

'You sound disappointed,' I said. 'Did you expect pentangles on the floor and reversed crucifixes on the wall?'

'Maybe. Look around, but don't touch anything.' Peter didn't see the humour in my comment. I needed to be normal and make light of things. The morning's events had put me into shock. My head ached and my eyes hurt.

The apartment was spacious. There was a lounge with a small kitchenette at one end and a balcony at the other. The bedroom had a double bed, a dressing table and a chest of drawers. There were fitted wardrobes on the wall opposite the bed. One of the wardrobe doors was open. It was empty. There were no clothes hanging up, no dresses, jackets, skirts, blouses, or shoes. Even the hangers were missing. She had a large television set on the drawers and there was a used cup from McDonald's next to her bed. The whole place was bland and nondescript. If we were to discover anything about Fabienne's personality, then we weren't going to find it here. The place felt like it had been cleansed.

In the living room was a three-piece suite in white leather. The cheap, wooden laminate floor was featureless, and the walls were magnolia. There were no ornaments or photographs. She had no books or DVDs and there were no magazines or personal stuff. The kitchen was new and spotless and looked as if she never used it. The cooker gleamed and the kettle was empty. No one ever switched it on.

'This place looks like a show home,' I said. 'Apart from the coffee cup, there's nothing here.'

'It looks like it's been cleaned recently,' Peter said. 'Sterile.'

'Why would anyone do that?' I asked. I could understand why a gangster, or a hoodlum, would clean a crime scene, but this was a young woman's apartment. What was the point?

'To remove any evidence that Fabienne may have left behind,' Peter shrugged. It was a mystery. 'Maybe she hasn't been here for a while.'

'I can't see how you will learn anything about her unless she tells you herself,' I shrugged. 'You need to get her to talk to you.'

'That's proving impossible at the moment.' Peter opened the bathroom door and revealed more of the same: nothing.

'Look, I know it's a bit odd, but if Fabienne is telling the doctors that she wants to talk to me, why don't you let her?' I looked out of the balcony window at the marina below and wondered how long it would take to fall into the water. Although it was a ground floor flat, the sea was way below the balcony. I have a real fear of heights, so it pops into my mind when I look over the edge of a drop. I don't like driving over bridges or even climbing a ladder. As I looked over the balcony, I decided it would take about four seconds for me to hit the water if I jumped. I wonder what goes through someone's mind when they jump. Do they have second thoughts? I can't imagine being desperate enough to jump. I watched the poor souls trapped in the Twin Towers, faced with the choice of burning to death or jumping to certain death. Can you imagine fate landing you with that choice?

'What do you have in mind?' Peter put his hands in his pockets while he listened to my idea. His trousers had dull patches where they were worn from sitting down and his black shoes were ridiculously shiny. He leant against the doorframe while I spoke.

'I don't have a clue how it would work, but she might talk to me. I know a little bit about satanic cults, maybe she'll open up.' I moved away from the drop. 'What have you got to lose?'

'Well the doctors are getting nowhere. I can ask if we could set up an interview with me as lead detective and you as an observer. Might be worth a go.' He looked me in the eyes, searching for something. Was he looking for my motive? Why would I want to get involved after all the trouble it had caused so far? If he was looking for the answers to those questions, he wouldn't find them because I didn't have them.

Every bone in my body was screaming at me to run a hundred miles an hour in the other direction, but I wanted to talk to her. I wanted to help her. I had another idea, too. I was going to write to Eddie Duncan in prison and ask him if he would speak to me. He was protesting his innocence about the murder of Pauline Holmes, and Fabienne Wilder was equally as adamant that she hadn't murdered Caroline Stokes. The police believed that they were murdered by the same killer, so by hearing his side of the story I may have been able to help Fabienne. I decided not to discuss my idea with Peter, not yet anyway.

'I think it's worth a try. You might not be able to use any of it in court, but at least we could learn about her. It could shine some light on the murder.' I tried to sound convincing.

'I'll make a call and set it up. Are you busy?' He took out his mobile. I shrugged and smiled. What else would I be doing?

CHAPTER 9

Eddie Duncan – Risley Remand Centre

Peter dropped me off at home an hour later, and on our journey, I had casually asked which prison the original suspect was being held in. I think my interest appeared to be innocent and Peter didn't ask any awkward questions. When I got home, Evie Jones made a big fuss and it was a struggle to switch on my laptop and write a quick letter to Eddie Duncan while she was demanding attention. I made it brief and to the point. Fifteen minutes later the letter was posted and on its way to Risley Remand Centre. We were never destined to meet, but he called me from prison.

From talking to Eddie Duncan, I knew that as he sat in his cell, he felt helpless. I knew what it was like to be arrested and locked up for something I hadn't done, so I had sympathy for him as his situation was a thousand times worse. He was looking at a murder charge and he'd already been locked up for over a month. How he coped, I can't imagine. He was a tough man, a survivor from the back streets of Moss Side in Manchester. As a boy he ran with a bad crowd and many of his friends didn't make it to school-leaving age. Some of them were shot dead by the teenage gangs that controlled the drugs in the area, and some of them joined the gangs and ended up in prison.

Eddie was gifted with a good business brain and he realised that running with a gang would never make him wealthy for life. The profits from selling drugs from a gang were huge, but the downsides were numerous and the pension scheme non-existent. He branched out on his own, dealing a few ounces of weed here and there before moving up into the lucrative hard drug market. Hard drugs are chronically addictive and very expensive, and he used the nightclub scene to sell his wares.

He was a good-looking guy with a nice smile and a charming personality to match. Eddie soon had dozens of female customers who needed the drugs but didn't have the money to pay for them. Sex was often the only currency they had. He didn't want sex with most of them and so he turned into a pimp almost by accident. He moved away from the city to Llandudno but kept his business interests separate from his private life. The drugs and prostitution worked side by side, and he made a good living. Pauline Holmes was different, though.

When he met Pauline, she was working near to Piccadilly station on her own. Other working girls often attacked her for straying onto their patch, and without the support of a good pimp she was at their mercy. When Eddie first set eyes on her, her looks stunned him. Much the same as Fabienne had done to me. He approached her and they got chatting. He took her for some food and by the end of the night he'd agreed to look after her. Pauline liked Eddie. She hoped that one day he would tell her to stop working the streets and move in with him. She wanted children, Eddie's children. Eddie wanted her too, except he couldn't ruin his street cred by shacking up with one of his girls.

As he lay in his prison cell, he wished a million times that he had swallowed his pride and taken her off the streets. If he had, she would be alive now and he would be free. He was looking at life in jail until they arrested Fabienne Wilder for a similar murder. Eddie's solicitor jumped on the arrest immediately and there was suddenly a light at the end of the tunnel. If Eddie didn't kill Pauline, then who did? That was the dilemma that the Nine Angels had. Eddie's arrest meant that their involvement would never be investigated. If Eddie was freed the police would reopen the Fabienne Wilder investigation, and that would cause problems for the Niners. Eddie Duncan could not leave prison. I knew that if he was released in the light of new evidence, he would never talk to me on the outside. I didn't realise it then but asking him for that meeting was like signing his death warrant. I may as well have slit his throat with my own hands. Four hours after calling me, he was dead.

CHAPTER 10

Blood Ties

After posting my letter and walking the Staffie, I grabbed a few hours of broken sleep. Peter called me and said that the interview was on and that I had to meet him at Denbigh Hospital as soon as I could. I arrived at the asylum later that day and parked the truck in the same spot as I had on the previous visit. The weather had cleared, and the sun was trying to break through the clouds, though the light was fading as the day came to an end and night-time approached. The building was not as frightening in the daylight, but it still looked like a lunatic asylum. There was an aura of malevolence about it. I think it's the wire and the fences. There's something not right about enclosures built specifically to keep humans in rather than out.

I walked into the reception and waited for Peter. He came from the corridor where the interview rooms were and waved me over.

'Okay, the doctors have agreed to let me talk to her. You're an observer. At the first sign of her being aggressive we pull the plug on the interview, okay?' Peter was talking at a hundred miles an hour. 'Before we begin, I need you to see the pictures of the victim, Caroline Stokes.'

'Why do I need to see them?' I'm not squeamish, but I knew there was a reason why he wanted me to see them before I spoke to Fabienne. I had my own opinion on the subject of her guilt. I could tell by the way he looked at me in her flat that he had concerns about my interest in her. 'Is this to make me realise what a monster she is?' I joked.

'I need you to have no doubt in your mind that she is the chief suspect in a terrible murder,' Peter said with a stern face. Looking back, Peter always exaggerated his facial expressions, like a bad actor in a low-budget soap opera. 'They found her next to the body with the victim's blood all over her face and hands. I need you to remember that when we talk to her.' He opened a door and ushered me into an office which the detectives had borrowed temporarily. There were two other detectives there already and neither of them looked pleased to see me. Both men nodded silently when we entered. I pulled up a chair and sat down.

'Take a good, long look at them.' There were four glossy photographs, each six by five inches. Some were close-ups of the victim's face. She was a pretty girl, but she looked older than her years. Her eyes were blank and staring. There was a savage rent in her throat reaching from her windpipe up to her left ear. I had seen crime scene pictures before, but the victims were anonymous then. This victim seemed different because I was familiar with the case. Knife wounds vary according to the shape and type of blade used. The wounds in the victim's throat were ragged. The edges of the remaining flesh looked ripped and torn rather than cut. Other photographs showed her blood-soaked chest with the satanic symbol etched into it. The murderer had crushed her ribcage. She was wearing a white blouse, a pair of black high-heeled boots, white briefs and bra, a black leather miniskirt and a denim jacket.

'There was hardly any blood left in her body. Pauline Holmes was the same. Now that's not all that surprising considering that they'd been stabbed in the chest and throat, but there wasn't much blood on the ground where we found the body, and like I said, Fabienne's clothes were clean.' Peter tapped the photograph. If things were not so weird, I may have made a vampire jibe, but the demeanour of Peter and his detectives was not akin to making jokes just now.

'Okay, I get the message. I thought suspects were innocent until proven guilty in this country.' I smiled but they did not return it. The detectives looked at me as if I had taken a dump in a church. 'That was a joke.' Nobody laughed.

There was a knock on the door and a guard poked his head around it. 'She's secured in room F. We're ready when you are.'

'Okay, thank you.' Peter tapped me on the arm. 'Let's go. We're on.'

'Nice to meet you,' I said to the detectives as we left. They didn't even look at me. 'Nice to meet you too, Conrad,' I muttered sarcastically.

Peter threw me a withering glance as I followed him out of the room and down the corridor. My heart was racing at the thought of seeing Fabienne again. I wanted to know who she was and what her involvement with the victim was. I was convinced she'd not murdered her. The lights were bright, and I was tired, and I think the adrenalin in my bloodstream made me dizzy. My knees seemed to buckle. I wobbled and shut my eyes, and suddenly I was looking down at the body of the victim, Caroline Stokes. It was as if I was there. Something or someone had taken control of my mind.

She was right there in front of me, looking straight back at me. She was dying, but there was life in her eyes. There was a man kneeling over her, sucking on the wound in her throat. His eyes were dark circles. He turned to me and smiled. Blood ran from his chin and his teeth were smeared red. He beckoned me to drink. He was no vampire from a movie set, nor was he a monster. He was human. He was a feeder. Somewhere in his twisted mind he believed that killing an innocent victim, looking into their eyes as they died and drinking some of their blood would help him to become immortal. I didn't know how I knew, but I did. I have a vivid imagination, all writers do, but this image was as clear as day.

'Are you okay?' Peter's voice interrupted my thoughts. He grabbed my arm and stopped me from toppling over. I felt like I had fallen back into my body and the image was nothing more than a fading memory, like a dream just before you wake up. My head was fuzzy, and I felt weak. The hallucination had left me exhausted.

'Yes, sorry, I was miles away there,' I answered, embarrassed. 'I'm tired. I think this morning is catching up with me.' I felt like a light had switched on in my head, but what could I say to Peter? He is a hardened detective who deals in black and white, guilty or innocent, and I didn't think that telling him I'd just had a hallucination would be the best way to start an interview with a woman who was locked up an asylum. 'I'm just tired and nervous, I think.'

'Are you worried about talking to the girl directly?' Peter asked, concerned.

'Sort of, I'm all right though.' I smiled. I had to talk to her. 'I think we should give it a try.'

'Are you sure you're up to this?' Peter frowned.

'I'm fine.' I nodded and smiled again. This time it was more convincing. Peter opened the door to room F, and we stepped into the small interview room. It was nine feet square, and the floor was covered in brown carpet tiles. The table was bolted to the floor and the only light came from a powerful fluorescent tube, protected by a wire mesh. Inside the room, the two-way mirror was unnerving. Knowing that people were watching your every move from behind it was unsettling. Fabienne was sitting on a chair and her head was on the table, resting on her arm as if she was sleeping. Her wrists were manacled to a thick leather belt around her waist. She raised her head and looked at us when we walked into the room and her face lit up like a Christmas tree.

'I knew you would come. I knew it.' She reached out her hands as far as the straps would allow her to. I smiled back at her nervously. Her eyes held me in a spell. 'The doctor told me all about you. You were here the other night, you're the writer; you've written about them, haven't you? I knew it. I knew I was right.' she babbled excitedly.

I looked at Peter for an explanation. I wasn't happy with too many details being handed to a murder suspect, even if I did think she was innocent.

'The doctor had to apologise for ignoring what Fabienne told him about the observers behind the mirror. He has told her your name and that you are indeed a writer,' he explained. I swallowed hard. My throat was dry and tacky. I tried to smile at Fabienne without looking too concerned that she knew all about me.

'He's a prick. The doctor, I mean, not you,' she said to Peter. 'I knew you were a writer and I got the first letter of your name. I guess things sometimes; sometimes I know things that I shouldn't. I don't know how I know them, but I do.' Fabienne giggled. Her black eyes sparkled. 'You look a little shocked; maybe even a bit scared.'

'I'm okay. I'm tired, that's all.'

'No, there's something else in your eyes.' She frowned and stared into me. Her expression changed to one of realisation. 'You saw him, didn't you? I know you saw him.' She pointed to my head. 'I was thinking about him and you saw him too.'

'Who did I see?' I asked. She stopped smiling immediately. Her expression darkened.

'Don't treat me as if I'm stupid, Conrad. The doctor doesn't understand me, but you do. You do because you have an imagination.' She leaned forward and lowered her voice. 'We are similar, you and me. You see imaginary things in your mind, whereas I see things that are real, and I know you saw him, but we see them.' She pointed to her head again. 'You saw him in your head, didn't you?'

'Okay, I understand what you're saying, but I'm not sure what is real and what isn't. My imagination is working overtime today. Things have been a little strange, so forgive me if I seem confused.' I smiled at her.

'You have a nice smile.'

'Thank you.' I blushed.

'You definitely saw him, didn't you?' She lowered her head and looked up at me with those eyes. It was as if she was looking into my mind for the answer.

'Yes, I saw him,' I replied.

'Wait a minute. Who did you see, exactly?' Peter asked, confused.

'He saw the feeder; the man who killed Caroline Stokes.' She looked Peter in the eye. She seemed to be as sane as the next person was.

'You saw the man who killed Caroline Stokes?' Peter asked, incredulous.

'I didn't kill her, he did.'

'When did you see him?' Peter emphasised the word 'when' and sounded very sceptical as he looked at me.

'Just now, in the corridor,' I confessed. 'I thought it was the memory of the photographs replaying in my mind or my imagination playing tricks until Fabienne asked me about it.'

'Really, and now what do you think it was?' He raised his eyebrows.

'It was your imagination,' Fabienne butted in. 'But this time you imagined the truth. You saw what really happened not a story.'

'Okay, if you believe I saw him, describe him to me.' I wanted to know if she really knew what I had seen in my mind. I'm as sceptical as the next man when it comes to things like visions or premonitions. People with the power to speak to the spirits of the dead are something that I cannot accept easily, although the weight of evidence would suggest that there is something to it. I can't explain it and I can't understand it, therefore it's not true. My sister, Libby, is a medium and she knows things about our late father that she shouldn't know. He didn't bring her up and she had no contact with him from about the age of six, but she knows things about him that that I can't fathom.

'Wait a minute,' Peter interrupted. 'Write down what you think you saw on here.' He passed me a pen and a sheet of paper and I scribbled three lines on it. Peter looked at it, making sure that Fabienne couldn't see it. 'Okay, Fabienne, what did he see?'

She didn't hesitate. 'He saw a man in a grey suit feeding on her. He was bald on top with grey hair around the sides and he wore a blue tie with a horse on it.' She smiled at me because she knew it would shock me. 'The horse was rearing-up. Am I right, Conrad?'

'I didn't see colours, Fabienne,' I answered, after glancing at Peter for permission to reply. 'I saw a bald man in a pale suit and tie, but I didn't see any colours. I saw it in black and white.'

'Some people only see shades. He was feeding though, right?' She leant her head to the side childishly.

'Yes,' I answered.

'Was she still alive?' Fabienne asked quietly.

'I think so,' I whispered.

'That's what they do, you see.' She turned to Peter as if he needed an explanation. 'They believe the ultimate thrill is to look into their victim's eyes as they die. They capture their soul, their strength and life force.'

'What is a feeder, Fabienne?' I asked. I didn't know how long Peter was going to go along with this, so I wanted answers to the questions that we had asked ourselves repeatedly.

She looked down at her hands and her mind seemed to drift away. When she looked up at me again, she had tears in her eyes.

'What do you know about the Nine Angels? I know that you wrote some stuff about them in one of your books, that's why I recognised your name. They've talked about you before, you see. They hate you because your book caused them problems. But what do you really know?'

'I know they were a satanic cult,' I shrugged. 'And I know they were fascists and that they were founded by important people.'

'Why do you say 'were', past tense?' Fabienne asked seriously.

'Because I believe the founder renounced the organisation, moved to Canada and they disbanded,' I answered. I wasn't sure if that was the truth, but I wanted her to tell me about them, not the other way around. I didn't want to give her anything she could twist into a story. 'Am I wrong, are they still a functioning organisation?'

'They are very much a functioning organisation.' She looked at me with teary eyes. 'There are millions of them and they're everywhere. They go under many different names and guises, but they are the same.'

'They began as different groups, though?'

'Oh yes, many different groups.' She smiled again. 'Some are idiots looking for something different in their sad, mundane lives, but some of them are very real and very dangerous. The Nine 'Angles' were real and then the Nine Angels broke away from them.'

'Why?' Her use of the word 'mundane' hadn't gone amiss, although it didn't register with Peter.

'Power.'

'I'm sorry, I don't follow.'

'The founder of the Angles left for America, where people are easier to find, if you know what I mean.'

'Not really.'

'They need followers to join their sinister and they need the mundane to sacrifice and feed on.'

'The mundane being anyone not in the group, yes?'

'Sort of.'

'Do they worship Satan?' I asked. Some experts that said the Nine Angels were a Gnostic religion, not devil worshippers, but their websites told me a different story.

'Yes, they worship Satan, sex, violence, and money. They believe humanity is heading for extinction on this planet and that their beliefs will make the shapeshifters and planet-jumpers take them with them. They have a different way of life,' Fabienne began.

'Shapeshifters and planet-jumpers?' I looked at Peter briefly. He rolled his eyes towards the ceiling. Satanic cults were difficult enough to believe, but planet-jumpers and shapeshifters were too far from his reality to entertain. 'Let's say Peter and I don't accept that side of things. We need to know about what the human members are doing.'

'Trying not to be human, basically.' She laughed.

'What do you mean?'

'You must see how those spoilt little bitches go mad for the *Twilight* vampire and his nemesis the werewolf? Their panties are wet for them.' She made her fingers into a claw shape and laughed. 'They want a real handsome bloodsucker to fuck them and change them into immortals, don't they?'

'I suppose they do, in a romantic way.'

'These people have the same desire. They want to be more than human, and they genuinely believe that they are, too. Some of them are.'

'Tell us about it.' I sat back fascinated by her eyes and her voice. I didn't know whether what she was saying was true. It didn't matter to me. There was an underlying truth in her analysis of the human mind. 'How will the things they do here, save them?'

'The Nine Angels believe civilisation as we know it will end in a world war, centred in the Middle East.'

'Like in the 'Book of Revelations'?' I asked.

'Yes. They think the world will go to war over oil and the West will grind to a halt. Anarchy will reign and only the organised will survive. That's what they do. They organise. They're building a global network so huge they'll be able to rule when Armageddon comes. They'll use the mundane as slaves and treat them like sheep waiting for the slaughter. The feeders think human blood will take them to another level and bring them closer to dharmakaya.'

'What are feeders for, exactly?' I repeated the question. I could understand the concept so far, but not all of it. I hadn't heard the word dharmakaya before in any of my research. I had no idea what dharmakaya was. I had to pick it apart one thing at a time.

'Feeders are trusted by the nexion to which they belong. They have proven themselves to be trustworthy by embracing the sinister and living by its code. Sacrifice and blood, enables them to be taken to the next level.'

'What was that word you used, 'dharmakaya'?' I pretended not to remember it properly to prompt an explanation.

'it's the meaning of cosmic evil. As some believe in an almighty good, they believe in an evil which runs throughout the universe.'

'And if they gain the trust of their nexion?'

'They promise all the pleasures that society finds taboo. Sex with anyone you want, no matter what their age or if they're consensual. They practice indulgence, not abstinence. They give money and power in return for loyalty. They do not tolerate other cultures or religions, and they encourage the ultimate sin: murder. The feeders are the members they use to assassinate those who get in the way of their plans. They kill their victims and drain their blood. They do it for effect to frighten others. That's how they maintain their secrecy.' She pressed her finger to her lips and made a gentle *sshhh* noise.

'Do you believe that?' Peter asked.

'Do you?' Fabienne snapped her reply.

'Of course not.' Peter sounded flustered. This was not the type of interview that he was used to. 'It's the biggest load of crap I've ever heard.'

'Are you a Christian, Sergeant?' She tilted her head and looked into his eyes.

'Yes, sort of.'

'Then you will know that the Lord God accepted human sacrifice from the Jews.' She smiled. 'In the 'Old Testament', the 'Book of Judges', the Israelite warrior Jephthah is about to set off to make war on the Ammonites. In payment for victory, Jephthah promises God he'll sacrifice the first 'whatsoever' that comes from his house to greet him upon his return. His daughter greeted him first.'

'What has that got to do with anything?' Peter snorted.

'I'm trying to explain to you that human sacrifice to whichever god you believe in is as old as the hills.'

'So, do you believe that their sacrifices and rituals are acceptable?'

'No, don't be ridiculous,' she said sharply. 'They're perverts who justify their behaviour by saying that they believe. I'm giving it to you from their perspective. They farm us for their rituals.'

'What do you mean?' I asked. All of a sudden, she was associating herself as a victim. I'd believed all along that she was innocent and now she gave me something to latch on to.

'They groom us as children. They scour the care homes, correction facilities, special schools, and hospitals for potential prey.' She made her fingers into claws and laughed. 'They groom children to take to their little services. They groom the children for their orgies, and when they grow up, they become like them.'

'Did they groom you?' I felt sick inside. I can't abide paedophiles. I would gladly put a bullet into the back of their head rather than release them from prison. 'Were you involved in their rituals?'

'Yes, from a very young age. They had some of my brothers and sisters too. We were all in care, you see,' she replied calmly. Her eyes reflected the sadness inside her as she thought about her siblings. I wanted to hold her tight and keep her safe. "They're intelligent people with normal personas. They do not walk around with horns on their heads or tridents in their hands.'

'They befriended you first?' I asked the obvious, but I wanted every detail.

'Yes, of course.' Fabienne frowned. 'Do you think we would have let them abuse us just because they wanted to?'

'No,' I stammered, embarrassed by my clumsy question. 'Who were these people, Fabienne?'

'I don't know their real names.'

'Where are they, then?' I wanted them locked up. 'Tell us where they are.'

Peter kicked me under the table. He was investigating Fabienne on suspicion of murder and I was trying to find out who had allegedly abused her. She could have been making it all up, but I doubted it. He wanted me to steer the conversation back to the murder.

'Let's get back on track. You said the feeder killed Caroline Stokes,' Peter asked impatiently. He was annoyed. She'd hypnotised me to the point that I had forgotten he was there.

'They did.' A tear ran from her eye and rolled down her cheek.

'How do you know?' Peter pressed.

'They wanted me to become a feeder because I see things, but I refused.' She tried to wipe her eye, but the straps held her. I took a tissue from a box on the table and leant over. As I wiped her eye, she smiled. She was no killer. I could see a little lost girl in there behind the mask. 'They have controlled me all my life, but I refused to join them completely and so they killed her.'

'They killed Caroline as a warning to you?' I asked.

'No, she was sport.' She turned to Peter defiantly. 'I saw the mark on her. She was cut with the culling mark, wasn't she?'

Peter didn't answer her question. 'Are you telling me that this cult, the Nine Angels, murdered Caroline Stokes as a warning to you?'

'No, you idiot.'

'Then who did they kill as a warning and why?' Peter asked angrily.

'They didn't want me to run away and follow her.' She sounded like a little girl. Another tear ran from her eye and trickled down her cheek.

'Follow who?' I asked.

'Pauline Holmes,' she sobbed, and her voice broke. Peter looked at me and raised his eyes to the ceiling as if he didn't believe her. Then she dropped a bombshell: 'Pauline Holmes was my younger sister.'

CHAPTER 11

The Order of Nine Angels

When I left the asylum, I headed home in a state of shock. Fabienne had remained rational throughout the interview and the information she gave us was mind-blowing. If it was true, then organised evil really did exist on our doorstep. I wasn't sure back then how much credence I should give to the Niners, but now I've no doubt in my mind that they're powerful and dangerous. I listened to Fabienne with an open mind, knowing she may be delusional but not believing that she was a killer. After speaking to her and listening to her story, I was convinced that she was both innocent and sane.

Peter followed me home and we arrived at the same time as my partner. She'd finished a long day at the office and seemed surprised to see Peter. They'd worked together many years before. She looked smart in her business attire, both professional and attractive. Her long dark hair was pulled back from her face and fastened in a bobble at the back. All the reasons that I was with her flooded back to me in a wave of emotions, tinged with sadness because I hadn't tried as hard as I should have to keep the relationship alive. I had taken her for granted for far too long.

'Hello, Peter.' She smiled. 'Is he in trouble again?' she added, eyeing me coolly. My night in the cells had not been explained away yet and she wanted answers.

'No, it was all a misunderstanding.' Peter patted my back again and I winced with pain. 'Conrad is helping me with a case. It's all above board, honestly. He gets to follow an investigation and I get to pick his brains.'

'I see.' She walked in through the side gate and upstairs to the flat without saying a word to me. 'You'd better be careful what you pick from his brains because I don't know what's been going on in there lately. His head is full of nonsense'

Peter looked at me and grimaced at the dig, which had been aimed at me. 'Look, if you're going to have a domestic, I'll leave it until tomorrow if you like. Do you need some time alone?'

'She'll be fine,' I whispered, so that she couldn't hear me. If the truth be known, I thought that his presence would avert any fireworks, for a while anyway. We followed her into the flat and I closed both front doors behind us, ensuring that Evie Jones didn't bolt for the beach in all the excitement. She didn't know who to say hello to first, running from one person to the other, her claws skidding on the laminate, trying to find purchase.

'Are you setting up your laptop?' she shouted from the kitchen.

'Yes, we'll be in the dining room if that's okay,' I replied, making a fuss of the Staffie. 'Come through here.' I invited Peter into the back room.

Peter followed me into the dining room, which led off the hallway. It was a through room which led into the kitchen. A large picture window looked out onto the mountain, and the long oak dining-room table, which we never dined on, took up the centre space and doubled as a desk. We used to eat there in the early years of dating and share our tales of the day at work over a bottle of wine. It had been a long time since we had done that, and a twinge of guilt gripped me. I spent too long working or on the golf course and in the pub nowadays.

'Do you want a beer while you work?' she called.

'Yes please.'

She walked in and plonked two bottles of Bud on the table. 'I'm going to have a shower and clear some e-mails,' she half smiled at me. 'I presume you'll be sleeping at home tonight or are you planning on assaulting anyone else?'

'Yes, I'll be sleeping here.' I smiled back, although another spike of guilt stabbed me. I've been a fighter all my life, and I'll be the first to admit there have been occasions where I've used my fists first and ended up in trouble. She hated that side of me. The truth hurts sometimes. 'I'll explain everything later as best as I can.'

'You better had.' She left and I could hear her padding up the hallway with the Staffie bouncing along behind her.

'Sounds like you're in trouble.' Peter winked.

'I'm always in trouble,' I replied, swigging half the Bud in one go. 'It's the secret of a good relationship.'

I fired up the laptop and began searching for information. We talked in hushed voices as my partner worked in the next room. I didn't want her frightened by what had happened over the last forty-eight hours. We found page after page of satanic blurb and I tried to explain their mindset to Peter in the space of a few hours.

'Here, listen to this.' I pointed to the screen. 'They call themselves the Drecc, followers of sinister and occult rules and laws. They live by their own laws and we, the mundane, are nothing more than the cattle they prey on. Our belongings are theirs to take and our lives are theirs to extinguish any time they please.' We looked at each other and I could tell from his expression that he still thought it was nonsense. One site explained the history of the Nine Angels and it was just as I'd explained it to Peter earlier. I let him read it and digest the information.

'You can see from this that the Nine Angels is the most important British, neo-Nazi, satanic order currently still communicating on the Internet. I say British because there are thousands of foreign sects with similar methodologies, but their sites are based here. I can tell from the English that they're here in this country.'

'How can you tell the difference?'

'Look how they spell *colour*. The Americans spell it *c o l o r*.'

'I get it.'

'Look here. It says that the 'Angles' formed as a fusion of three other satanic orders: Camlad, the Noctulians, and the Temple of the Sun. The order presents Satanism as a path of self-overcoming in a chaotic, amoral universe. The Satanists must break through their own mortal limitations through acts considered illegal and evil, including murder, to expose them to the 'acausal'.' I looked at Peter to see if he was following me.

'What's the 'acausal'?' He obviously wasn't.

'The acausal are the sinister magical forces which give unknown strength and power to the achievers.'

'Sounds like crystal meth,' he joked.

'Here's the hierarchy. There are seven degrees of rank: Neophyte, Initiate, External, Internal, Master of the Temple, Magus, and Immortal. Now, Anton LaVey was a Magus because he founded the Church of Satan. Obviously, an Immortal is the next step up the ladder.'

'What, like *Highlander*?' Peter scoffed. He was taking the piss because he didn't understand or didn't want to understand. But the facts were there to see. The information backed up everything Fabienne had told us and more.

As the reader you must be sceptical too. Google those right now if you don't believe me and you will be amazed at what these crazies think. The problem is, they're not wrinkled old crones dancing around a boiling cauldron, making up spells. They're intelligent, articulate people. They're lawyers, bankers, judges, police officers, soldiers, doctors, and nurses. They're everywhere you go, and they are in the millions, watching and waiting, killing and feeding, but always in the shadows.

'See here how they encourage their members to act independently and to use society's frailties to cover their activities.' I pointed to a chapter ahead of where he was. 'Do you know how many people go missing every year? Well, so do they, and what if they use that fact to select prey?'

'I don't follow you.' Peter took a mouthful of beer and shook his head.

'Read this,' I said, taking a slurp of cold beer. I read it out to him so that I could be sure that he understood the magnitude of the issue. 'In 1988 the British Press began to carry allegations that children were being sexually abused and murdered by secret organisations during rituals variously known as black magic, witchcraft or Satanism.

At an international conference, the founder of a British children's charity expressed her belief that up to 4000 children a year were being sacrificed in Great Britain alone. British psychiatrist, Norman Vaughton, was reported as saying that there were over 10,000 cases a year in the United States. The Adam Walsh centre in the US claimed that there were over 10,000 children involved in demonic cult activities and over 200 unsolved murders attributed to satanic cults. *The Times* (Gledhill 1990) asserted that there was proof of an international conspiracy involving thousands of similar cults.'

'Fucking hell.' Peter frowned and shook his head in disbelief. I googled the original reports and the links that came up were endless. You can find them in seconds, try it. 'I can't get my head around this,' Peter said.

'Is it really that surprising?' I asked. 'We both know that thousands of normal people go missing every month, right?'

'Right.' Peter shrugged. 'Our missing person teams are deluged with cases. You're not going to tell me that the Nine Angels are taking them all, are you?'

'No, but where do they all go?' I looked at him and smiled. 'Are they all living in cardboard boxes under the railway arches or pushing shopping trolleys around, pissed out of their skulls?'

'No, I didn't say that.' Peter sounded offended. 'Some people just choose to drop off the radar.'

'What, all of them?' I asked incredulously. 'I've done a lot of research into the number of missing people every year and they can't all just disappear. Maybe they're cattle. Picked and slaughtered by the dark ones, the feeders.' It was my turn to make my hands into claw shapes and I pulled my lips back to expose my incisors. 'Seriously though, hundreds of them must wind up dead. Where else can all those people be?'

'This is crazy,' Peter said, reading some of the information we had found. 'How the hell do they get away with posting this stuff?'

'You're the policeman, you tell me.' I finished my beer and walked into the kitchen. 'Do you want another one?'

'One more. I'm driving, remember.'

I nodded and drank my new beer as I walked back to the table. 'Can I talk this through with you, because I want to know that you fully understand what they're all about. I know it's difficult; sometimes I can't get it straight in my own mind,' I said.

'I'm listening.' He frowned and looked offended. I wasn't insulting his intelligence; I was questioning his ability to be open-minded.

'Fabienne was talking about human sacrifice as if it happens every week. She said she'd seen dozens of people sacrificed.' I drank again and the beer hardly touched the sides. Evie Jones bounded down the stairs and skidded through the door, running right past me on the way to the dog flap in the kitchen.

Peter laughed and looked confused. 'Where's she off to?'

'She's sensed someone walking their dog past the flat. She'll bounce off the fence and frighten the life out of them until she's sure they're gone.'

'She's a good guard dog, I bet.'

'She is indeed.' We laughed, not realising how good she would prove to be. 'Look, when Fabienne said that the Niners regularly murdered people I was sceptical, but everything she said was plausible, even if it was shocking.' Peter nodded silently in agreement. 'Who wouldn't be sceptical until you really see the proof? Would you believe millions of people were exterminated in the Nazi death camps unless you had seen the bodies on television? I doubt if I would. I would think that the numbers had been exaggerated but the evidence is clear.'

'I see your point. I remember hearing something on the news about a lake in Africa somewhere that was so full of human bodies that the water had been poisoned and all the fish had died.' He was recalling the story of the Tutsi massacres. 'I didn't believe that until I saw a film crew reporting with actual footage of the bodies in the lake. Like you just said, I wouldn't have believed it unless I'd seen that documentary.'

'There you go.' I raised my bottle and we clinked them. 'It's the stuff of nightmares and horror books until you see it with your own eyes, and then it becomes real.'

'Do you believe her?' Peter looked tired. Dark circles sat beneath his eyes. He drained his beer and went to the fridge for another one for me. I'd finished it without stopping for breath.

'Yes, I do.' I took the full bottle from him and drank greedily. My throat was still sore from the pepper spray. 'I don't know why, but I think she's telling the truth.'

'I think that she believes what she's telling us is true, and there's a big difference,' Peter said. 'But I also believe that she's deranged and delusional. This satanic order stuff is nonsense. I'm sorry but I just can't accept it. They may well exist, and I believe what you have told me from your research, but I still believe that she killed that woman in the park and I think she's manufacturing the whole thing to avoid prison.'

I felt totally deflated. I thought he was on the same wavelength as me, but I had read it all wrong.

'You told me I could never be a police officer because I'm too soft, right?' Disappointedly, I emptied my beer in two slugs.

'Right.' Peter guzzled his and went back to the fridge. 'I think I'll risk another.'

'Well, you could never be a writer because your imagination doesn't stretch far enough. Where do you think all this stuff has come from?' I pointed to the screen. 'Look at all these websites. They're not all created by one little computer troll off his head on acid.'

'Okay, let's say I'm keeping my mind open for a moment.' He twisted the top from his bottle with strong, gnarled hands. 'But my opinion hasn't changed a bit.'

'Well, imagine she is telling the truth. Imagine they do scour care homes for vulnerable children. Imagine they do worship the dark arts and they do sacrifice humans. You have two dead bodies in the morgue that back up her story. Look at the pictures of their injuries. They were slashed and torn apart; no knife made those neck wounds on its own. They were carved with demonic signatures.'

'Maybe, but until we can prove that Pauline Holmes is her sister, the story is a nonstarter for me.'

'Look at her eyes. We both said they had the same eyes before we knew any of this, right?' I insisted. He didn't want to believe it because it was too scary. 'They even look alike physically.'

'They do look like sisters; I'll give you that. I'm being sceptical, Conrad, because in my experience of interviewing murderers, they tend to tell lies and make up stories.' He shrugged. Evie Jones rattled through the flap and made a beeline for me. She jumped up at me and bit my hand gently, mouthing the skin. It was obvious that the danger from the passing dog-walker had subsided and she was letting me know that we were now safe.

'What if it's all true?' I sighed and swigged my beer. 'She said that the temple leaders gain strength from human sacrifice and that they aim to become 'Immortals', the highest degree that they can reach.'

'I'm not following you.'

'Read this bit here. It's a set of instructions on how to carry out a ritual sacrifice. People are being slaughtered by these lunatics.' He couldn't believe what he was reading, but it was there in front of him. 'Read it carefully because it's there. You can't ignore this.'

'Do you really believe in Satan?' Peter hiccupped and shook his head. The beer was beginning to get to him.

'I believe in evil. Just watch the news and you see it every day.' I flicked down the page and saw a link relevant to my point. 'Listen to this.' I clicked on the link and began to read the information. 'In ceremonial rituals involving sacrifice, the Mistress of Earth usually takes on the role of the violent goddess, Baphomet.' I looked at Peter. He was listening intently. 'It sounds like they're publishing a recipe for soup, it's so blasé.'

'What kind of women get into this shit?' Peter grunted.

'Evil ones or women who are coerced into joining in.' I slurred a little on the word 'coerced'. 'Listen to this shit: The Master of the

Temple takes on the role of either Lucifer or Satan. They regard the sacrifice as a gift to the Prince of Darkness. This gift, however, can be offered to the dark goddess, the bride of our Prince,' I continued. 'They're talking about the sacrifice as if it isn't a person. Human life means nothing to them. Now that makes them dangerous.'

I remember our conversation that night as if it was yesterday, and I can also remember how frustrating it was trying to get Peter onside. I realised that night as we researched the subject that we had stumbled on a minefield. 'Listen to me, O9A and their followers believe that the act of human sacrifice manufactures powerful magic. The ritual death of an individual does two things: it releases energy and it draws down dark forces or 'entities' to them.'

'Now you're asking me to believe in a load of old bollocks.' Peter scowled and shook his head. 'It draws down dark forces?' he scoffed. 'Where, from Mars, Jupiter, or the planet Zog?'

Evie waddled off because she wasn't the centre of attention. I heard her sigh as she marched up the stairs to seek it elsewhere. 'You're missing my point completely.' I raised my hands to my head in frustration. 'It isn't that long ago that people believed their Gods lived on Mount Olympus and shaped their fate by playing chess. The Egyptians buried slaves alive to look after their dead masters on the other side. The Norsemen thought thunder was made by Thor smashing his hammer against the clouds. The fact is that they believed what they were told to believe.'

'No, I'm not missing the point.' Peter was sticking to his guns stubbornly. He pointed to the laptop. 'Some of it I can just about swallow, but that stuff about dark entities is a load of old bollocks.'

'You're right, Peter,' I nodded and stared into his eyes. 'You're right, it's a load of old bollocks and we both know that but – and here is the point, listen carefully.'

'I'm listening.'

'We know that killing people to release dark magic is bollocks, but these sad, silly, demented fuckers believe that it does.' I banged the table. 'Do you get it?' Peter looked at me blankly. 'They believe that killing people makes them powerful and magical because their teachings here on the laptop right in front of us – their Bible, their Koran, their encyclopaedia of evil knowledge – tells them that it does, get it?'

Peter coughed and cleared his throat. 'Of course, I get that bit, but that's why I think Wilder is delusional.' Although he pretended that he understood my point all along, his facial expression told me different. It was as if a light had come on inside his brain. 'It's just hard to accept that thousands of people actually follow this shit.'

'Why, when millions of people like me and you go to church every Sunday believing that it will give them eternal life?' I stood up and walked to the window. 'Do you think your local vicar will live forever?'

'Of course, not.' Peter looked away sulkily.

'Do you believe that devout Muslims go to a place where they're surrounded by virgins?' I turned and stared at him.

'No, of course I don't.'

'Well, three-quarters of the planet think that they will and they're prepared to go to war and sacrifice their lives for their beliefs, and a shitload more are christened and live by the Bible because they all believe in some form of religious shit.' I laughed and finished another bottle. 'Now you tell me who is talking a load of old bollocks, Peter.' He looked at me blankly. 'Go on, you tell me who is telling the truth, then. The Christians, the Muslims, the Jews, or the Nine Angels? They can't all be telling the truth, so who exactly is talking bollocks then?'

'All of them.' Peter finished his beer and laughed. 'Okay, so you think that there is something in this then?' He pointed to the Niners website again. 'Convince me.'

'Are you two arguing?' I was so lost in making my point that I hadn't heard my partner coming down the stairs. 'You haven't got him onto religion, have you?' She rolled her eyes at Peter. She'd showered and changed, and she was wearing baby pink house pants and one of my old shirts. Her hair hung loose in all its shining glory and the smell of Armani 'She' followed her into the kitchen along with Evie Jones in tow. 'Don't mind me, I'm just getting a coffee and then I'll be out of your way.'

'I'll have one too, please,' Peter called. 'So, will he. He's getting a bit argumentative after a few beers.'

'I'm not arguing.' I sat down, exhausted from the day. 'I'm trying to show you that there are other points of view to consider.'

'There are always other points of view to consider, Peter,' she said sarcastically from the kitchen. I could hear the chink of cups and the kettle boiling. 'You have to remember that the most important one is his.'

Peter grimaced again and smiled. 'Come on then, tell me what you think.'

'I don't know what to say apart from keep an open mind,' I began. 'I'm not religious but I've always wanted to go to Jerusalem. When I got there, I realised what an amazing place it is. Don't get me wrong, most of it is a shit-hole, but it has major religious significance to the three mainstream faiths; Christianity, Judaism, and Islam.'

'What has that got to do with it?' Peter moaned.

'What was it like there, in Jerusalem?' I shouted to my girlfriend.

'It was amazing, he's right about that,' she backed me up.

'The history there is almost comical. The Muslims built their mosque, the Dome of the Rock, on top of the Wailing Wall to piss the Jews off, and then they sealed up the Golden Gate and buried their dead in front of it to stop the Messiah entering the city, all because the scriptures said that's where he would arrive. Millions have died there fighting for that city, before the Crusades and since. Why?'

'You tell me.'

'Well, they must have believed that the son of God could actually return from the dead as the scriptures foretold. They believe, Peter, and that's the point, they truly believe.'

'So why did you go there, then, if you think it's all bollocks?' My partner plonked two cups of steaming hot coffee onto the table, kissed me on the forehead and disappeared up the stairs again with the Staffie panting after her.

'Curiosity, Peter.' I shrugged. 'I've always been interested in religious iconology and religious wars. I wanted to see what all the fuss was about.'

'Were you disappointed?'

'No, quite the opposite.' I gave a wry smile. 'It's one of my favourite places ever.'

'You talk in riddles sometimes.'

'I went to the Wailing Wall and touched it. I wrote a wish and rolled up a tiny piece of paper and placed it with the millions of other wishes that are stuffed between the huge building blocks, and then I visited the Church of the Holy Sepulchre. The rock where Jesus was crucified is in there and you can queue up to touch it.'

'Did you?'

'Yes, behind a line of tiny nuns and priests from all over the Christian world. I put my hand into the hole and touched the rock where they crucified the son of God.'

'And what happened?'

'Nothing.' I laughed. 'There was no epiphany or lightning bolts, but I'll tell you something about the city. There is an electric atmosphere there. You can feel it everywhere. I can't explain it, but there is an energy there which all three faiths will claim belongs to their God. There is something that we can't explain emanating from every brick and stone.'

'Did you use the 'force', Luke?'

'Piss off.' I laughed again. 'I don't do religion, but scientists know that certain things in nature can absorb energy, such as crystals and batteries, right?'

'Now you're talking my language.'

'Do you remember vinyl records?'

'Just about, although I'm not as old as you.'

'Well, I think that certain elements retain echoes of the past within them, just like a vinyl record does, except, rather than a stylus needle picking it up, some people's minds do it. When they see a vision it's a replay in their mind, and I think that the same thing happens with these forces or energies. They're all around us, but some people feel them, and some people don't.'

'I can accept that as a theory.' Peter smiled and slurped his coffee. 'So, you think that there is good energy and evil energy?'

'No, I don't.' I laughed at his confusion. 'I believe that there is energy around us and that it's people who are good or evil. They use the energy to suit them. The followers of Satan believe the evil force released in a murder can be absorbed by the killer, like a vinyl record absorbs music.'

'That makes sense to a degree, but I'm not going to get it by the governor.' Peter paged down on the laptop and clicked on a subsection entitled 'enemies'.

'Listen to this. This is really interesting.' He nudged me. The piece related to sacrificing enemies and specifically mentioned journalists and writers. 'For Satanists, not only the manner of living is important, but also the manner of your death. We will not tolerate the writers who interfere with our work. We will eradicate them. We must live well and die at the right time, proud and defiant to the end – not waiting to become sickly and weak. If you find them, kill them. The mundane scum of the earth wail and tremble as they face death: we stand laughing and spit with contempt at those that mock us or seek to expose us. Thus, do we learn how to live, and when we find them, they will learn the pain of death.' He looked at me and grinned. 'That's you fucked, then.'

'It's no idle threat.'

'They're crackpots,' Peter gasped.

'Yes, but they're real,' I insisted as I read on. 'Listen to this piece about killing writers and journalists. Fabienne said they hated writers, didn't she?'

'Yes, she did say that. This is getting weirder.' Peter frowned. 'Go on, then. Read it.'

'Great care is needed in choosing a sacrifice: if the object being disposed of is a difficult individual or individuals, then they must be disposed of without arousing undue suspicion. A temple or group wishing to conduct such a sacrifice with magical intent must first obtain permission from the Grand Master or Grand Lady Master. If this is given, then detailed preparation must begin.'

'Do-it-yourself sacrifices?' Peter scoffed.

'It's a 'how to' guide for selecting a victim.'

'They're fucking nuts.'

'Listen, though.' I held up a finger and read on. "First, choose the sacrifice, those whose removal will actively benefit the Satanist cause. If candidates are zealous, interfering Nazarenes, for example journalists and writers, attempting to disrupt us in some way, then they must suffer horrific pain. Use sacrifice to protect established Satanist groups and orders. Find them and kill them.' I made the claw hands again, although the chapter disturbed me. I tried to make light of it. 'Doesn't look good for me, then.'

'I can't believe this is on the Internet.' Peter shook his head in disbelief. 'I'm going to look into getting this site blocked. That has to be illegal.'

'I haven't got a clue about the legalities, but it's frighteningly close to what she said.' I looked at him for agreement, but he was having none of it.

'She could have read the same shit that you have.'

'Fabienne said they hated writers before we read any of this. This backs up her story, Pete.' I appealed to him to keep an open mind. 'Either she has done a lot of research or she was a witness to their meetings.' I was adamant she was a victim, not a murderer. They'd abused her from a young age. They were monsters and I was going to help her. At least that's what I thought then; of course, all I did was make things worse.

CHAPTER 12

Constable Knowles – 6540

Back then I didn't know why Constable Knowles had targeted me. Since then I've had time to look at his police records and to listen to the recordings that he made. I'll explain them as best as I can because his fate was forged by his own hands, not mine, although I don't think that a Crown Court judge would see it that way. They will say that I went too far or that I used excessive force. I'll let you decide.

Ged Knowles joined the police force four years before our first encounter. He attended the police training academy at Bruche, Warrington, where his employee records show that he was unpopular with the instructors and the recruits. His probationary notes show that he was recommended as a fail and yet he passed and was deployed onto the streets. Every note on his file shows that he was an unpopular, racist, sexist pig, yet his superior officer waived disciplinary action on numerous occasions. When he attacked me, he was already on his final written warning for misconduct; being suspended for excessive use of force during my arrest and a pending serious assault charge would be the final nails in his coffin as far as his career went. At least that's what I thought at the time.

Soon after graduating, another police officer had introduced him to the Nine Angels purely because, after spending many long night shifts in the same patrol car, he saw that Knowles was naturally violent, racist and sexist. His colleague teased him with tidbits of his secret organisation to test the waters and see what his reaction would be. As soon as he mentioned their liberal attitude to violent sex, Knowles wanted in. Over a period of months, the officer weaned him into the O9A. Once he'd been accepted, they regularly attended their ceremonics, which turned into a seething orgy of violent sex. That suited him down to the ground. Ged thought the religious stuff was bullshit, but he went along with it for obvious reasons.

When he joined the Nine Angels, they promised him a promotion at work and a pay rise, and all he had to do in return was lean on people when he was told to. People like me, writers, journalists and other police officers; people who got too close to the Nine Angels. He was a violent, aggressive, bigot anyway so he enjoyed it. The problem was, the O9A demanded secrecy and discretion, especially the senior members that held important positions in respectable organisations and businesses. Most had families and friends who would disown them if they discovered their true religion. Ged Knowles was in serious trouble at work. His position as a police constable was fragile at best. The fact he'd received a final written warning months before – for assaulting a reporter while off duty on a night out in Manchester – didn't help, and his excessive use of force during my arrest had put his behaviour under the microscope.

He was suspended on full pay and I heard later on, that he was calling in favours from members of the senior hierarchy within the force. There were sinister members all the way up to the top, but they didn't want to cover for a rogue officer who had overstepped the mark in public. He was making waves, attracting attention, and becoming a liability. The North Wales Police were keeping a lid on the incident as far as the Press were concerned, but I wasn't. Despite being warned that I may still be charged with the mysterious assault on the beach warden, I told my side of the story to anyone who wanted to listen. I wasn't guilty of any crime and the level of violence used to arrest me was unacceptable. That was my side of it. The police would have to respond on behalf of their suspended officer.

Looking back, the story made a few of the middle pages of the regional publications and then fizzled out completely. It was another indication of how wide and high their connections are. They had the power to stifle the Press. Not completely of course, but they can ensure that an unsubstantiated allegation is treated as just that: unsubstantiated. A couple of the stories hinted that I was once a Thai-boxing fighter and that my novels are graphically violent. The readers could read into that whatever they wanted, but it made sure that I didn't appear to be a completely innocent victim of police brutality. There's no smoke without fire.

While Knowles was on suspension, he tried to call in favours from his fellow Niners. Many tried to distance themselves from him, but Officer Knowles was pedantic. He felt that he had gone out on a limb to ward me off and as such the Niners owed him. After a barrage of telephone calls, a senior member of the order contacted him and summoned him to a meeting. I know that he met with a senior officer and the nexion leader. Knowles was on the periphery of the order back then, a Neophyte; he was at the bottom of the hierarchy. But he was full of self-importance and would go to any lengths to achieve promotion within the police force and the O9A. In his mind, he was a superior being, an alpha male, and he deserved to be promoted. He wanted to progress, and he knew that his suspension was a serious blow to his career in law enforcement. He needed to know what the Niners were going to do to support him. Progression would bring him power and he was desperate to embrace it, but he couldn't progress until he was deemed ready by the order.

What happened before that meeting can only be guessed, but I know that he met with a man who was, a local Justice of the Peace. He was a council member, a member of the Masonic Lodge and, unbeknown to his family and friends, the Master of the Temple in his sinister tribe. That's how they function. They integrate into all sections of the community and spread their evil subversively, constantly looking for new members. That's why I know they'll find me eventually.

How do I know all these details about Knowles? Because he was a clever man who trusted no one. Knowles recorded his meeting with the Niners. He knew that the recording could be used to leverage promotion or to blackmail the attendees at a later date. He had several meetings recorded and he kept them on a memory stick, which I took from his pocket when he died. If I sound like a ghoul or a despicable thief, before you judge me, read on. The recorded conversation goes like this, and bear in mind that Knowles sounds drunk on the recording:

'*What happened, Knowles?*'

'*I had that fucking writer bang to rights on an assault charge, but a do-gooder constable turned up at his house at the same time. It kicked off and things got a little bit out of hand. I sprayed him and roughed him up a bit. The constable reported me for assaulting him. I had him for assaulting a warden; she's a Niner too, but another patrol turned up and screwed it all up.*' Knowles can be heard laughing as he brags to the Niners, although the two senior members can't be heard laughing at all. '*He went down on his lawn behind a fence. I thought he was out of view of any witnesses, so I kicked his head like a football. He's an arsehole; no one will listen to him and his whining. It will blow over.*'

One of his colleagues, snorts. He sounds angry. '*It won't blow over, you idiot.*' His voice is crisp and well-educated.

'*Don't call me an idiot,*' Knowles snaps. '*You told me to warn him off. You told me to sort him out.*'

'*I told you to lean on him, not to kick his face in on his front lawn in front of other officers.*'

'*Okay, you two, calm down,*' a second voice pipes up. He sounds more mature than the others, and from the recording it's obvious that he's in charge. '*Blaming each other is not going to get us anywhere. Ged thought he was acting on our behalf, so we need to come up with a plan to resolve the problem.*' The last sentence sounds patronising, as if he thinks that Knowles is of low intelligence.

'*You don't understand how an internal investigation works,*' the first voice says, concerned. From his knowledge of internal affairs and the language he uses, I deem that he's a senior police officer. '*The assault charge is not going to disappear. The main witness is a well-respected police officer and there are two other independent witnesses. This will not go away.*'

'*You need to encourage Wright not to give evidence against me,*' Knowles demands in a slurred voice. '*With him out of the picture, it's just Jones and his fat mate we need to worry about.*'

'*And how do you think I should go about encouraging a decorated police officer not to give evidence?*'

'You're the governor, so act like one and tell him.' Knowles growls disrespectfully. 'If I go down, then I'm not going alone, I promise you that.'

'Your threats to expose another member of the order will be dealt with, Knowles,' the senior officer retaliates. 'This is all your own doing and Jones is a high-profile victim of a serious police assault. There are two clear choices here …' He pauses. Knowles remains silent. He must have realised that his veiled threat was a mistake.

'What do you see as the options?' the older voice asks.

'We need to shut Jones up.' He pauses. 'Or we need to shut Jones and Knowles up permanently.'

'What are you doing?' Knowles sounds panicked at this point and there are other people in the room, moving about. There is the sound of a scuffle or a chair being dragged. Although I've listened to his recordings a thousand times, I'll never know exactly what happened. 'Okay, okay,' Knowles bleats. 'I'm not going anywhere.'

'I agree,' the older voice says. 'You need to shut him up, Knowles. If you fuck this up, then we'll eradicate you along with the writer, understand?'

'Yes,' Knowles replies sheepishly, all his bravado gone. Then there is a loud cracking sound, like a whip almost, and he moans. 'Okay. I said okay.'

'How far has this mess gone?' the older man asks, ignoring Knowles's distress.

'We know he has spoken to the girl, although I haven't heard the tapes yet so I don't know what she's told them. It doesn't matter, he must be silenced.'

'How did he get to the girl? I thought she was sectioned.'

'Sergeant Strachan from the murder squad arranged it, from what I believe.'

'What a tosser. If I had my way, I'd shut him up for good, too.' Knowles sounds like he is talking through clenched teeth.

'Do it and do not mess it up.' The older man sounds weary with it all. 'He caused us no end of problems with his infernal books. We were under scrutiny for months while investigative reporters searched for evidence that we exist. I cannot allow that to happen again. Kill him and you will be advanced, fail and you will suffer.'

The recording clicks and comes to an abrupt ending at that point. I think Knowles was using a watch or pen with a small memory to record, but there is enough there to explain what happens next. I didn't realise that in writing my books, I had put the spotlight on them. The buzz around the storyline sent journalists scurrying everywhere looking for evidence that they existed. Most people start with the Internet and the investigators bombarded sites with hits. The unwanted attention caused many of the order's members to defect for a while to hide their identities. Apparently, that was my fault, and it was only a matter of time before they murdered me.

CHAPTER 13

Fabienne Wilder

Fabienne tried to explain things to me as simply as she could and I accepted the things she told me with an open mind, although I wanted to believe her anyway. I was smitten with her. I wish that I could say it was all sympathy, but it wasn't. She fascinated me physically, mentally and – although I tried not to be – emotionally, too. I kidded myself that it was about protecting her because there was a mental connection between us. I don't profess to be psychic, but she was, and I think that she used my imagination to communicate certain pictures from her mind. Maybe it was her looks, maybe I was smitten to the point of believing anything that she said, but the plain and simple fact was that I did. The Order of Nine Angels was daunting and shrouded in mystery and bedevilment, but I genuinely believed I could protect her from them. How wrong can a man be?

I knew that the moon cycle had an effect on the crime rate, but she told me how their strength increases during the full moon and how much more aggressive the females become. I had no problem believing that; it definitely affected my mood. It always had. I realise not everyone is going to believe it though, right? How can a lump of rock circling around the earth possibly affect the actions of the billions of humans going about their business far below? Most scientists will laugh at you if you were to suggest that the moon has a direct effect on the abhorrent behaviour of humans. Is it physical? I don't know, maybe. Fabienne will tell you it is – she experienced their sexual violence for nearly a decade, and it was far worse during the full moon.

There is enough basic research to show that there is a statistically significant increase in criminality during the full moon. Many people have a gut reaction about the moon, accepting without too much thought that they tend to get drunk easier when the moon is full or that they're more likely to get into an argument. Women say their period pain can be worse during a full moon. As I said earlier, there is a theory that says the effect of the moon on women is tidal, that it has the same pull on the water in our bodies as it does on the planet's oceans. Water accounts for more than eighty per cent of our bodies, so it's possible that the pull of the moon affects the concentration of the chemicals in the body. Fabienne's gift became ultrasensitive when the moon was waning.

The next day, the moon was doing just that and Fabienne was causing all kinds of problems at the asylum. She was demanding to speak to Peter or myself and said it was a matter of life or death. Peter rang me, explained that his caseload was massive and asked me if I would go and see Fabienne as a visitor. I couldn't get there quick enough. The story of her childhood and the abuse by the O9A was eating away at me and I didn't need an excuse to want to speak to her.

I parked in my regular spot and scanned the car park for patrol cars. There was no sign of any policemen and no sign of Peter's Citroën either. It was going dark when I walked into the reception area, and the same security guard booked me in. I signed in and waited for a flustered-looking nurse who took me into a visiting Wilder. They were similar to the interview rooms in size but for a Perspex screen between us. A male nurse stood behind her as she walked into the room and sat down. She didn't look pleased to see me this time. She was not pleased at all.

'Hi, Fabienne,' I said. Her eyes looked into me and there was concern in them. She looked tired and sad as if she'd been crying.

'Hi, Conrad; where is Sergeant Strachan?' she asked abruptly, looking over my shoulder at the door as if she was hoping he would walk in. I was a little disappointed that she didn't seem as glad to see me as the last time we met.

'He's on another case,' I smiled, but she didn't return it. She appeared cold and distant. 'What is the matter?' I asked.

'Touch me,' she mouthed. She sat down and placed her hands flat on the screen. I touched the Perspex on my side. There was a tingle of electricity, static maybe, but maybe it was something more. The nerves down my spine glowed warm and my mouth started to water. 'Can you feel that?'

'Yes,' I answered honestly. Have you ever been close to someone that you really wanted to kiss but daren't, that you desperately wanted to grab hold of and embrace? Multiply that feeling by a hundred and that's how her touch felt. The tension was incredible.

'If you can feel that then believe me when I tell you that you're in danger, Conrad, and so is the Sergeant.' She leaned closer to the screen. 'I've seen it. They're coming for you and they're coming now. Do not go home to your loved ones; leave now or they'll be hurt, too.'

The warning hit me like a freight train. I felt as if a giant hand had twisted my guts. I had researched the Order of Nine Angels for days and the more I learned, the more frightened I became. They were real and they were powerful. If Fabienne said they were coming for us, then I believed her. The night that Peter had been at my house, I found four incidents where journalists investigating them disappeared and another where a female reporter was found raped and murdered in a terrible manner. God knows what the poor woman suffered before they finally killed her. One of them was Malcolm Baines, and now that I've had the time to look into their deaths, there is no doubt in my mind that they're connected to the Niners. There was no solid proof that they were real, but I knew they were.

'What do you mean they're coming now?' I asked. I wasn't sure that I wanted to know, but how can you pretend your life is not in danger? 'Have they contacted you?'

'No, but I know they're coming. I do not know who they'll send or when it will be, but trust me, they're coming.' She spread her hands open and moved her lips closer to the screen. I wanted to touch her, kiss her, and a voice in my head wanted me to hurt her. My mind was spinning like a top. Hurt her? Where had that thought come from? 'Do you have a crucifix?' she whispered through the screen, shaking my thoughts into whispers.

'Yes.' I laughed. Believe me, it was a nervous laugh. I wear a silver cross from a holiday in Jerusalem. I'm not religious, but I liked it. As I explained, I like iconology. I also have a crucifix tattooed on the triceps of my right arm and another huge one on my back. I showed her the chain and the tattoos. 'Will they protect me?'

'No, Conrad, they won't protect you.' She looked at me as if I was stupid. 'This is not a Dracula movie, it's real.'

'I know. It was a joke.'

'Save your jokes. You are in danger.'

'How can you know unless they've told you?'

'It's not your soul that I'm trying to save. It's you.' She pointed a finger to her heart and smiled. Her smile made me melt to the middle. 'Tell the world my story before they come for you. You don't have long, Conrad. Tell the world about them. They'll take me, too, so tell them now. Make people look for them. Make them scurry for the dark corners where they deserve to be, Conrad. Slow them down. Stopping them is impossible, but you can slow them down for a while …' She closed her eyes and tears spilled from them and ran down her cheeks. Her chest shook with sobs and she kissed her right hand. She blew the kiss through the Perspex screen and then stood up and walked out of the room without looking back. I called out to her to come back several times, but she was gone. I was completely numb.

CHAPTER 14

Sergeant Strachan

As soon as I got out of there, I ran to the truck in a panic. My head was all over the place. What exactly did she mean? Who was coming for me? Was she a total basket case? As I said, I'm a sceptic, and I was panicking about the ramblings of a murder suspect who was being held in a high-security mental hospital. I smoked three menthols one after the other to stop my hands shaking, but it didn't work. I was a mess. I was questioning everything that I put value in. It wouldn't be the first time my head was turned by a pretty face, and my late father always joked that my brains were in my pants. He was pretty much spot on, to be honest. Would I be listening to her if she was a fat bloke in his fifties? The answer is no. I was letting my mind run away with me because I was so attracted to her, and that was the truth.

I called Peter and he sounded harassed when he answered. A babbling phone call from me was the last thing he needed when he was working. 'Can you talk?' I tried to calm myself down, but it wasn't easy.

'Make it quick, I'm working on a case on the outskirts of town near the power station.' Workers from Wylva Power Station had found a body near Cemaes Bay; water from the sea supplies the giant cooling system and one of the inlets became blocked. Anyway, I needed to warn him about what she'd said.

'Look, I've just seen Fabienne and she's really upset because she thinks the Niners are coming after us.' I sounded ridiculous and I knew it. There wasn't a shred of proof for anything that this mysterious woman had told us from day one, but I believed her. I was behaving like an adolescent with a crush.

'What makes her think they're coming after us?' Peter sounded disinterested at best.

'She's seen it.' I thought about what I'd said and how feeble it sounded. 'Well, she said that she knows that they're coming for me and you and probably her, too, but she's absolutely convinced that we're all in danger.'

'She's seen it?' Peter exaggerated the word 'seen' to let me know that he thought I was talking rubbish and panicking for no reason. He worked in the real world where evidence talked and facts were currency, whereas I was standing in a dark fantasy land – in more ways than one. 'Seen it in a dream, I suppose?'

'That's what she said.' I swallowed, feeling a bit silly as I analysed my own words. It's almost impossible to relay a conversation as powerful as the one I'd had with her, and I failed miserably. I wish now that I could have found the right words to convince him, but my mind was awash with emotions, not facts.

'Has anyone from the Niners contacted her?'

'No.'

'Did she have anything of substance to say?' Peter wanted to get off the telephone and get on with his work.

'I know it sounds weak, but if you'd seen her, you would understand. She was terrified and really upset.' I reached for another menthol and tossed the empty packet across the truck. Now was not the best time to run out of cigarettes. 'I think she's telling the truth,' I added feebly.

'She's a murderer clutching at straws, and the only person that's swallowing any of this is you.' There was a tortured silence – I couldn't think of anything to back up what she'd said. There was nothing to back it up with. He was right. 'If you're worried about her devil-worshipping friends coming to drink your blood, then go home and put plenty of garlic in your tea, mate.' Peter laughed bitterly. I couldn't understand why he'd want to belittle me like that, but I guess he was trying to shock me back to reality. He wasn't having any of it. 'Listen, I'm snowed under here, but I'll give you a call in a couple of days when we know if she's to be charged or not. Take it easy, Conrad. It'll be something to laugh about the next time we have a few beers. Just wait until I tell the lads that you fell for a nutter in the loony bin. She's not the first bunny-boiler you've fallen for, and she won't be the last. I have to go. Speak to you soon, mate.'

'But listen.' The line was already dead. He was right, though. My track record for meeting anorexics, bulimics or psychologically disturbed females was legendary, and the sad fact is that I usually fell head over heels in love with them a week before their true colours showed. I'm a sucker for a pretty face, and I can't see past that until it's too late. I suppose that makes me shallow, but my feelings are what they are, and you can't change that, can you?

I didn't expect Peter to drop everything and come running to protect me, but I didn't expect him to be so candid either. The truth hurts, I suppose. I was worried sick that another Constable Knowles would be on my case, and more than a little perturbed that Peter had bummed me off the phone as if I was selling timeshares or guttering. I redialled his number and it flicked straight to answering machine. 'Bollocks.' I punched the dashboard and started the engine, gunning the revs much further round the dial than was necessary.

I drove home feeling drained and empty. I knew then from Peter's reaction that Fabienne was gone. It occurred to me that all they'd wanted was an insight into my research, and now that they'd decided that Fabienne was a crackpot, I was a hindrance. He wouldn't let me anywhere near the investigation if he thought that my judgement was impaired. The brief time that she'd been in my life, she'd turned my world upside down. I wasn't sure if I was on my head or my arse, but I knew something bad had entered my mind. The strength of the desire I'd felt in that one visit to Wilder was abnormal. I'd wanted to help her more than I'd wanted to help any woman before.

When I got home, the evening news carried the story of the murder that Peter was working on. Engineers at the power station had investigated a blockage in one of the cooling vents. When they checked the outlet, they discovered a body. The victim was male, but decomposition was so advanced they couldn't identify him.

At least Evie Jones was pleased to see me, and she sat with her head on my lap as we watched the news. My partner was working late again, and I opened a bottle of red wine while I waited for her to get home. I remember finishing the wine and drinking half a bottle of a second before conking out drunk and exhausted, both mentally and physically.

I dreamt that Peter and his team had finished with the basics at the scene, then went for a quick beer in town after work to discuss their next steps. It had been a testing few days for the murder squad and they needed to unwind. A few beers turned into ten beers and tequila slammers, and then they went for a kebab. I wasn't there with them in the dream, I was an observer. I knew something bad was going to happen.

A big man approached them outside a kebab shop. He had wild dreadlocks and a bushy beard. He was wearing a denim bomber jacket and leather jeans and there was a motorcycle club emblem on the back of his jacket. As he neared them, they figured he was drunk, and they parted to let him pass. The man seemed high on something and he was looking around as if someone was chasing him. He was breathing heavily and sweat ran down his brow. He reached inside his jacket and looked at the group of men. When he removed his hand, a blade flashed in the street lights.

Peter shouted a warning to the others, 'He's got a knife.' He dropped his kebab and grabbed for the man's arm. He swore and pulled it away and then slashed it across Peter's arm. It was razor sharp and it sliced through the sleeve and into the flesh. The blood on the blade seemed to glow in the dark. He drew back and then plunged the knife towards Peter's chest. Peter moved away from the thrust and the knife hit the wall. There was a metallic grating sound and sparks glinted like tiny fireworks. Four police officers pounced on the big man as he waved the knife blindly.

They grappled him to the ground, despite his incredible strength. They managed to restrain and handcuff him and held him down until a team of uniformed officers arrived and carted him off to the station in the back of a white van. Peter and his colleagues talked briefly to the arresting officers and then drifted off in separate directions to get taxis home. I watched them all leave, one by one. As the last taxi drove out of sight, the street lights flickered and fizzled out, leaving me in darkness.

In my dream, I was left alone in town. Time had moved forwards. It was pitch-black and raining heavily, and everywhere was boarded up and derelict. The kebab shop sign was hanging loose and swinging noisily in the wind. It had been closed for years and the writing on the sign was hardly readable. When I looked around, I was huddled in a doorway, wrapped up in a stinking sleeping bag, which I instinctively knew belonged to me. I could smell my body odour and it was clear that I hadn't washed for months. My bones ached and my joints were painful when I moved. The cardboard beneath me was the only mattress that I owned, and there was a deep sense of loss and longing in my heart. I knew that decades had passed, and I'd lost everything and all that I had to my name was the bottle of cheap vodka in my hand.

I heard footsteps walking down the street towards me and I heard voices and laughter. I recognised my partner's voice and her laugh. I could smell her perfume on the breeze, and I looked out of my makeshift home to see if it was really her. She was older, much older, but she was still beautiful. I didn't recognise the man that she linked with her arm, but she looked happy as they approached. I called out her name, but she glanced into the doorway and walked on as if I were just a voice on the wind. She hadn't seen me or heard me. I saw the wedding ring glinting on her finger. It wasn't one I'd bought her. Tears ran down my filthy skin into my matted beard. I felt my heart being torn from my chest as she walked on with her new husband, and I knew that I was damned to a future which didn't include her.

'Conrad.' My partner's voice woke me from my nightmare. 'I'm going to work and the dog needs walking.' She sounded mad. 'I'm getting a bit sick of waking you up from a drunken stupor, if I'm honest.'

'What time is it?' I mumbled. I sat up and my head felt like lead, but the pain of loss was still inside me. 'God am I glad to see you. I must have drunk too much wine and fallen asleep.'

'There's nothing new there then, is there?' I watched her walk out of the living room towards the kitchen. I knew that I'd better make an effort, or I was in trouble. 'At least you weren't in the cells this time, so I suppose I should be grateful.' She picked up her work bag which contained her laptop and auditing equipment. Her business suit looked immaculate as usual. 'We need to talk. I'm the only one who's pulling my weight around here. I don't know what planet you're on anymore.'

'I'm sorry but things have been a bit weird lately.' I reached out to her for a hug; the memory of my nightmare was still fresh in my mind and I needed her to hold me tightly. I needed her touch to reassure me that everything would be all right, but she recoiled and the look on her face made me feel sick inside. I knew then that I may have pushed her too far. When you know that someone you love has lost their feelings towards you, the world's a desolate, hopeless place. Once those feelings have gone, they never come back.

'Like I said, I think we need to talk, Conrad,' she said in her business voice. Her voice changed when she was talking to her subordinates on the telephone, and when she used that tone with me it really pissed me off. 'You're too drunk to get upstairs most nights and I'm getting a bit tired of your excuses, to be honest.'

'I'll make tea for us tonight and we can talk.' I smiled and tried to think of the words to make things right, but they escaped me. 'I know I've been preoccupied with work, but I'll take a few days off and we can spend some time together.'

'I'll be home about eight o'clock.' She marched towards the front door knowing full well she was in control of the situation. Aren't they always? Weaker sex, my arse. 'I think you need to move out and get your own flat for a while; that way you can drink yourself stupid and not get on my nerves.' The door opened and I heard her stop for a moment. 'Evie needs to go out, don't forget.'

I wanted to tell her about my dream and how I felt about her, but I missed the chance. Something inside me told me I never would get the chance again.

CHAPTER 15

Facebook

I was dehydrated and feeling peaky. The residue of the red wine was making me sluggish and I had a sickly sensation in my guts. My relationship with my girlfriend was precariously balanced and looking back it had been that way for a long time. There was no one to blame but myself. Although I loved her, we'd become like brother and sister instead of lovers, and that's when you take people for granted. It's easy to take people for granted when you think they'll always be there, but take it from me, nothing lasts forever in love unless you're prepared to make an effort every day, and I didn't. Getting drunk with my friends in the pub after work was becoming the norm, and my excuse that working at home all day meant that I needed a break in the evening was wearing thin. I was going out earlier and coming home later. Socialising to relax was my excuse, but the truth was, drink had a hold on me. Your friends at the bar are not really your friends. They're just like-minded men that want to drink every day. Life through the bottom of a pint glass looks fun until the money runs out or your liver packs in then it's last orders for good. Once your glass is empty and you have to go back to the real world, reality can be stark.

Anyway, Evie needed walking and I decided that the fresh air would do me good, but I needed to fire up my laptop and check my e-mails and e-book sales before we set off. As my computer loaded, the Facebook tab was indicating that there were over forty notifications on there. The last time I'd seen that many was on my birthday. Curiosity got the better of me and I logged in to see what all the commotion was about. What I saw took my breath away. I couldn't believe my eyes.

Earlier that morning, a window-cleaner had found Peter's broken body lying in the gutter at the side of some shops on the edge of the town centre. From the comments and postings on the link, it wasn't far away from the kebab shop in my dream. As I explained previously, he'd married into a big family, and our circle of friends who we had worked with over the years reached into the hundreds. Facebook was buzzing with the news of his death. Of course, the first thing people ask is why and how he died, and one of the comments from a colleague in the force was that someone mowed him down in their car and left him for dead in the road. 'It was a hit-and-run.' That was what they said but I knew it was bollocks.

I sat and stared at the growing list of condolences and I had to physically stop myself from telling everyone that it wasn't an accident. He'd been murdered by a satanic cult known as the Order of Nine Angels. Can you imagine the reaction that I would have received if I'd gone ahead and posted that? His family and friends were devastated and in the early stages of grieving. I knew how stupid and irrational and downright disrespectful it would sound.

I didn't know what to do or what to think. I needed to speak to someone who would have the details of his death without rocking the boat and upsetting his family. Calling his wife was out of the question, but her brother was a good friend of mine back then. We went back a long way in our previous careers. I decided to call him and pass on my condolences and dig for a little information at the same time. His phone switched over to answering machine a few times, which I'd expected, but on the fourth attempt he answered. He was shell-shocked when we spoke, but he told me confidentially that one of Peter's colleagues had taken Peter's brothers aside and told them that his injuries indicated that the vehicle reversed over him several times to make sure he was dead. Although they hadn't officially announced it, they were treating it as a murder inquiry.

He told me that the CCTV tapes taken by the police showed a vehicle in the area where he was found and that they were almost certain it was the car which had killed him. It would be a week later when they found the stolen vehicle burnt out on the other side of Manchester, and his death remained a mystery to his family until the whole thing blew up in my face. Now I think some of them still believe that I had something to do with it, and in a way, I did, but not the way that they think.

The visit to the asylum the previous day and Fabienne's foreboding prediction shook me to the bones. She'd said that we were in danger and now Peter was dead. In my mind I was next, and I flipped my lid. For a few hours, I was a nervous wreck. I called my partner and left several garbled messages asking her to call me back as soon as possible, but she was in meetings all day and probably thought that I was either drunk or calling to make an excuse about going to the pub again. Between calls I received a call from Peter's wife. She knew we were working together in the days before his death, but she had no idea what we were working on. It was a short call and I didn't tell her that I'd already spoken to her brother. She told me that Peter had died in a hit-and-run accident and that she would tell me when the funeral arrangements were set. I was so shocked at that stage that I just thanked her for letting me know and hung up. Seconds later I realised this wasn't a coincidence that could be fobbed off. I had been right to believe her all along. Fabienne was innocent and she was right about the Niners. They were coming for us.

CHAPTER 16

Deleted

When it had sunk in about Peter's death, I went into a blind panic. It couldn't be an accident. It was too much of a coincidence. I couldn't get hold of my partner and I knew that she wouldn't be back until later that evening. I also knew that if I did get through to her, she would think that I'd finally lost my grip on reality. There was nothing else to do except go to the person who knew the most about everything that was going on. I needed to talk to Fabienne again. I had to gather as many details as she could give me to hand over to the police. Mistakenly, I thought that they would automatically connect his death with the investigation around Fabienne. I was certain that Peter's superior officers would want to talk to me about our interviews with Fabienne. I was right that the police would soon be looking for me, but not for the reasons that I thought.

I jumped into my truck and grabbed my laptop bag. I needed my notes from the research I had done the previous night and now I had dozens of questions to ask her. My plan had been for Peter to accompany me to the hospital to see her that day, but he was already dead, assassinated. That left Fabienne and me as their next targets and I felt alone and frightened.

When I reached the asylum, the car park was full. There were three marked police cars in the ambulance bays and it soon became obvious that something was wrong. I gave up looking for a space and parked on the grass verge. I was in such a flap that I virtually abandoned the truck in the first available spot that I could find. The reception area was busy when I walked in and I sensed that the atmosphere was dark. I waited my turn for the reception desk to clear and then asked the desk clerk if I could see Fabienne Wilder. On my previous visits it had been security guards who I spoke to, but this was within office hours and different protocol applied. The receptionist asked me if I was related to her.

I stopped for a second and thought about the question. Why would she ask that? I lied and said that I was her next of kin, which caused a raised eyebrow from the woman, but I had my story mapped out. I had to talk to Fabienne no matter what. She asked me to take a seat at the side of the reception area and I sat nervously and waited. Policemen were coming and going, and in my mind, I hoped that they had connected Peter's death to Fabienne's story. I was way off the mark, but at the time that's what I wanted to believe. It was the longest forty minutes in history.

Eventually, a young doctor in a white coat approached me and took me into a relatives' room, which was down a corridor in the opposite direction from the interview rooms. We walked in silence and he opened the door and allowed me to enter first. He was a young man in his twenties, and he looked harassed. He removed his glasses and rubbed his eyes before he spoke.

'May I ask who you are?' he frowned and looked me up and down. I'm the wrong skin colour to be related to Fabienne genetically but he couldn't say that outright.

'I'm her stepfather,' I lied. 'She's been missing for months. I've travelled up from London overnight and I need to speak to her urgently,' I said sternly.

'That won't be possible. Take a seat.' He gestured to a couch beneath a window which looked out over the grass towards the new housing estate nearby. 'Look, this will come as a shock to you and there's no easy way of telling you this, but I'm afraid Fabienne took her own life last night.' The doctor put his hand on my shoulder, and I felt my knees go weak. Tears filled my eyes and I could feel my lips quivering. Fabienne was the only person who could help, and she was dead. It wouldn't sink into my brain. All I could feel was an overwhelming sense of loss. She'd been in my life for a few days, yet I felt devastated. I also felt fear. Stone cold fear. Had they got to her too?

'What happened?' I stuttered.

'She hung herself.'

I don't know whether it was the shock or the stress of the previous days catching up on me, but I began to faint. I literally felt my body sagging and slipping down the upholstery. I looked to the light outside and remember feeling the doctor's hands steadying me. I could hear his voice, but I didn't compute exactly what he was saying. As I looked out of the window, an image came into my mind. It was Fabienne in my head. I was looking at the world through her eyes, but everything was in black and white, like an old film. She was lying in a hospital bed. The room was painted white and the walls were bare. The smell of disinfectant drifted into my consciousness. I didn't understand how it had happened, but they had restrained her. She was strapped to the bed.

I sensed her fear as she lay there, helpless. She was scared and she couldn't move. I could feel her fear. She was calling for help in her mind. She was calling for me. They'd strapped her hands and feet to the bed, and she called out for help repeatedly. Screams for help are commonplace in an asylum and they ignored her. I saw the shadow of a man looming over her and I felt a sheet slipping around my neck as if I was there inside her body. The cotton sheet began to tighten and cut off her air supply. I felt what it was like to be strangled to death and I felt her desperate struggles as the oxygen in her lungs became exhausted. I felt her eyes bulging out of their sockets, and the pressure in her brain felt like the blood vessels were about to explode. Death approached quickly. I sensed that despite everything, she'd suffered; she didn't want to die. She clung on and struggled for as long as her body allowed before the darkness descended and her struggles became twitches. As the twitching finally ceased, I felt a flash in my mind and the image faded and disappeared.

'Are you okay?' I snapped back into reality. The doctor looked into my eyes and placed a paper cup of water to my lips. I sipped it and waited for my head to clear. I must have been gone longer than I thought, as I didn't see the doctor move to fetch the water. I was confused and frightened. The news of her death sapped my strength, and combined with the loss of my friend, it was a shattering blow. Experiencing her final tortured moments was the icing on the cake. The world had finally gone mad around me and I felt like I was drowning in a sea of confusion. Nothing made sense.

'When did they find her?' I asked the question without thinking about it. The answer was irrelevant. She'd been murdered. I knew that much for sure. Fabienne had shown me the last moments of her life; the moments when they sent someone to erase her. As I thought about her, I felt a tingle of static in the tips of my fingers where we had touched through the Perspex, and the hair on the back of my neck felt like a breeze was touching them. I was playing things over in my mind. Peter was dead – an accident. Fabienne was dead – a suicide. What would my death be? Would they find my body at all? Would I spend my final moments on this earth fighting for my life, or would it be worse? Would they make it slow?

'Mr Jones?' A different voice disturbed my thoughts. I looked up and saw a policeman in the doorway. He was youngish and his spotty face made him look more like a student than a serving police officer.

'No,' I lied. 'I'm Michael Wilder.' I didn't know why I lied at that point, but I did. It didn't matter anymore who I was, relation or otherwise because she was dead. Maybe Fabienne put the name in my mind, a message from the other side to protect me, but it worked. It bought me vital minutes to get out of the hospital without being dragged into a complicated investigation. Later on, I discovered that her stepfather was indeed called Michael, but it could have been a fluke, who knows? The police officer frowned and was about to speak when the doctor butted in.

'Do you mind, officer?' He turned and walked towards him. 'The man has just lost his stepdaughter. Please show him some respect, he's obviously badly shaken by the news. Whatever you need to talk to him about, it will have to wait.' The police officer sheepishly closed the door and left the room, but he gave me a nasty look as he went.

The doctor held his chin between his finger and thumb and gave me the cup of water to hold. 'Are you feeling strong enough to hold this?'

'Yes, I'm okay,' I replied although my hands were trembling.

'Look, Mr Wilder, I'm not sure what is happening here, but the police have seized your stepdaughter's body.' He lowered his voice as he spoke. 'it's most peculiar, and they're asking some unusual questions. I'm not sure if talking to them right now is good for you.'

I didn't want to talk to them for my own reasons. Trying to bluff my way into an asylum would take some explaining anyway, especially when the person who I was trying to see was dead.

'You're right. I can't talk to them right now. Is there another way out of here, Doctor?' I asked. My spider senses were tingling. They'd killed Peter and Fabienne in one night and what the doctor told me set the alarm bells in my brain ringing. I had to assume that the police were involved, or at least some of them were. I was guessing at that point that Officer Knowles was not the only one involved with the Niners. I was in trouble because they knew I was there. The officer had asked if I was Mr Jones. How would they know that I was there unless one of them had spotted my truck, and how would they know it was my truck unless they wanted to find out what vehicle I drove? Why would anyone want to know what type of vehicle I drove? The questions were rattling around in my head like a tornado in a tin can factory. 'I really need ten minutes to gather my thoughts before I speak to the police.'

'Of course, I understand. Come this way.' He led me through a door at the rear of the room, which opened into a toilet corridor. 'There is a fire door at the end of the corridor. Take your time before you come back in, I'll tell them you're to be left alone for a while.'

'Thank you, doctor.' I shook his hand and darted through the fire door. He smiled thinly as he pulled the door closed. He knew that I wasn't going back through it. I ran as fast as I could across the lawns to the truck. When I reached it, there was a large box van stopped behind it. The driver was stood on the grass talking into his mobile phone. A police officer was talking to the driver of the car behind him and I realised that my truck was blocking the entrance to the car park. A saloon car could squeeze by, but the delivery truck was too wide.

I stopped running and walked to the driver's door. The van driver was open-mouthed as I casually climbed into the truck and slammed the door. Luckily, the engine started at the first ask. I heard a torrent of abuse though the glass, but I didn't have time to swap insults. I wanted to be away from the asylum and the police. As I pulled off the verge, the police officer was shaking his head but made no attempt to stop me. I drove past two officers who were stood there near their patrol car on the car park, but they didn't even look in my direction. I began to think that I was being paranoid. No one was chasing me, and two minutes later I was on the main road and heading back to the island.

I arrived home confused and frightened. As I said earlier, when it comes to physical conflict, I don't have a fear gene as long as I can see who I'm fighting. But the Niners were not going to send someone to stand toe-to-toe with me. I wouldn't know who it was or when they would come, but I knew it would be soon; very soon. Fabienne and Peter were already dead and that was too much of a coincidence. The dreams and visions that I'd had could be nothing more than my vivid imagination working overtime, but they added credence to my fears. Everything seemed real.

I walked into the house and listened for any hint of danger. I heard Evie Jones burst through the dog flap into the kitchen and I could hear her claws scratching along the laminate towards me. She was excited but her behaviour was normal, which allowed me to relax a little. I went to the kitchen and put the kettle on. I needed coffee and a cigarette. I actually needed a drink, but the conversation I'd had with my partner that morning put the brakes on that idea. She hated me smoking, but I was tense, and I needed the nicotine. I made a fuss of Evie while the kettle boiled, and for a few moments, things seemed normal. I made my brew and unlocked the back door, lighting my last menthol on the balcony. The caffeine and nicotine intake made me feel better. As I thought about things, I made a plan in my mind. I had to talk to my partner first.

I called her at work again, which was a huge no-no, but this time she answered. I was expecting a frosty reception, but I was surprised how warm she sounded.

'Are you okay?' she asked, concerned. 'I've heard the news about Peter; it's all over the office.'

'I really need to talk to you properly. You need to come home as soon as you can.' I couldn't tell her why she had to come home in a few sentences on the telephone. She would think that I'd lost all my marbles, so I waffled that it was dreadful news but that there was more to it.

'You know that I'm working.' She used her business voice again. 'I'll see you later and we can talk then.'

'Listen to me.' I was trying to remain calm. 'We're in danger. There's more to Peter's death than meets the eye, but I can't explain it on the phone.'

'What do you mean?' She sighed. I knew I was flogging a dead horse. How could I expect anyone to believe me? 'Sorry, I'll be back in a minute.' She covered the handset and called to a colleague in the background. 'Look, they're restarting the meeting. I'll have to go.'

'Peter was murdered,' I blabbed. I regretted saying it immediately, but I felt as if no one was listening to a word that I said. 'They've made it look like a hit-and-run, but I know who killed him.'

'And how would you know that, Conrad?' She was at her limit with me. I could tell.

'Trust me, I know it's them, and they're coming for me next. It's all to do with that policeman who beat me up and the murder investigation Peter took me on.' I was desperate to explain everything, but it had to be done face to face. I was concerned for our safety and I needed her help.

'So, you think that officer is coming back for you?' she sounded incredulous. 'Why, what have you done? If you're seriously worried then call the police, Conrad. I'll have to go; they're waiting for me.'

170

'Look, it's complicated,' I stressed 'There's more to it than just one policeman going off on one. There are thousands of them and they're everywhere.' I was trying to communicate my point without sounding like a fruitcake, but I must have sounded pathetic.

'Thousands of who, Conrad?' she snapped. 'I hope you're not rattling on about those satanic cults or whatever it was you were looking at with Peter. It's one thing writing a storybook about them, but you're beginning to sound deranged.'

'Why won't you listen to me?' I shouted this time, which just made matters worse. 'Peter is dead and so is the girl we interviewed. She told me that they were coming after us and now they're dead. I'm not the one who is deranged.'

'Don't raise your voice to me.'

'Well, you're not listening to me.'

'I'm at work and you're talking rubbish. Have you been drinking?'

'No. I haven't had a drink.'

'I need to go.'

'Do you think the world of burgers, milkshakes and chips could survive without you for a few hours while we talk about this and sort out what we are going to do?' I was angry now. What did I have to do to convince people?

'Sort what out?' she scoffed. 'What do you think we're going to do?'

'We need to get away from here until everything is out in the open. They know who I am, and they know where I live. We need to get away today.'

'Have you been drinking?' she asked again, ignoring my rant. 'I'm going to stay at my mum's tonight. I'll call and grab some things tomorrow. I can't deal with you right now. We need some time apart.' The call ended, but I held the phone next to my ear for a while before I put it down on the kitchen worktop. Evie Jones tilted her head and looked at me. She sensed that I was upset, and she licked my fingers to let me know that she wasn't leaving.

I felt drained by it all, but I was almost relieved that my partner wasn't coming home. I wouldn't have to explain it all to her while she looked at me as if I was bonkers. She would be safe at her mother's for now. I had to make sure that Evie and I were safe, too. By the time the kettle had boiled again, I was packed and ready to go. I could see Snowdonia through the kitchen window; it was a thirty-minute drive away and there are plenty of campsites and guesthouses to stay in. Whichever direction I chose, I knew that I could become anonymous within a few hours.

I dressed in my camping gear, water resistant cargo pants with large pockets on the sides and a Gore-Tex jacket. They were green and brown, which wouldn't catch the eye, especially up on a mountain. I had bought a neck knife and a belt knife a few years earlier from the Internet while researching a book about drug dealers and concealed weapons. The neck knife consisted of a black cord that looped over my head like a pendant chain and dangling from it was a stainless-steel scorpion pendent about four inches long. It looked innocent enough at first glance, until you pulled the tail of the scorpion and a four-inch stiletto blade slides out of the body. It cost me nine-pounds including postage and packing, and for an extra five pounds they included the belt knife as a bonus buy. It was an experiment to see how easy it was to buy lethal weapons on the Net. I never thought I would wear them, let alone need them for protection. I've always been a keen clay-pigeon shooter and I owned a Remington pump-action shotgun and a Mossberg, which I took from the lockbox and cleaned. Taking the shotgun in a case was perfectly legal as long as I had my licence on me and I wasn't walking into a bank with it. There were plenty of farms who allow licence-holders and shotgun-owners to hunt rabbits on their land at night. I knew that I could take it with me without breaking any firearms laws.

I was nearly ready to go when my partner walked in through the front door. She hated guns in the house, despite the lockbox. When she saw me sitting on the bedroom floor next to a rucksack, with a loaded shotgun next to me, she thought I had lost the plot. Can you imagine the conversation we had? It was surreal. I was explaining to my partner of eight years that a satanic cult was trying to kill me. I had interviewed a murder suspect who was psychic and had been sectioned into the local asylum. It was research for my new book, and now everyone involved was dead and I was next. It didn't go down well at all; I remember the look of disbelief in her eyes and it cut me to the bone.

She offered to call me an ambulance as she packed her bags. There was no way she was staying in the house while I had a loaded shotgun; especially when I was talking gobbledygook. The more I tried to convince her, the madder I sounded. How could I possibly convince anyone of sound mind that I was telling the truth? She left in a rush and I haven't seen her since. I miss her terribly, but I don't blame her for leaving me, how can I? Put yourself in her shoes, what would you think? She lived in the real world where percentages and profits were kings; I was in a world of demons and death where nothing made sense. She was right to go even though it broke me inside.

As she walked out of the door, I felt numb, but I was resigned to the fact that no one would listen to me until the police realised the deaths were linked to the Holmes and Stokes murders. I decided to take the Staffie and the truck and head for the hills, although I hadn't decided which hills at this point. There is a Tesco garage a few miles away in Holyhead and I needed to fill the truck with diesel. I didn't want to stop on the way. I took the gamble to fuel the truck up first and then come back for the gun and the dog. It was daylight and I didn't think they would try anything in the open.

I fed Evie Jones and then walked out of the front door while she was distracted with her food, locking both doors behind me. The roads were busy, which gave me some comfort, but the thought of police cars arriving spurred me to hurry. The Navara started first time and I drove as calmly as I could to the garage, although my nerves were at snapping point. I pulled in and waited for a pump to come free. The Tesco garage is a nightmare, as people fuel up and then go shopping for their tea while you wait for them to move their vehicles from the pump. It can be frustrating at the best of times, and today was not the best of times. I'd been waiting an age and I was tetchy. I wanted to honk the horn, but I didn't want to attract attention to myself. It seemed like forever until the owner returned with his shopping and a stupid grin on his face.

'Sorry.' He waved, as he put the bags into the boot of his car. 'I won't be a second,' he said. He closed the boot and jogged back to the shop. I couldn't believe my luck. It seemed like an age before he came back holding a loaf of bread. 'I'd be in trouble if I'd forgotten the bread.'

'Are you sure you haven't forgotten anything?' I called out of the window. He looked at me confused.

'Sorry?' he said.

'I said have you forgotten anything? I wouldn't want you to get home and realise you've forgotten the milk or teabags. Feel free to nip back inside and browse the magazine rack, or better still, move your car so I can get some diesel.'

'Charming,' he muttered, as he got in his car.

'Just move, please.' I was losing it. The Navara is a big truck and I felt like driving over his car to the next pump. After arsing about with his seat belt for another few long seconds, he pulled away and I jumped out and waited a few minutes for the attendant behind the counter to activate the pump. I filled up the tank, locked the cap and walked to the cash point. It was busy and I was paranoid. Everyone was a threat. Every glance was an assassin coming for me. I slid my card into the machine and entered my PIN. The screen informed me the number was incorrect. I was stressed and, in a rush, so I tried it again, slowly this time. The same message appeared on the screen: incorrect number. I've used the same number for decades. I tried it again with the same result.

Someone had blocked my account. I knew without trying again that they'd done it. They were trying to stop me running. They were more powerful than I imagined, and I was blown away. I hadn't seen anything yet.

CHAPTER 17

That Night

I knew that if I was going to run, I needed money. I went home after pleading with the Tesco garage employees to take my name and address, and I promised to return with the money as soon as possible. Of course, I never did. Serves them right for making me wait at the pump. After everything that had happened, I was in a paranoia bubble. I drove past the side of my flat where I've parked my car for the last fifteen years and pulled into a caravan site a few hundred yards up the road. I turned it around so that it was facing the exit, anticipating that I may need to make a quick getaway. My imagination was running wild, but what was the alternative? Act normally and wait for someone to take me out? I couldn't do that.

I had to look out for me and the Staffie; it was us against the world now. When we first brought Evie Jones home and realised that she was a danger to passing dogs we secured the balcony, making sure that there were no gaps in the fence where she could wriggle out and down the stairs to attack a poor, defenceless Labrador. The only breach in the fence was a weak panel. The panel separated our balcony from the next flat behind us, and I wedged an old sun lounger against it and then heaved the wheelie bin back so that she couldn't fit behind it. As I walked home, the weak panel became our escape route in my mind. If danger came to our door, we could leave through the back, push the bin a few inches, move the sun lounger and slip onto our neighbour's balcony without being seen from the main road. Part of me was impressed with my ability to plan with such detail and another part of me questioned my sanity. If you could have heard the conversations going on in my mind that day, you would have too.

The coast road at the front of the flat was busy when I walked up the side path to the front door. Knowing that dozens of normal human beings drove by every hour gave me some comfort. It would be a different story once the teatime traffic faded. The population of Trearddur Bay goes through the roof during the daytime as visitors take the coast road to enjoy the views, but by eight o'clock it turns back into the sleepy village it really is; in the holidays, all the properties are full but by October, it's a ghost town with no lights on anywhere at nigh time until the weekends when the tourists come back again.

I locked both doors while the Staffie whirled around my feet. There is no command that you can give to an excited dog welcoming you home. You have to face the barrage in the knowledge that it will eventually subside. I checked all the doors and windows, knowing that they were secure, but paranoia forced me to check them anyway. My mind is so full of imaginary goings-on when I'm writing a book that I forget whether I've left the iron on, if the front door is locked and where I'm supposed to be going in the first place. I had to check them a second time just to be sure.

With the Staffie settled and the kettle on, I called the Santander customer service line. A very helpful lady with a Scottish accent looked into my account and informed me that a petrol station close to Birmingham had reported that someone had tried to use several debit cards in different names to pay for a tank of fuel, and that one of the names was mine. The bank quite rightly put a block on my card until I contacted them. It sounded like a perfectly believable scenario which could happen to anyone at any time, but in my mind, it was them. The Niners had done it to stop me running. I had to make a contingency plan to stop them from doing it again. I needed more than one way to access money and it needed to be as anonymous as possible. I logged in online and pulled up a prepaid MasterCard site, which I had used for a while when travelling abroad. I used the card to buy stuff online, and for travelling, they're perfect. I swapped my payment details from my Amazon account so that my e-book money went direct to the prepaid card rather than my bank account.

At the time, we both had a personal drawer in the kitchen units, and I rifled through them, my brains running at warp speed. My partner had left a Barclaycard which I was authorised to use. I didn't know it was there and she must have kept it from me in case I used it to fund my crazy marketing ideas. She was very frugal with money but I'm the opposite. I'd give my last pound away without thinking about it so, she didn't trust me with money and looking back she was spot on. She'd forgotten all about the card in her rush to pack, so I activated it online and took that too. For a moment, I felt like I had one over on the Niners. I was wrong, as usual.

The sun was going down and I wasn't finished swapping money from my accounts yet, so I logged onto a *We Buy Any Car* website and asked for a cash price for the truck. There are too many cameras on our roads to hide for long. If they had access to police cameras, and I believed they did, then it wouldn't take long for them to track me down. With all that organised, I tried to think how else they could find me. The obvious way was my mobile phone. I printed off all my numbers from my Samsung, put them in my laptop bag and then stashed all my notes on Fabienne into a small safe, which we kept in the loft. I planned to buy a number of prepaid SIM cards from the shops the next day. They would keep me in touch with the people I trusted, though God only knows who I could trust.

It took me the best part of three hours to sort everything out and the sun was gone from the sky. I began to think that I'd missed my window of opportunity to travel in daylight. I watched the roads around the flat through the kitchen window, looking for any suspicious vehicles approaching. When you're in that frame of mind, they're all suspicious. I decided that it was safer to stay at the house for the night and leave in the morning when there was more traffic on the roads. There was more chance of them ramming me off the road in the dark. My run-in with Officer Knowles was still on my mind too. It would be easy for a rogue officer to pull me over at night. I had to start thinking like a man on the run.

I locked all the doors and closed all the curtains, setting the burglar alarm to hallway so that I could move from bedroom to bedroom at will. All the windows and doors were renewed fairly recently, and they had good locks fitted. If anyone tried to break in, they would have to smash a window. I felt as secure as I could be under the circumstances. As well as all those locks, I had the shotgun and the Staffie. At the time, I fancied my chances to get through the night safely.

I resisted the urge to drink myself to sleep despite being home alone, although I took the liberty of smoking my head off. My eyes were burning, and eventually I nodded off into a dream-filled slumber. I didn't sleep long. Evie Jones woke me. It was three o'clock in the morning when she started barking. I was tired and my head was aching. There was a rattle from the backyard, and I rushed into the back bedroom to investigate. I was amazed to see a figure struggling over the back-fence panels. They're six feet high and the intruder was considerably shorter than that. A layer of gravel covers the backyard and they landed with a crunch on my side of the fence.

My heart was in my mouth. Although I knew I was in danger, I was still shocked to see an intruder climbing the fence. Evie Jones kicked off and she was bouncing off the window, her snot and saliva smearing the double-glazed panel as she tried repeatedly to charge through the glass. The figure heard the Staffie and looked up at the window and smiled. It was an evil sneer and I recognised her immediately. It was the beach warden.

The light from the bedroom illuminated the yard to a degree. I couldn't believe her nerve, but I was almost relieved to see that it was her. If that was the best that the Niners could send, then I would live forever. Once again, I was wrong.

As I watched her to see what she was planning to do, she took a small haversack from her back and quickly removed a glass bottle. She fumbled in her jacket pocket and then stuffed a rag into the neck, tilting it so that the flammable liquid soaked into it. The flat below mine was a holiday home and rarely occupied. I realised then she was going to firebomb the building. I had double-locked the doors and none of the windows opened wide enough to climb out. If she threw the petrol bomb through the window downstairs, then we would never make it out of the front door. A judge may see it another way, but I had no choice but to do what I did. Honestly, I didn't.

CHAPTER 18

The Niners

I understood the consequences of what I was about to do, but it didn't matter. It was me and Evie Jones or her. I grabbed the Staffie and pushed her out of the bedroom onto the landing. She was snarling and scratching at the door, but it would hold her long enough. Closing the door so that she couldn't get in, I turned the butt of the shotgun and smashed the bedroom window with it. The double-glazed unit exploded into tiny pieces. If the Staffie had been in the room, she would have jumped through the opening and broken her bones in the fall. Time slowed right down as the beach warden held the petrol bomb away from her body and lit the rag. I held my breath as I pulled the stock into my shoulder and aimed the shotgun. It was a stance that I had taken a thousand times before, except that this time my target was not a clay disc; this time it was a human.

Without a second thought about the implications of my actions or where I would end up, I squeezed the trigger and the Remington kicked in my hands. The lead shot smashed her wrist bones to pulp and shredded the flesh around them. Only a few strings of sinew attached the hand to her arm. She looked shocked. She stared at the ruined appendage and looked around for the culprit. 'Where had the gunshot come from?' was written all over her face.

'You never expected that, did you?' I muttered under my breath as I squeezed the trigger again. The second blast ripped a massive chunk of her bicep from the bone in the upper arm and blood splattered across her neck and chest. A plume of white gravel shot skywards as the pellets smashed through her flesh into the yard.

Her evil smile was gone, replaced by a 'little lost girl' expression. She looked scared for a moment as the burning bottle fell from her ruined hand. Her fingers could no longer grip, and it smashed onto the floor at her feet. The burning rag ignited the petrol and the flames engulfed her in seconds. I felt no remorse as I watched her knees buckle and her clothes melt around her body. The blackened material mingled with her burning flesh as she turned into a human bonfire. I could hear her hair crackling as it burned and the skin on her face seemed to blister before it blackened and burned. She stared at me with accusing eyes. The Remington had another shell available and I could have put her out of her misery with a shot to the head, but part of me wanted her to suffer. I wanted to watch her die in agony. If you think that that's sick, then so be it but the feeling didn't last for more than a few seconds. I couldn't watch her suffer. The shape of her skull replaced her facial features as the flames devoured her. She screamed like a banshee until I fired again and put her out of her misery; her body finally toppled over, and she twitched for a long few seconds before she was finally still.

'I hope that really hurt,' I said to myself. I heard my voice and it didn't sound like me. I felt relieved that I'd shot her before she could pitch her incendiary through my window. It hadn't occurred to me at that point how I would explain the charred remains in my garden of a woman who had recently accused me of assault. If the Nine Angels were right in their belief that you gain the strength of your victim if you look into their eyes when they die, then I was 1-0 up at that point.

Even now, years on, I feel nothing but contempt for her. I hope she gets everything she prayed for from her dark lord and that she burns in his hell for eternity. I leaned against the window frame as the adrenalin dissipated and I allowed my small victory to blind me from any other danger. I said that they wouldn't come in ones, and they didn't. I was still gloating when the bathroom window smashed and the Staffie went ballistic on the landing.

CHAPTER 19

Officer Knowles

I ran for the bedroom door, slamming fresh shells into the shotgun. I nearly spilled them onto the carpet in my panic. I should have realised that the warden had made it too obvious that she was in the backyard. She'd virtually announced her arrival to me and the dog. She was acting as a diversion so that I wouldn't see someone else climbing on top of the balcony walkway. She'd drawn my attention away from the easiest access point. The kitchen had a walkway outside, which gave access to the flats further along the building. If you stood on the walkway, the window ledge was at knee height, and with the glass smashed it was a simple case of stepping into the house.

As I reached the back-bedroom door, I heard the Staffie go into attack mode. It sounds like a sports car going into top gear. Her growling drops an octave or two as she launches into an attack. Evie Jones bears the scars of being a fighting dog in her younger years, and had we not taken her from the rescue home they would have destroyed her because of her aggression towards other animals.

I heard her snarling change tone as she attacked the intruder, and there was a cry of pain as she latched on to a limb. I could hear her thrashing about in the bathroom and there was a tearing sound of material and flesh. A guttural growling noise came from her throat. A man's voice was cursing in a language I didn't recognise. I reached the door and flung it open.

Officer Knowles was wearing a balaclava, but I immediately knew that it was him. The lights were on and I could see his eyes. I would recognise them anywhere. When he saw the shotgun in my hands, his eyes widened with fear and he found the strength to break free of the Staffie. If he had done his homework at the police station, he would have known I had had a shotgun licence for ten years. Evie fell away, bounced off the toilet and attacked again. She attached her teeth to his right hand. He was holding a Beretta and somehow, she knew that he meant to do me harm with it. The Staffie was swinging from his arm as he thrashed about, but she wouldn't let go. I aimed the shotgun at him, but he was spinning around too much for me to take a shot without hurting Evie.

Knowles stumbled through the bathroom door onto the landing, and I stepped back quickly, hoping that he would fall to the floor and drop the weapon. He panicked and swung her body against the banister rail. The blow winded Evie Jones and she crashed to the floor as Knowles raised his gun and blindly squeezed off a round. Blood poured from his arm and splattered up the wall and I could see that there was a ragged tear in his forearm. A flap of skin the size of a cigarette packet was missing. I made a mental note to buy her some lambs' liver as a reward – if we made it through the night.

Knowles fired again and the bullet smashed into the doorframe, splintering the wood and showering me with shards. I fired at the ceiling, blasting Artex and plaster all over us. I wanted him to run away from the Staffie so that I could shoot him. He ducked and stumbled in the darkness towards the top of the stairs, and as Evie readied for another lunge, I tripped over her and the shotgun roared again. A large hole appeared in the bathroom door, but thankfully she was unhurt. There was one cartridge left in the Remington, and without taking aim I fired from the hip. The shot sprayed the landing with deadly lead pellets, some catching Knowles in the shoulder. The force slammed him into the wall, leaving bloody smears on the magnolia, and he squealed like a girl as he threw himself out of the way.

Evie Jones was up on her feet snarling like a pit bull, but I couldn't risk her being shot by the Beretta as she ran down the stairs. The burglar alarm sounded as Knowles hit the sensors, and I grabbed her collar as she set off in hot pursuit. She licked my hand as I shoved her into the spare bedroom and shut the door. I could hear her running onto the bed and hurling herself at the door. She wanted to finish what she'd started, but I had to think for both of us and keep her out of the line of fire.

I loaded three new shells into the shotgun and looked over the banister. As I did so, a bullet whistled by my ear and crashed into the ceiling above me, showering me with more plaster. It crossed my mind that if my partner had returned home and seen the bullet holes, she may have believed what I had been saying. I heard Knowles moving into the back room, which meant that I could make it down the stairs. Then it dawned on me that the electric box was in the dining room and I could hear him fumbling about. He was going to kill the lights.

I was halfway down the stairs with my back pressed against the wall when the lights went off. I stopped suddenly and backtracked up the stairs with my head down. The street lights on the car park provided a dull yellow glow through the curtains and they would silhouette me if I ventured downstairs. I would have been a sitting duck if I had carried on.

I crouched down next to the baluster, my breathing laboured and beads of sweat trickling into my eyes. There was silence for a few moments, then muffled thuds and raised voices drifted through the walls from next door. It wasn't the first time I'd woken up the neighbours, but this time would be the one that they'd remember the most clearly. I wasn't sure what to do, but Evie's protestations gave me an idea. Despite the street lights it was dark at floor level all the way down the stairs, and she was much faster than me. I reached for the bedroom door handle and let her out.

She didn't hesitate. She knew where he was, and she pelted out of the bedroom towards the stairs. As she reached the top of the landing, I fired a shot over the banister towards the dining-room door. It blasted a huge chunk of plaster off the wall and I heard Knowles gasp in the darkness as wood and plaster hit him in the face. I heard her padding on the carpeted stairs and then her claws scratching the laminate as she reached the hallway at the bottom. I replaced the spent cartridge and followed Evie Jones at full tilt. Turning the power off is not a good idea when a Staffie is on your case. She could see in the dark far better than Knowles could. Bull terriers were bred for their aggression and Evie Jones is at the extreme end of the scale. They're powerful fighting dogs and fear nothing, especially if their loved ones are under threat.

I didn't have a clue where Knowles was hiding and every piece of furniture became a bunker that he could shoot from, but Evie Jones knew exactly where he was. She ran snarling into the back room, and I heard Knowles shouting. There was a muzzle flash as he fired wildly into the darkness and then a scream as she latched on to her target again. As I turned the corner at the bottom of the stairs, I could see him thrashing about wildly. The flames in the backyard were dying down, but they illuminated the room enough for me to see him. The Staffie had him by the right calf, and as much as he kicked her, she wasn't letting go. They don't let go. I watched him point his weapon at Evie and my jaw clenched tightly at the thought of a bullet hitting her. There was no choice but to take him down.

In a split second, I shouldered the shotgun, aimed carefully and pulled the trigger. I aimed for his upper central mass, knowing that at that distance the deadly spray wouldn't hit the Staffie. The roar of the shotgun drowned out her snarls for a second, but she didn't relent from her attack. The blast knocked Knowles off his feet onto his back and the Beretta clattered across the wooden floor. Evie saw the opportunity to switch her attack to his head. I could hear his muffled screams as she ripped at the soft flesh of his face. It sounded like he was drowning. Pointing the shotgun at his legs, I picked up the pistol and left her to it while I switched the power back on. Evie had ripped the balaclava from his head.

With the lights on I could see that Knowles was in trouble. He was mortally wounded. Blood was pooling from beneath him; the lead shot had mangled his insides. It took me a while to calm Evie enough to release her jaw. A fellow Staffie owner had told me that a sharp smack on their anus is the only way to encourage them to release. It didn't work. When I finally pealed Evie Jones off his face, she'd ripped a ragged hole where his nose and upper lip should be and his left cheek was hanging like a piece of raw steak, exposing his teeth and gums in a macabre grin. I bundled her into the kitchen under protest and shut the door. She sat next to her water bowl and wagged her tail as if she knew that she'd done something good. If only she knew just how important it was.

When I returned to Knowles, he was crying like a baby and his breathing sounded laboured and wet. His chest hissed every time he took a breath as air leaked through the holes in his punctured lungs. The shotgun blast had smashed his ribs and ripped holes in his vital organs. There wasn't much time left for him. He looked at me, his eyes pleading. 'Help me,' he hissed. Crimson air bubbles appeared where his nose once was.

'You're a bit fucked up.' I snorted. I took a deep breath to calm myself and wiped the sweat from my forehead with the back of my hand. I knew that the police would be on their way and I didn't have long. I put the shotgun over my shoulder and smiled. I had nothing but contempt for him. There was nothing inside me but hatred. If Fabienne was right, then he was a rapist of men, women and children. He had threatened me and spat in my face. He sprayed me with pepper spray and kicked me unconscious. I was betting that he ran over Peter too. 'I guess what goes around comes around,' I said. In a morbid way I found his situation very sad; how had it come to this?

'Help me,' he hissed again. He had no lips, so it sounded like *helppsssssh me*. Blood dribbled from the side of his mouth and it reminded me of a scene from *Saving Private Ryan*. At this point, I may have been able to claim self-defence, but then again, I doubted it. If he stayed alive long enough to tell them otherwise then they would lock me up until a jury decided if I had used reasonable force to protect my home. Looking at Knowles and watching the flames flickering outside, 'reasonable' was not an adjective which sprang to mind.

'Help you? You came to my home to kill me.' I said. 'What should I do, call you an ambulance? Or do you want a couple of ibuprofen out of the cupboard? I don't think so, do you?'

'Please help me; I'll make them leave you alone.'

I thought about that for a moment. There was nothing that I wanted more than being able to return to my boring old life, but I didn't trust him. He didn't look like he would survive the journey to hospital and what were the chances of him sticking to his side of the bargain? None. Something told me that he couldn't stop them anyway. How could one man influence an organisation founded on evil? 'Why would I trust you?'

'I can get you money.' His words were slow in coming and his chest was spurting blood as he breathed. He hissed like a punctured inner tube in a bowl of water.

'Stuff your money,' I said. 'I'll tell you what I'll do,' I said slowly, thinking as I spoke. 'If you tell me where and when you meet with the Niners, I'll call you an ambulance before I leave. Otherwise, I'll let the Staffie back in to finish eating your face before we go. What do you think of that?' I figured that if I could pinpoint where they met then the police could wait for them and arrest the entire nexion, which would vindicate me and allow me to return to the normality that I so desperately craved.

He shook his head and tried to cough. Blood sprayed from the rent in the middle of his face. He groaned in agony. 'They'll kill me,' he said.

'They're the least of your worries,' I took the Remington and aimed it at his left ankle. His eyes widened in terror and I asked him again. 'Where do they meet? You're going to die anyway. All you have to do is decide how much of you there will be left to put in the coffin.' I looked out of the back window at the smouldering remains of the beach warden. 'I don't think your friend will fill an ashtray, to be honest. Now, where do you meet?'

The Staffie howled in the kitchen and I knew we were pushing it. The next-door neighbours would have called the police when they heard the first gunshots and saw the flames in the backyard. The burglar alarm was blasting too. The only reason the police weren't there already was the fact that firearms had been discharged. The regular patrols would be standing back from the scene until they could deploy an armed response team. If any of the armed police were Niners I was a dead man.

As I aimed the Remington at his leg, Knowles closed his eyes and cried. Each sob forced a bloody mist to rise from the holes in his chest. I felt no pity; his tears only served to anger me. I squeezed the trigger and the shotgun kicked. Knowles screamed as his foot flew across the room and landed with a splat in the far corner. A black hole appeared in the laminate flooring and blood from his stump poured into it. He grasped his thigh, lifted his leg and stared wide-eyed at his missing boot. His body heaved and an unearthly scream echoed through the house. 'Fusssssck yousshhh, you'rssse a deassshd man.'

'Look who's talking,' I answered. 'Where and when do they meet?' I pointed the shotgun at his remaining ankle. His eyes were wild and panicked. He knew I really didn't care how much pain he was in. He stopped being a human being when he came to kill me. Blood bubbles were grouping around his exposed teeth. I reckoned his lungs were filling with blood and he wasn't long for this world. 'I've got at least five minutes by my reckoning. This is your last chance.'

'Fuck you.' he hissed in agony.

He closed his eyes as I squeezed the trigger again. His remaining foot slithered across the laminate at high speed and stopped against the skirting board. Knowles screamed even louder and it was like music to my soul. 'Does it hurt?' I asked as I replaced the used shells. 'I'm going to blow your knees off, then your hands, elbows, and so on until you die, or you tell me, so it really is up to you.'

'No,' he screeched. The prospect of more pain broke him.

'Stop. Brunt Boggart, they meet at Brunt Boggart Farm near Benllech,' his voice was a whisper now.

'When?'

'Three days before the full moon.'

'Are you telling me the truth?'

'Yesssssh,' he whined, but I didn't believe him.

'Are you telling me the truth?' I asked again. He blinked and looked upwards. I wasn't sure if that meant that he was lying or not, but

I wasn't bothered either way. I squeezed the trigger again and blew his right knee to smithereens. Blood and bone sprayed across my face and splattered the ceiling. Knowles wailed and I liked his pain. I heard sirens in the distance and knew it was time to go. I aimed the barrel below his waist and put one of the remaining shells into his groin, which ripped off his genitals and left a gaping bloody hole between his legs. His body twitched and bucked, but his agony had no impact upon me.

'That one's for Fabienne Wilder,' I said. Then I fired the other shells into his lower face and blew his head clean off. It rolled across the laminate and thudded against the brick hearth. 'And that one is for Peter.'

A second and then a third siren spurred me to move. I needed to know what was going on outside before I could make any decisions. If the armed response units were already surrounding the building, then I would muzzle Evie Jones and we would walk out together and take our chances with the judicial system. I wasn't about to take on a siege of armed police. I ran upstairs and peered through the front bedroom curtains.

Two patrol cars were blocking the entrance roads onto the car park and a third was parked in the lay-by to my left. A uniformed officer was talking to a gaggle of my neighbours who were dressed in a mishmash of pyjamas and tracksuits. There was no sign of an armed unit. I sprinted to the back bedroom and looked outside. There was one uniformed policeman stopping traffic coming down the roads at the side of the flat. The roads were dead at that time of night and a lone taxi which he had stopped did a three-point turn and went in search of another route. The exit road from the caravan site where the truck was parked was clear, and it was hidden from view by overgrown hedges.

I ran downstairs and grabbed what we needed. Knowles's body stunk of excrement. The cloying smell of blood filled my senses. The scene was horrific, and as I looked at his dismembered body parts scattered across the room, it was blatantly obvious that Knowles wasn't shot and killed in self-defence. Forensic officers would look at the evidence and establish that he'd been debilitated by a shotgun blast and suffered a sustained attack from a dog before being systematically tortured, prior to the final lethal shots being fired to his head. I had watched enough episodes of *CSI* to know that, despite being attacked in my own home, reasonable force was not used. In fact, it looked like a mad man had been let loose. A court would crucify me and in hindsight, so they should. I had lost my mind.

I used my feet to prod Knowles's feet back to his body and the butt of the shotgun to nudge his head closer to the corpse. I positioned them as close to where they once were as I could. I ran into the front room and switched on the gas fire without igniting it and then repeated the process in the dining room. I opened the oven door and switched on the gas and then did the same with all four rings on the hob. I ignited one of the rings and then grabbed the Staffie. I hooked Evie to her lead, and we crept unnoticed across the balcony, down the stairs and behind the cover of the high fence panels. The wheelie bin groaned as I put my shoulder to it and heaved, but it was compliant and slid across the gravel enough for us to disappear through the fence. We tiptoed across our neighbour's rear lawn and I unbolted their garden gate. It took us into an alleyway between two rows of caravans and an indoor swimming pool. Apart from half a dozen grey wheelie bins and a rotting Talbot campervan, the alley was empty. We reached the truck and I managed to get Evie into the back without too much noise; then I hid the Remington behind the rear passenger seat. I stashed Knowles's Beretta under the driver's seat where I could reach it. If we were stopped by the police, there would be no gunfight. I had no wish to go down in a blaze of glory; that's Hollywood bullshit. I wanted to live, but if I got a sniff of any Niners, uniform or not, then they would get a bullet in the face. As we neared the exit to the caravan site, the escaping gas ignited and there was a thumping whoosh as the windows on the upper floor of my home exploded outwards. It had been my home for a long time and I'm not sure if it was the sadness of torching the house or the horror of what I'd just done to two human beings that made me cry, but I sobbed uncontrollably. Evie tried to console me, but I needed more than a lick on the face. I had to wipe the flood of tears from my eyes before I could see well enough to drive. Evie Jones and I were a mile up the Porth Dafarch road by the time the armed unit arrived at the inferno.

CHAPTER 20

On the Run

Heading straight for the A55 was the right thing to do, although we would need a lot of luck to put some distance between us and the bloody scene we had left behind. I hoped that the fire would destroy enough evidence to gift me a chance in front of a judge, but my priority now was anonymity. Arterial roads and two bridges were the only way off Holy Island onto Anglesey. It was obvious I would head for one of them to get out of town, but I was convinced that no one would be looking for me until they'd figured out what had happened at my house. The fire would confuse the scene enough to cloud what had happened and who was to blame. I figured they would think one of the bodies was me and the other was my partner until a detailed investigation could be carried out. By that time, we'd be long gone.

Ged Knowles was proof enough that the Nine Angels had penetrated the police force. Obviously, I had no idea how far their reach went, but I had to assume that he wasn't the only one. One thing was certain: when the fire was extinguished and the bodies were found in the ashes, they would blame the carnage at my home on me. They would arrest me and put me into a remand prison while they conducted the interrogation process, which would make me a sitting duck for bad cops and prison inmates alike. The other factor that I had to consider was Evie Jones. There was no way I would let anybody put her back into a kennel. Her hatred of other dogs would make it a living hell for her. I knew that I had to write this book and put my side of events forward in the only way that I know, then disappear. It would take me a while, but I knew that criminals remained undetected for years if they had half a brain and focused their minds on it. I had more than half a brain most of the time and my desire to remain alive and retain my liberty was intense. We take both for granted, but it has become my main focus in life.

I decided to head for the mountains and drove through Valley to the expressway. As I accelerated down the slip road onto the main carriageway, the heavens opened. The wipers squeaked noisily as they struggled to clear the torrent of water from the windscreen. I tuned the radio to Mon FM, Anglesey's local station, and sure enough, within twenty minutes, news of the fire and reported gunshots were the lead bulletin. The newsreader informed listeners that there was at least one fatality at the scene and that there was growing concern about the whereabouts of the property owner, Trearddur Bay – based author Conrad Jones. I'd turned my Samsung off earlier, so if the police had tried to reach me, I didn't know about it. The radio didn't mention my partner, so I had to assume that they'd tracked her down to her mother's and spoken to her. The fact she'd left me would only muddy the waters – 'Estranged husband goes on the rampage'.

Despite the furore, I was desperate to let her know that Evie Jones was with me. I didn't want her to think that she'd been trapped in the fire. But I guessed that if they were looking for me then they would be monitoring her calls. I hoped that she would figure out that the Staffie would have used the dog flap to escape the fire or she would be with me. It was weird: I had shot two people and set fire to my home, and my number one regret was not being able to tell my partner that the dog was okay.

I had no idea where we were going exactly, but I was acutely aware that the description of my truck would be circulating the traffic police bands pretty soon. I had to reach the section north of the A55 which filtered off to Bryngyran before I could exit and disappear onto the remote minor roads. I flicked stations trying to get a better picture of what the police were releasing to the Press, but the same bulletin was repeated on a loop. It wasn't long before my next-door neighbour's voice was added to the newsflash. She'd been interviewed at the scene and was describing how they'd heard a number of gunshots before the explosion.

'I felt like I'd woken up in Beirut.' The high-pitched voice was undeniably hers. I wondered how long it would be before other voices were tagged onto the piece.

The news was vague, which was positive for now. At least they weren't broadcasting that there was a reward on my head, dead or alive. I analysed every word they said about it over and over. The severity of what I'd done wasn't lost on me. I knew that I had crossed the line and that my life would never be the same again. A huge flash dazzled me for a second as thousands of volts hurtled towards the earth. The thunderclap rumbled over a few seconds later and the rain began to batter the windscreen. The downpour ricocheted off the tarmac, creating the image of a wall of water two feet high. My head was spinning as we reached Caergeiliog. We were nearing the quieter stretches of the motorway when I spotted blue lights closing on us in the far distance. Evie Jones was exhausted and sleeping peacefully on the back seat. The truck was cruising at seventy, which is quick for me. I really am Captain Slow. The only time I go over eighty miles an hour is on an airplane. I was on the run, but still couldn't drive over seventy without breaking into a sweat and envisaging that one of my tyres would blowout at any second. I gripped the steering wheel and pushed my foot down hard. The truck accelerated easily, and the speedometer was showing ninety before I felt any vibration in the vehicle. The extra speed didn't help; the police interceptor was gaining ground on us fast.

The blue light was closing quickly, and I figured it was about a mile behind me. I had to make a decision: stop and hope that my bizarre version of events would be believed or run and let things come out in the wash. The next exit was five minutes away and there was no way we would reach it before they caught up. The truck simply couldn't go much faster, and as I said earlier, I don't do fast. I couldn't outrun a high-powered police interceptor on a two-lane stretch of expressway, but the steep banks on either side gave me an idea. I decided to see how effective the four-wheel drive was. I'd used the truck in the snow many times and it stuck to the road like shit to a blanket when the four-wheel drive was engaged. If I couldn't outrun them, maybe I could out-think them. I waited for the ideal stretch of expressway, where the grassy banks veered steeply up from the tarmac and there were gaps in the hedgerows and treelines beyond.

I slowed down and turned off the headlights. Selecting low-ratio four-wheel drive, I steered the truck up the steep incline. Despite the cloudburst, the fat tyres gripped the slope and the truck climbed the bank with ease. I pressed the accelerator and it roared up the slope without slipping once. When I reached the top, I could see the police car screaming to a halt on the motorway. I saw them leaning across the car to get a better look, talking frantically into their radio as they watched me smash through a fragile three-rail fence with ease. Calling for aerial support was out of the question while this storm raged. As I took the truck over the crest of the hill, I saw them attempt to drive their Volvo up the bank, but it only climbed a few yards before the wheels stuck in the mud. Soil and stones flew in the air as their wheels spun uselessly. Evie slept on through the panic. We'd had a lucky break and I patted the steering wheel lovingly as the truck ploughed onto remote farmland unhindered.

I drove across open farmland, which, from the number of fluffy white animals that I had to circumnavigate, I surmised was used for sheep-grazing. It was undulating, but no problem for the Navara. I carried on for fifteen minutes before turning the headlights on and our progress quickened. Five minutes further on there was a five-bar gate, which took me onto a farm track. Staying on the fields wasn't an option. The rain was hammering down and the already sodden ground would soon turn to impassable swamp. Sooner or later we would come to a stone wall or deep water and we would have to travel miles in the wrong direction to avoid them. Eventually the police would realise that my whereabouts were not only a concern but a priority, and then every available resource would be thrown at finding me. I couldn't risk the weather breaking and a police helicopter finding the truck on open land. We wouldn't stand a chance of escaping that. The farm track was the best option and the farmer had considerately left the gate unlocked. As I steered the truck out of the field, I could see the lights of Llangefni in the distance and I drove the truck towards them. Heading back to the main roads or the motorway was too dangerous. If I could get through Llangefni town centre, the roads beyond weaved their way across the island to the mountains of Snowdonia. The roads there were narrow and unlit. We could blend into the night and lie low in the daylight hours. All we had to do was find our way off the farm and we'd be travelling at speed again.

The Staffie woke up and sensed my relief, and she sat between the front seats and licked my face. At that point I thought we had outrun them, but I underestimated the power of the Press and the influence that some news programmes have. Every mistake is a learning experience, but you can't make mistakes when you're a murder suspect. As we reached the end of the farm track, we approached the farmhouse and the outbuildings which surrounded it. The track weaved through the farm and was the only way that we could reach the roads beyond. The farm buildings were in darkness as we drove through the farmyard, but as we reached the entrance to the yard, a huge dark shape blocked our path. The Staffie suddenly pricked up her ears and I knew she sensed danger. A deep growl came from her chest.

I stopped the truck but left the engine running while I assessed the situation. A massive combine harvester blocked our path to the road. The truck's headlights picked out the shape of a man wearing heavy overalls and a black donkey jacket. There were two black and white mongrels sat at his feet. He levelled a single barrelled shotgun at the windscreen. I had to laugh to myself. I envisaged him shouting, 'Oi, gerr orrff my land.' But something told me it wouldn't be that simple. I'd driven roughshod across his land and he would have seen the headlights coming across his fields. He was protecting his farm, that's all; or so I thought.

I had hidden my shotgun behind the backseat, and I couldn't reach it, but I thought an explanation would be more appropriate than the Remington. Thieves steal thousands of pounds worth of farm equipment every year and I had driven my truck across his land in the middle of the night. How could I expect anything else? I opened the door and stepped out. The rain soaked me in seconds. Evie Jones was snarling at the mongrels, so I had to close the door to stop her jumping out and attacking them.

'Hi, I'm sorry I came across your land, but it was an emergency. I was trying to get away from someone on the motorway,' I lied. 'I need to get into Llangefni. Can you tell me the best way to go?'

'I know who you are,' the farmer growled. 'You're that writer fella they're talking about on the television. Turn off the engine and put your hands up.'

'Okay, take it easy,' I said. I swallowed hard and debated my options. Was the farmer one of them or had he seen me on the news? If he was one of them then I was as good as dead. If he wasn't, I was looking at a long stretch behind bars and Evie would get the needle. I couldn't let that happen either way. My mind conjured up too many scenarios for me to make a rational decision. Were the police officers who chased us Niners? Could they have traced the landowner and contacted him? Was that feasible?

'Look, you don't need to get involved in this,' I said calmly, although I didn't feel that calm. 'Just let me by and I'll be on my way.'

'I don't want to shoot you, but I will.' He cocked his head and winked in a 'stupid uncle' type of way. 'They asked me to keep an eye out for a truck crossing my land. They told me that you're that writer fella who everyone's after.'

'Who asked you?' I was losing my cool. I was losing my mind if the truth be told, but I didn't want to fight with this man if he was just protecting his land. 'The police?'

'I pay no heed to the police, young man. Don't matter to me if you're alive or dead when they get here, so I'd be turning off that engine if I was you,' he winked again.

'Doesn't matter if I'm alive or dead?' I muttered his words under my breath.

'Nope. Don't matter to me. Turn the engine off before I blow a hole in you.'

Now I was worried. He sounded like he had a vested interest in capturing me but for who? The police or the Niners? My head was spinning.

'There was no need to threaten me, but I'll open the door and turn the engine off, okay?'

'Do it slowly, like I said. I don't want to shoot you, but I'm not bothered either way,' he warned with his irritating wink. I was getting sick of being threatened and I needed to get away from there. Once again, I was left with no choice. I opened the driver's door and the Staffie bounded out of the truck like a whirling dervish. I turned off the headlights and dived behind the truck. The farmer fired his shotgun at me as his mongrels met Evie Jones. If he really wasn't bothered whether I lived or died, then I owed him the same respect. Flight was no longer a valid option, which meant only one thing.

I could hear Evie tearing into the yelping mongrels. There was only ever going to be one winner, and she tore into them and tossed them around the farmyard like rag toys. The farmer kicked out at Evie trying to save his dogs; he stumbled and grabbed for a drystone wall to catch his balance. He broke the gun to discard the empty cartridge and scrambled for another one. His stumble cost him valuable seconds and I bolted from the back of the truck towards him. In a few strides, I closed the gap between us and pulled out the blade from my neck knife. He was closing the barrel as I reached him, but I was travelling too fast.

I gripped the knife in my right hand with the blade pointing outwards near my thumb and slammed it into his temple. I was running at full speed when I hit him; the tungsten blade pierced the side of his skull as if it was made from eggshell; his eyes rolled into the back of his head as his body went limp and collapsed onto the floor in a crumpled mess. I couldn't let go of the knife for some reason. Blood pumped down my hand and trickled around my wrist. Its warmth had a creeping, repulsive feeling. I wanted to wipe it off as quickly as possible. His mouth was moving slightly and his tongue lolled from the side of his lips. His legs muscles went into spasm. It's strange what you learn about the human body when you're so close to death.

I released my grip on the handle and wiped the blood from my hands on his jacket. I felt the urge to wash them thoroughly, but that would have to wait. Taking the shotgun from his hands, I turned to see how the Staffie was doing. It was clear to see that one of the dogs had fled and she had the other by the throat. She was dragging it like a toy and flinging it from side to side. There was no fight left in it, but Evie was making sure that it was defeated. I should have done the same.

I tried to recover the knife, but it was wedged deep into the skull and it wouldn't budge. I put my foot on the farmer's head and pulled with all my strength. There was a slushy noise as the blade came free. Using the sleeve of his jacket, I wiped the blade clean on one side and then the other before sliding it back into its sheath. Blood flowed freely from the wound, but there was a rhythm to it. Every heartbeat increased the flow slightly. I should have realised then that he wasn't dead.

Suddenly, his eyes cleared, and he grabbed for the gun. I was so shocked that I slipped on the saturated grass and fell awkwardly onto my elbow. I was almost on top of him. His strength surprised me. He scratched at my eyes with one weather-beaten hand while he tried to wrestle the gun from me with the other. I broke free of his grip and managed to kneel up. I twisted my body and slammed the butt of the gun into the bridge of his nose, smashing the delicate bone and slicing a rent across his cheek. He released his hold on the gun and I brought the butt down again, onto his forehead this time. His damaged skull cracked and imploded, spraying me with grey brain matter and pink goo. It splattered onto my face and neck, and a globule of grey tissue dribbled off my nose onto my lips. I spat it out in disgust and slammed the gun into the remains of his face again. His body twitched as I rammed the heavy stock into his head again. It was as if I was in a bad dream and nothing was real. There was no rhyme or reason to what was going on; the world had become a dangerous game where the aim was to survive no matter what it took.

I was soaked, my muscles ached, and I knelt on all fours, gasping for air. Sweat mingled with the rain. It poured down my face and trickled down my back. As I looked at the dead farmer, I felt bile rising in my throat and my stomach launched its contents back up the way it had come. I retched until there was nothing left, and the stomach acid stung the back of my throat. In the space of a few days, the world had become a surreal nightmare. I had killed three people in one evening and had no qualms about it. What had I done? The Staffie ran over, licking the blood from my hands and face. I patted her for saving me again, but I needed to catch my breath. I gathered my nerve and stood up, but my body was trembling with shock and exertion.

'Good girl.' I held her head close to my chest. 'What the fuck are we going to do now, Evie Jones?' I asked her. I heard my voice breaking and knew that tears were not far away. Evie Jones licked my face and she took my right hand gently into her mouth. Whatever it means to her, it made me get a grip on reality. There was no time for self-pity or self-recrimination. If we were to remain free, then we had to move.

I looked around before we climbed back into the truck and I found a weak point in the farmer's perimeter fence. I bypassed the harvester by forcing the truck through the hedge to the left of the big machine. I had not seen the gap as we had approached earlier. If I had, the farmer and his dogs would probably still be alive, but we all have choices to make and he made the wrong one.

I could no longer take anything for granted. I'll never know if he was one of them or if he was an upright citizen trying to apprehend a suspected murderer. Once he had fired that shotgun, it made no difference to me. I had to treat everyone as my enemy. My lesson learned I placed the farmer's shotgun on the front seat where I could grab it quickly. My cache of weapons was growing, as was the number of pursuers. I drove down the access road and joined the main drag towards town. As we trundled through the empty streets of Llangefni, Evie Jones stretched out on the backseat, panting. She was knackered. So far, it had been a long night.

CHAPTER 21

Facebook

We encountered no problems as we crossed Llangefni and headed along the quiet backroads towards Menai Bridge; we crossed the straits using the old bridge and then took the Caernarfon road, before turning off to Llanberis heading towards the mountains. I stuck to the quiet roads and avoided the tourist town; some of the back roads don't even show up on a map. We travelled all night without seeing another vehicle on the road; I wanted to keep moving. The rain stopped as dawn broke and I pulled the truck into a small car park on the edge of the river Llugwy. It's an isolated spot, unfrequented by most tourists. More people view it looking down from the peak of Snowdon than from the road where we were. There are no rowing boats, swans or nearby chip shops, just the river and surrounding peaks. A single-track road hugs one bank of the Llugwy; grass and weeds form a living green line along the middle of the tarmac. The far bank rises into almost vertical slopes which are dangerously loose. Extending the length of the south-east side of the river are the Screes, consisting of millions of fragments of broken rock. Rising from the river to a height of almost two hundred feet. The shale slopes offer no solid foundation to walk on.

It's a place which has inspired poets and painters for centuries, and the peace and tranquillity was a startling contrast to memories of the previous night. The river lake was as smooth as a mirror and the hills reflected from the water as if you could walk on the surface itself. It's such a peaceful place to be and considering what had happened over the last few days, it was exactly where we needed to be. The mountains had a humbling effect on my soul, and although I had lived through a gruesome nightmarish night, the beauty of the mountains wasn't lost on me that day.

I washed the dried blood from my hands in the freezing water and I looked at my reflection. I hardly recognised the man that I saw. He frightened me. I looked like a maniac. My eyes were sunk deep into my head and my face was smeared with blood and brain matter. I remembered the horror movie *Dawn of the Dead*. It frightened the life out of me. I looked like an extra from the film. If I'd held out my arms and walked like I'd crapped in my jeans, I would have made a great zombie, no doubt about it.

The blood would wash off and the horrific memories would fade, but what was I going to do now? My life as it was had gone. I had killed three people, one of which could have been a perfectly innocent farmer. His remains would shock the most hardened forensic team, and where was the evidence that he'd fired at me? There wasn't a scratch on my body and none of the shot had hit the truck. The evidence would tell the police that I'd bashed his brains out with my bare hands. I was a killer on the run, and I was armed. They would shoot me on sight if I didn't surrender.

No one would believe my version of events. A random case of research working alongside a murder detective had mutated into a brutal killing spree – why? Because of Fabienne Wilder, the suspect in yet another brutal murder. The authorities had sectioned and detained her in a secure mental health unit, but I had believed she was innocent when no one else would listen. They would think that I needed to be sectioned. They would either shoot me if I resisted arrest or lock me up and throw away the key.

There was no easy option and no magic solution. I had to wait and see what the next few days would bring. I wasn't thinking clearly enough to construct a solid plan of action. I needed some sleep and Evie Jones needed feeding. She was pottering around at the edge of the river, lapping thirstily at the water. Every now and then she'd come running back to me before scooting off again. It suddenly occurred to me that she wasn't on her lead. I looked around and the nearest sheep was half a mile away up a mountain. She deserved a little run after what we'd been through. The dog had saved my life several times in one night. I wouldn't have made it this far without her. She waggled over to me and rolled over onto her back, wriggling her hips against the grass. We were on the run from every police force in the British Isles and we were being hunted by a murderous satanic sect, but obviously it was tummy-tickling time. She had her priorities right.

The next few weeks were a blur. We spent the first three days in lodgings behind a pub called the Miners' Bridge. I was wary about using public places because of the news coverage my plight had received. But we met the landlord by chance. We'd parked near a river which we used to bathe and keep Evie's water bowl full when we met a ruddy-faced man walking along one of the footpaths. He made a huge fuss of her because she reminded him of a dog that he'd had for seventeen years before it died. Apparently, her markings were identical. He introduced himself as Graham and asked me where we were staying. I mumbled something about needing to be away from other tourists and dogs.

Despite having a no-pets policy, he offered me a room in a converted outhouse on the proviso that none of the other guests saw Evie. I agreed but told him that I was hiding from my ex-wife who was suing me for every penny that I owned, and that I would have to pay cash. He laughed and told me that he'd bought that particular T-shirt himself, and we signed in under the name of Eris Jones. That suited me, and we had a few days of warm water, good food, and comfortable beds. I spent the time writing on my laptop, stopping every hour to watch the news updates. The news wasn't good. I was now the main suspect in a triple-homicide investigation, and the police were warning the general public not to approach me as I was armed and extremely dangerous. My photograph was all over the nationals, as was a description of the truck. They used photographs of trucks the same make and model. I'd parked it out of sight behind the outhouses so that none of the guests would see it. Graham had seen it though and that bothered me.

I didn't know where to turn, and I was thinking about turning myself in when he tapped on the door late one night. To be honest, I thought it was the police and I hugged the Staffie before opening the door, but it was Graham and he was alone.

'I wondered if you fancied a few quiet drinks and some company,' he asked. My first instinct was to refuse, but he held up a bottle of single malt and two glasses. 'I think we need a chat, Eris,' he added seriously. 'I mean you no harm and your business, is your own, but I think you're in trouble and I may be able to help.'

I'm not sure why I trusted Graham, but I did. Maybe he reminded me of my father in some ways. I let him into the room, and we cracked open the whisky. He made a proper fuss of Evie Jones, and after a few drinks he asked me outright if I was the man that the police were looking for. There didn't seem to be much point in denying it. I told him that I was indeed Conrad Jones and that I had killed those people, but I explained my reasons and told him most of the story. He listened intently and nodded his head as I explained the events of the past weeks. The whisky had loosened my tongue and the whole saga came out. After an hour or so, Graham frowned and rubbed the grey stubble on his chin.

'You're going to have to get rid of that truck if you're to have any chance of hiding from the law.' He lowered his voice as if someone was listening at the door. 'Listen, I know a lot of travellers who go to and fro from Ireland and they're always on the lookout for dodgy motors, especially four-by-fours. I'll do you a deal.' He raised a bushy grey eyebrow. 'Wait here a minute.' He tapped the side of his nose with his index finger as he got up and left the room. Evie sniffed at the door as it closed. If she liked him then I couldn't go far wrong; I trusted her judgement.

When he returned, he had a carrier bag stuffed with some of his belongings. He pulled out a flat cap and black rimmed reading glasses. I had already let my hair and stubble grow attempting to change my appearance. Combined with the glasses and cap, they aged me by ten years at least. The stubble on my chin was nearly silver in colour, and although it itched like crazy, it was the best disguise I could come up with.

'I've shaved my head for years, so a wig would be good.' I laughed as I put on the cap and glasses. It was a simple disguise, but they aged me enough to make me look like any other middle-aged tourist in Snowdonia, and there were thousands of them.

'I've never had much call for a wig.' He chuckled, rubbing the wiry mop of grey hair on his head. 'Where would you buy a wig in the Snowdonia? The cap will have to do for now. I'll get you a few grand for the truck as long as you promise to put my pub in the book.' I laughed and gave him the keys. I'd hidden the weapons days ago in the woods behind the outhouse.

How could I refuse his offer? His kindness will stay with me as long as I live. The next day he knocked on my door and brought out a brown envelope full of cash and a set of car keys. 'Here's three-grand for the truck and here's the keys to my Land Rover. I don't use it anymore. If I'm truthful with you, I lost my licence last March driving pissed-up and I was going to sell it anyway. I've taken three hundred quid out of your money for the Landy if that's okay with you.' I thanked him and shook his hand warmly. 'I'll call after closing and we can have a few drams if you like. I've got a lovely bottle of Talisker which nobody likes.' His eyes smiled but there was sadness in them, too. He knew that he wouldn't see us again. 'Look after him, Evie Jones.' He patted her one last time and left. His kindness will stay with me forever. With the truck gone, he was implicated in aiding and abetting a known criminal. If I stayed around, he would probably lose his pub, and I felt that it was time to move on.

Confident that my disguise had transformed me enough not to get recognised and with a new vehicle, we drifted from one guesthouse to another. Using the Internet to search out the most remote, dog-friendly places, we stayed on the move. I began to think that we'd cracked it and I was tempted to call my partner and explain everything. Half of me wanted to hear her voice, but the other half knew that the call could be traced. And I wasn't convinced that she would be sympathetic to my version of events anyway. I continued to write about the Niners and the story of Fabienne Wilder, but sometimes I would start to shake and cry. As the days and weeks went by, post-traumatic stress began to bubble to the surface. I was plagued by nightmares of the dead; their faces haunted me and still do. I began to question myself. Did they really need to die? Could there have been another way? The true horrors of the violent deaths at my hands were seeping into my soul and destroying me.

I drove into Betws-y-coed one day, which is a beautiful place. I bought SIM cards from one of the supermarkets and put them into my Samsung. I was itching to call home and speak to my partner, my mum, my brother, and my friends, but I dared not. Isolation and anonymity were good therapy, and they were keeping my liberty intact.

I bought a red top newspaper which was carrying the story of the hunt for me. No one was actually saying that I was the murderer, but the police weren't seeking anyone else to help with their enquiries. In my mind, that means, I'm guilty as charged. The entire story had finally come out, which I thought would help me, but it hadn't. It sounded like I had suffered a mental breakdown and turned into a violent killer. My whereabouts were a total unknown. The Press were reporting the story of the crime-thriller writer who had gone on a killing spree with a shotgun following the mysterious death of his friend, a serving officer in the murder squad. Some reporters were linking other recent victims to the story, while others were toying with the theory that, unable to cope with the murders, I may have taken my own life.

It was big news. They plastered it across the newspapers and local and national television. Despite the fact that my appearance hadn't raised an eyebrow for weeks, we had to pack up and move on as frequently as we dared. My picture was being broadcast daily. If they'd concentrated as much attention on the description of my dog, then we'd have been spotted weeks before, but no one knew for sure if she was with me. The forensic details from the farm hadn't disclosed that his dogs were savaged to death. Had those details been released, I think I would be in a cell and Evie Jones would be glue.

I bought a two-berth caravan from a farmer for five hundred pounds. He allowed me to pitch it next to a stream on his land where he rented out pitches to the odd camper who couldn't get on the proper sites. Mould riddled the walls and it smelled damp, but it would become home for the next few months.

As I studied the newspapers it became obvious that some of the reports were being tainted by people who had it in for me. The Niners were trying to manipulate the news to suit them. They couldn't go public to find me, but they could use their influence to gain public opinion, so I decided to do the same. It was time to stick my head above the parapet and tell my side of the tale. When I wasn't writing, I spent every waking hour hammering the Internet with my story. My address book is full of Press contacts from my years of publishing books. I e-mailed everyone that I had in my address book and sent them my version of events. I used open Wi-Fi networks to message everyone that was important to me. I was touched by some of the messages of support that were posted on my pages and sickened by some of the derisory comments from those who didn't believe me, Peter's family included. Not everyone liked me enough to take me at my word and who could blame them?

The book forums and writers' groups on Amazon and Facebook were buzzing with my story, but a lot of people thought that my version didn't add up and it was just another one of my stories. Under the microscope, the facts were there for all to see. Three people were shot and killed, and I was on the run. Guilty as charged, Mr Jones. Many of my contacts shrugged off my Internet rants about the Order of Nine Angels as the desperate efforts of a condemned man to escape his fate. The Niners had members and casual sympathisers at executive level across the spectrum of the Press and they ensured that they painted me as a psychopathic murderer. Every chapter and word of my published novels were analysed, and because they are violent stories, general opinion was that my mind was already warped and that I had been a ticking time bomb waiting to go off. Maybe I am. Who knows?

Anyway, it was pleasing at the time that my Internet campaign was working to some degree. People were hammering Google and discovering the myriad of satanic orders that are out there. There was a wave of panic across North America in the nineties following the discovery of the sexual abuse of children and human sacrifice by satanic organisations, and the Press began to drag up cases from decades ago. Look it up for yourself. You may believe me if you do. Some of them have Facebook pages. How bonkers is that? *Hello, I'm in a secret satanic cult, so you can find me on Facebook if you want to chat about sacrifice, child abuse or how the dark arts are working for you today.* Is it me, or has the world reached a new level of madness since the worldwide web became established?

The beauty of it is that it works both ways. They can find each other, but you can find them in minutes. I've always used the Internet to its full capacity to market my books and clearing my name was no different. The sceptics among the Press were crawling all over their websites and people were beginning to ask questions about their identities; O9A was being scrutinised and they were squirming. The idiots who joined their Facebook forums were suddenly in full view for all to see, and their membership crashed overnight. Chat rooms were alive with discussions about my plight. After two full weeks of screaming my innocence, one of the big tabloids ran an investigative report into the Nine Angels and their sister groups, and because it was front page news the other red tops followed suit. The existence of dangerous satanic cults actively recruiting and operating both globally on the Internet and on the streets of the UK became an accepted fact. Some of their websites were shut down and some of them simply crashed beneath the wave of public pressure.

A friend of the reporter Malcolm Baines highlighted the fact that he had been working on a story about the Niners when he died. The newspaper ran a thorough investigation into his research and discovered that his work had been deleted. When they tracked down the computer terminal responsible for the deletion, Jason Clement resigned in shame and his face was plastered across the news. He was arrested by the police for possession of indecent images of children; the search of his home address and his personal computer uncovered thousands more. The investigation didn't end there. The Met's computer boffins traced hundreds of links and documents which had been sent to an address on their own server. A high-ranking officer, Inspector Woods, was dismissed in disgrace and later arrested for possession of child pornography. Woods hung himself before he went to court.

The arrests forced the police to reopen the investigation into the death of Malcolm Baines. A detailed search of his computer revealed that he had never joined any Internet gambling sites. His bank account, credit card and login details were all uploaded from Jason Clement's personal computer. Three months after his arrest for possessing child porn, he was rearrested on suspicion of the murder of Malcolm Baines and held on remand at HMP Brixton. On the morning of his second day of incarceration, his throat was slit by a fellow inmate. Like I said to Ged Knowles, what goes around comes around.

Cold cases from the eighties and nineties were scrutinised time and again. At last the world was listening to me, and as the clamour from the UK drifted across Europe and the Atlantic, law enforcement agencies worldwide began to look into the groups from a different perspective. Suddenly, their websites began to disappear and their profiles on the social networking sites vanished. Facebook and Twitter removed and blocked anyone connected to their pages. Photographers and reporters swamped the Brunt Boggart Farm near Benllech, and its dark past was investigated in-depth, which added to the intrigue of the entire backstory. The police searched the place in detail. I'd seen it on the news. What the police found, if anything, I'll never know; the Niners are not stupid. They would have cleansed the farm of any incriminating evidence as soon as Officer Knowles was found dead.

Detectives were receiving calls from thousands of parents and friends of missing people who they thought may have had links with the cults. It had worked. I had done exactly what Fabienne asked me to do before she died; I had succeeded in slowing them down. They'd been forced into the spotlight and like any creepy crawly, they were scurrying for the shadows. I was elated; I felt like I had won. It helped the guilt that was eating away at me.

When the newspapers launched their coverage of the story, I drove to Llangollen and bought Evie Jones some lambs' liver from a butcher's shop and a bottle of Jack Daniels for me. We had something to celebrate at last. They were under the microscope and I revelled in the discomfort I was causing them. There would be powerful people shitting their pants right now, and that made me laugh aloud. I gave her the liver raw and we spent a few days feeling like there was a light at the end of the dark tunnel we'd been travelling through.

My mirth was short lived. If they hated me before, now I was number one on the hit list for every would-be Satanist on the planet. Internet trolls began slating my books on Amazon. Dozens of crap reviews appeared overnight. My exposure to the Press had boosted book sales to new heights, but the deluge of one-star reviews brought them crashing back down. They began to use the Internet as effectively as I had. They set up a fake Conrad Jones profile on Facebook and began adding all my friends. Imagine you're one of my close friends and you know what has gone on from the newspapers. All of a sudden, you get a friend request from me. Then I ask you for help. They were fishing for information from my friends about my whereabouts, and they could tell from the replies who had been in contact recently.

The newspapers were hounding people that I'd worked with decades ago. I knew because of the ridiculous quotes that were being printed on a daily basis. A couple of ex-girlfriends were pictured in one of the Sunday papers. Of course, they couldn't believe what a lucky escape they'd had.

He seemed like such a lovely bloke.

I always knew there was something wrong with him.

I told my friends he was odd. All those scary books he writes, I mean, who thinks up things like that?

Weirdo, total weirdo. My mum hated him.

Fuck off; I hadn't seen most of them for twenty years. Looking at how some of them had aged, it was me that had had the lucky escape; as for being a weirdo, she might have a point.

I monitored the fake Facebook pages and tried to let people know that it wasn't me. I have no way of knowing who fell for it, but that's when my best friend Reece and an ex-girlfriend I was still close to disappeared. Ross was never found, but my ex turned up in the River Lune. They were upping the ante in their search for me. I desperately tried to warn everyone on my friends list not to talk to me – it wasn't me. I messaged everyone and deleted my friends list to protect them. They were attacking my close friends, and when I found out Recce was missing, I cried. They found his dog Alfie slaughtered. I knew that it wouldn't be long before they went for my family. My mother was seventy-two then and my younger brother lived close to her. If they identified them as my only close family, then they could kill two birds with one stone. I couldn't see any end to it. It was hard enough running and leaving my life behind me. Protecting myself and Evie was difficult enough. If they targeted my friends and family, then the rules had to change. Hiding from them was no longer an option.

I decided against all my better instincts that I would call my brother. I used a pay-as-you-go SIM card and drove north to Wrexham in case the police were monitoring his calls too. I was paranoid about giving my position away. When I got through to him, after an avalanche of questions about where I was and what was going on, we both broke down in tears. My family had been devastated by the whole dreadful episode. Apart from the Internet postings and the endless stories in the Press, they didn't have a clue whether I was guilty or innocent. I had to put him straight on that. I was guilty. I did kill those people, but I told him it was self-defence. My brother knows that I have a fiery temper, but he accepted my version of events without question.

He told me that the police had been pressing my partner and my family to appear on television to appeal to me to turn myself in. I asked him to make sure that the first thing he did when he got off the telephone was to make sure that everyone we knew stayed out of the news and off the television screens. I spelled it out to him: they were all targets. He told me that the vast majority of people were backing me and that the feedback they were getting from the police and the Press was positive on the whole. He asked me if there was any way that they could help, but I couldn't think of anything. I said that I would be in touch as soon as it was safe to do so, and we said a teary goodbye. It was good to talk to him, and for a few minutes I felt normal again.

On the way back to the caravan, I stopped at a small cafe to get some coffee and let Evie have a walk. It was on the shores of the Conwy and the clouds had moved enough to allow a view of the peak of Snowdonia. The sun was trying hard to warm the earth while the clouds were away. I paid for my coffee and picked up a newspaper before making my way to an empty picnic table outside. It wasn't really warm enough to sit outside, but I couldn't relax while people were around. Every second glance made me nervous. Had they recognised me as the monster that was running from the police?

When I picked up the newspaper, my heart sank. On the front page was a full-length photograph of a woman called Pamela Bonner. I recognised her eyes immediately. She had the type of eyes that made men go weak at the knees. We were serious for a few years and we talked about marriage, but our careers took us in different directions. I put my career first and sometimes, I wonder if we would have made it. A few years later, she married, and I was gutted. I wasn't thinking straight and started seeing a married woman. Some of you will judge me and that's fine, but we didn't mean to fall in love, it just happened. The rights and wrongs of the affair don't matter now, but if she'd left her husband and asked me to commit to her, I probably would have. She had eyes like Elizabeth Taylor in *Cleopatra*. Pamela was stunning when we were young; she didn't look bad in the newspaper either. The headline read,

WANTED WRITER IS THE FATHER OF MY DAUGHTER.

I laughed aloud, drawing curious glances from an elderly couple who were determined enough to sit outside too. I wondered how much the newspaper had paid Pamela for that load of lies. I hadn't clapped eyes on her for years, so how could I be the father of her child? She must have fallen on hard times to come up with that one, but she had no idea what she'd done. She'd ruined any chances of my partner coming back to me.

Yes, Conrad, I forgive you for setting fire to our home, murdering three people and having an affair, no problem. Oh, and by the way, when is your daughter's birthday? I'll put it on the calendar, so we don't forget.

I laughed as I read the in-depth article, but the more I read, the less comical it became. Most of it was true. In fact, all of it was true apart from the daughter bit. The front page gave a brief timeline of the affair and Pamela was quoted as saying,

'He must have had some kind of mental breakdown.'

How the hell would she know anything about my mental health? Inside was a two-page spread detailing our relationship, accompanied by a dozen photographs of us as a couple on various days out. Two of them clearly showed her wedding ring. They must have been photoshopped. A quarter of the page showed a pretty six-year-old girl. She was the image of Pamela. Her name was Constance, allegedly named after her father, Conrad. Bullshit. Pamela told the newspaper that she'd never told me that she was pregnant because she didn't want to split up with her partner at the time. She said, she knew that the relationship could never work because I was obsessed with my career.

My mind was spinning. At first, I thought that she was trying to make a few quid by selling her story, but the more I looked at Constance, the more I started to believe her. When we split up, Pamela left the company about six months later and I heard that she stepped down from senior management and took on a part-time job somewhere. That fit in with her being pregnant and leaving work to become a single mother. If Constance was six years old, then Pamela would have been pregnant immediately after we split up. Or she was already pregnant, and she was telling the truth.

The more I ran the dates through my mind, the more convinced I was. Constance could indeed be my daughter. The article made me do backflips in my mind. Was I her father? I could have been. The rest of the afternoon went by in a whirl. Although I was on the run, the news that I may be a father was earth-shattering. For some reason, it put me on a high and the next minute, I would be as low as a man could go. I took the chance of calling my brother back, which shocked him slightly, but I needed him to contact Pamela and find out the truth. It was three hours later when I called him back for a progress report.

My elation turned into bitterness, hatred, and anger. My brother had spoken to Pamela and she convinced him that Constance was my daughter. She said that when she'd first seen my books on the Internet, she couldn't bring herself to tell me about our daughter in case I thought that she was a gold-digger. That was hard enough to digest, but when he told me that Constance had been missing since the previous day, I knew that they'd taken her. Something snapped inside me.

CHAPTER 22

Snapped

I'd had enough. I thought long and hard about it, but the same conclusions sprang to mind. They were trying to get to me by tracing my friends and family. My ex was dead, and Reece was missing. Pamela Bonner had told the world that I had a six-year-old daughter and now Constance was missing. Whether she was my daughter or not was irrelevant; they thought that she was. Who would be next? My estranged partner, my mother or my brother could all be on their lists. I was debating how long I would serve for manslaughter. If they sentenced me to ten years, I would serve seven. But in reality, I was looking at spending most of the remainder of my life in jail, if I was lucky enough to face a lower charge. The alternative was that the Niners would eventually find me and torture me to death. When you look at it that way, my options were not great. If the law caught up me, Evie would be destroyed. If the Niners caught up with us, they would destroy Evie Jones, too, but in a less humane way. Whatever we chose to do, we were stuffed.

In my mind, something snapped. I wasn't prepared to sit back while they hurt the people that I cared about. I didn't know how I felt about Constance, but I did know that I had to do something to stop them hurting her. They were killing other people to get to me and there was only one way to stop them. I had to go to them. Don't get me wrong, I did not decide to give up or give in. I was not going to surrender myself to them or the police. I decided to go and find them. They were only humans after all.

Ged Knowles and his friend died easily enough. Knowles told me where his nexion was based. The newspapers hadn't published any blinding revelations about the search there, so I had to assume that nothing concrete had been found. It had been weeks since it was searched. If there was anything incriminating on the farm, it would have been all over the Press. They'd cleaned the place of any evidence; I was sure of it. Even if they had cleansed the farm, there would be some connection there which may lead me to their hierarchy. I intended to start at the top and work my way down until they got the message that my family and friends were out of bounds. I would cut the head from the serpent and hope that it didn't grow back.

The police weren't able to prove that there was a nexion at the farm, but I didn't need proof. I didn't have to work within the same constraints they did. Knowles was in agony when he told me where they met; I believed him. The police must have looked into the owners, but they couldn't arrest anyone without proof that a crime had been committed there. I didn't need proof to tell me that they were guilty, and I didn't need the courts to convict them. The Remington was a far better punishment than prison. I made the choice to take the fight to them, and if that meant that I had to die, then it would be my way, not theirs. Evie Jones would want it that way, too, and I knew she would fight them with me without batting an eyelid.

I was cool, calm, and collected as I doctored my shotgun licence with a false name and a new photograph. 'Danny Holley' made a trip to a sporting outlet and bought enough shotgun cartridges to start a war. With my ammunition bought, I cleaned both shotguns and sharpened my neck knife. I cut the photograph of Constance from the newspaper and folded it into my wallet. Then I needed to find out as much information as I could about the farm called Brunt Boggart.

CHAPTER 23

Brunt Boggart

My search was a quick one as the farm was easy to find. Brunt Boggart is old language for 'Burnt Witch', an apt name for the place. Google that too if you don't believe me. The farm that comes up is in a small village on the outskirts of Liverpool called Tarbock Green, and the history behind its name is as dark as the hearts of the people who gathered there. Google it if you're still doubting me. The farm on Anglesey has no Internet footprint anymore. They've found a way to remove it but mystery and myths shroud the history of the farm. Obviously, a witch met a sticky end there, and ever since then, bizarre things have happened. Open-minded folk will see it as a curse from the tortured witch, but the sceptics among us will say that place has merely suffered from a series of unfortunate events.

The old farmhouse stood for decades, but it became dilapidated and subsidence, caused by the deep shafts from the copper mines on that side of the island, affected the foundations, making it unsafe. Old Mrs Williams, the matriarch of the family, refused to move out of the building despite the structural damage. As senility crept up on her, she became frightened of an old woman who followed her around the house. Of course, nobody else could see her. She died there when a fire sped through the dwelling. In the early seventies, the Williams family built a new farmhouse on the same site and it, too, burnt down. During a ten-year period, they built another three houses on the site and all three burnt to the ground within months of completion. The family suffered from a history of tragic deaths and mysterious accidents before they sold the farm and moved away. Where else would you choose to worship Satan and his dark forces?

As I read about the history of farm, I felt numb. Some of the newspapers had made a lot out of its sinister past while others brushed over it, feeling that their readers would think the story was being dressed up by reporters. My opinion is that historians have documented the tragic events on that piece of land for years and the Order of Nine Angels wanted to tap into the evil forces entwined in its history. If you believe in spirits and such things, then it's not difficult to comprehend my theory. O9A believe the evil that haunts the site can be tapped. The tragic accidents and deaths which occurred left an energy there, which can be used by them. I do believe that's what they think to a degree, but I find it difficult to believe something which cannot be explained.

I'm not sure how it works, but my theory is that everything has the capacity to absorb energy. Energy makes the universe exist, right? Take crystals for instance, they absorb energy. Quartz is used for all sorts of things. What about vinyl records and DVDs; they can store hours of music and film and then we replay them on devices. Well, I think the elements around us absorb events that happen near them. Wood, bricks, tiles, and concrete absorb heat and radiation; they're forms of energy, so why can't they store information?

A ghost, for instance, is a replay of something that happened centuries ago. Mediums and spiritualists are just better at replaying the information than we are. Anyway, I think Brunt Boggart absorbed the evil of the witch and the elements there replay it for those who have the ability to channel it.

What does that mean to me? Absolutely nothing. I was past caring about the Nine Angels and what they believed in. I didn't care whether they had supernatural powers or not. I know they can't stop a bullet. They bleed, they burn, and they die the same as we do. They would never stop looking for me and I was tired of hiding. It was time to take my destiny in my own hands. I loaded up the truck with the shotguns and shells and realised that I might need a little more firepower. I also thought seriously about leaving Evie Jones in the caravan, safe and sound, but I did not think that I would return from this journey. She stresses when she's alone and I couldn't predict when, or if, I would get back to her. The thought of her trapped in the caravan, running out of food and water stopped me from leaving her. I decided we would travel together. We would fight together and probably die together. I can't think of anyone I'd rather have next to me when the time comes.

CHAPTER 24

Pipe Bomb

If you want to learn how to do something, the Internet is a wonderful tool. You can find out how to make anything you like. I wanted to build some grenades and I found several sites on how to manufacture pipe bombs. I found a very useful video, which explained the process in idiot-proof fashion. I'm not very good with tools and my abysmal record of failed DIY projects serves as witness to the fact. A local plumbers' merchant sold me a length of lead pipe and I bought two boxes of display fireworks from a garden centre. Using a hacksaw, I cut the pipe into ten-inch lengths and then hammered one of the ends closed. I then filled the pipe with gunpowder from the rockets and stuffed tampons into the open end as fuses. I made six in total. I didn't think that I would need any more than six and I didn't think I would live long enough to wish that I had made seven.

When I had finished making my pipe bombs, I bought two bottles of merlot and a large portion of fish, chips and mushy peas from the bridge chip shop in Betws. Evie Jones ate a full lamb's liver, cooked chicken mixed with a tin of tuna fish and a bag of doggy chocolate buttons. It was our version of the last supper. I took her for a long walk around Miners' Bridge and thought about dying. Somethings were worth dying for. I felt terribly guilty about taking Evie with me to find them. I had a choice to put my life in danger, but she didn't; she would fight to protect me and die without thinking about it. My conscience was wrestling with the idea, but the alternatives seemed worse.

There is a footpath which circles the river and the scenery around it is stunning. The mountains in the distance merge with the skyline and the views are breathtaking in the winter and summer.

Walking around there in the peace and quiet with the Staffie trotting beside me made everything that was happening seem like a bad dream. I still feel like it's a nightmare now, and I want to wake up, but I can't because it's real.

Evie Jones shattered the peace and quiet and brought me back to reality when she spotted a duck on the water and launched herself off the path in a valiant attempt to savage it. I learnt three things about mallards that evening. Number one, they're open to aerial attack from the bank; number two, they cannot outswim a Staffie over five yards; and number three, they're really crap at fighting. By the time I had pulled her extended lead in, there were blood and feathers everywhere. As much as I love her, she is nuts; the duck was another casualty to account for.

It was Friday and the full moon was due in four days. If the dust had settled at the farm, then the satanic order would be meeting the next night at Brunt Boggart and we would be there to greet them. I had no idea if they would take Constance there or not, but I had to start somewhere. If there were any Niners there and I got the better of them, I would make them talk. If they knew anything about Constance's disappearance, they would tell me. I packed up the Land Rover and changed the letters on the number plate using black vinyl tape. I decided to leave the caravan where it was in the unlikely event that we survived. I guzzled the wine from a plastic cup and the alcohol numbed my muddled mind and allowed me to sleep for a while. It's strange to think that my tortured dreams are not as bad as my living nightmares.

CHAPTER 25

Brunt Boggart

The journey back to the island was uneventful. We avoided the expressway and stuck to the back roads, so progress was slow. We didn't encounter any police cars, bad ones or otherwise. It was a two-hour journey that took three. When we arrived, we found that Brunt Boggart was set in a leafy greenbelt, comprised of farmland, woodland and sleepy livery stables. I used Google Earth to study the area around the farm and spotted an acre of woodland, which offered an elevated view over the farmhouse and its outbuildings. It wasn't far from the farm and it offered perfect cover. I could watch the farm unnoticed.

We drove by the entrance to the farm and I spotted something that hadn't appeared on Google Earth: the owners had erected a high perimeter fence made from corrugated iron sheets and there were padlocked gates across the entrance. The extra security reinforced my suspicions that they would return. I parked the Landy in a derelict petrol station on the edge of the woods. Opposite, there was an old pub called the Pilot Boat. The once white facia was tinged with green and slates were missing from the roof. It was boarded up and the wooden sign outside was blistered and peeling. It reminded me of the dream I had the night before Peter died. There was something about the village which felt wrong. Maybe it was my imagination, but I could smell decay on the wind.

With the Landy hidden from the road, I put the Remington into its case and hung it from my shoulder. This was farming land, and if I did encounter anyone in the woods, then I would fit right in with my shotgun and my dog. With a terrible sense of foreboding, we headed off through the woods to find a secluded spot where I could watch the farm. From the aerial maps I had viewed, I gathered that we would have to walk a mile or so. I kept Evie Jones on a tight lead as we followed a badger trail through the trees. The wood was comprised of oak and sycamore trees, and like the rest of the surrounding area, it had succumbed to subsidence caused by the mines. It was pitted with deep ravines and flooded sinkholes. We picked our way through the natural assault course disturbing the grey squirrels and rabbits that inhabited it. The closer we got to the farm, the less wildlife there was. That definitely wasn't my imagination. When we reached the edge of the woods, I crouched down in the long grass and watched the farm as the sun went down and the night closed in. The darker it became, the tighter I held the shotgun.

Two hours went by and nothing moved. It was getting cold and the air started to bite. Evie Jones was edgy. Every creaking branch or rustling pile of leaves made her stand to attention ready for action. She was prepared to fight anything that came near me. Her fearlessness made me feel humble. I'd explained to her the night before as we walked around the river that it might be our last day on this earth. She didn't seem bothered by the news and she licked my face.

It was nearly midnight when headlights weaved along the narrow lane to the farm. I looked through my binoculars and watched as a dark Mercedes pulled to a stop at the gates. I watched someone climb out. He pulled the collars of his black overcoat up to shade him from the cold. I watched him looking around furtively before unlocking the gates so his colleague could drive through. The vehicle stopped again on the other side while he closed the gates behind him, then fastened the lock. The track led about five hundred yards away from the road. I could hear the engine noise drifting across the field as they pulled the vehicle into the farmyard. As they stopped in the yard, the vehicle triggered a security light and the halogen glow illuminated the scene. The buildings hid the car from the road and the driver steered it under a lean-to built onto the side of a barn.

Four men climbed out of the Mercedes. They didn't look like farmers to me. They were smartly dressed and looked to be in their fifties. Their long winter coats gave them the look of undertakers. They walked to the back of the car and exchanged words before opening the boot. My heart was in my mouth. Every nerve ending in my body was tingling. I wanted to see them lifting Constance out of the boot alive. Whether she was my daughter or not, I wanted her to be alive. If she was in the boot of that car, then I would get her out and take her to the police myself. If the four men wanted to get in my way, then I would introduce them to the shotgun.

 I watched them reach inside and struggle to remove something heavy. They were blocking my view of the boot and I held my breath as they fumbled about with their load. Whatever it was, it appeared to be bigger than your average six-year-old girl. One of them stepped back, his arms wrapped around something bulky. He lowered his end to the floor as his colleague struggled with his end of the bundle. Whatever it was that they were lifting, it was moving.

 I focused the binoculars slightly, trying to get a clearer view. I realised that it was a woman. Her hands were bound, and she was gagged. Anger rose in my throat and I could feel my heartbeat quickening. The bastards had a woman in the boot of the car, and they were going to take her into the farm and do God knows what to her. I was pissed off that it wasn't Constance, but it didn't matter. They weren't going to rape that woman that night or any other night. My hands were shaking so much that I dropped the binoculars. I reached into the soggy leaves and grass for them and wiped them on my sleeve before looking again. I refocused on the woman and gasped at who it was.

 I had to look away and then look again as they bundled out the woman. I wasn't sure if I was imagining it or if I was mistaken, but my body turned cold and a shiver ran down my spine. I simply couldn't be seeing what I thought I was seeing. I looked again and swore under my breath. There was no way I could be seeing this. It was late and I was tired, but there was absolutely no doubt in my mind who it was. She twisted her head towards the woods and looked at me as if she knew I was there. I could see her eyes as clear as day. Fabienne Wilder looked right back at me.

CHAPTER 26

The Ceremony

I was in shock. I'd come here looking for Constance and found Fabienne instead. All thoughts about blowing the place up with her inside dissipated as I watched her being dragged into the door. She was alive. My heart skipped a beat, but my brain was telling me that it couldn't be her. Maybe she had another sister. The doctor at Denbigh told me that Fabienne had committed suicide and there were police officers all over the hospital. Was the doctor one of them? Why else would he lie? My mind went into overdrive. That's why he showed me the fire door when the police officer came in to speak to me. He wanted me to believe she was dead. They wanted me to believe that she was dead. They wanted me out of the way. I was beginning to think that I'd been stupid. The Niners spread far and wide and I couldn't fathom who was who. Had the entire thing been an elaborate hoax to throw me off the scent?

Why did they want me to think she was dead? So, they could take her to the farm to sacrifice her? Were they just waiting for her release so that they could shut her up? Maybe; I had no way of knowing the truth. They might try to convert her again in order to use her powers for their own benefit. Whatever they were up to, I was going to help her. I couldn't stand there while they hurt her. She'd been through enough abuse at their hands. I waited for the security light to go out, and then we set off across the field towards the farmhouse. I felt like a condemned man walking to the gallows. I knew that I could turn and walk in the opposite direction, but my conscience wouldn't allow me to choose that option. Fabienne was in dire trouble and I had to help her. I thought about calling the police, but my trust in them had gone. It was up to me and the Staffie.

My pulse was racing, and cold sweat coated every inch of my body. Evie Jones was panting and pulling like a shire horse; she wanted to be off the lead, but I couldn't let her go yet. She was about as subtle as a lump hammer in the teeth. Stealth was not her forte. We reached the perimeter fence and walked along it for twenty yards before I found a section where the panels overlapped. A few strong tugs bent the corner up enough for us to crawl underneath. There was a dull renting sound as the metal bent and I froze for a few seconds in case it had carried inside the house. I bent double and peered through the gap. There was nothing moving on the other side. The farmyard was in darkness now; the security light had automatically switched off. I wriggled under the fence, my chest and face flattened against the damp soil. The grass was wet and smelled of my childhood. Camping with the scouts and playing Cowboys and Indians flashed into my mind. Evie Jones made things difficult as she tried to wriggle through the narrow gap at the same time. She's loyal but she's impatient too.

We surfaced at the rear of the farmhouse and I ducked low as we skirted the building, keeping to the shadows. I didn't want to activate the sensor in the security light. There was a solitary light on inside the house. It appeared to be in the hallway or maybe the stairwell. The curtains were drawn, but the light seeped out around the edges of the material. We crept towards the window and I peered through a gap at the edge of the curtains. There was no sign of life. The house was empty of furniture and the room I was looking at had a door which led into the hallway.

Suddenly, two of the men walked past the door. They'd taken off their coats and were bundling Fabienne towards the rear of the house. They had stripped her to her underwear and tied her hands behind her back. The gag had been removed, but she wasn't shouting or screaming for help. She went by in an instant, but I swear she glanced at the window. I felt a prickle of electricity in my mind as I saw her eyes. I wondered why she wasn't screaming. In truth, the farm was too remote for anyone to hear her and her energy would be put to better use trying to fight them off. The other two men followed them a few seconds later. I could see them unfastening their collars as they walked. It was obvious what they had in mind.

I couldn't hang around any longer. It was obvious that they were going to gang rape Fabienne, but that couldn't happen. Not tonight, Josephine; while I had breath in my body, it wasn't happening, but I needed to act quickly. I let the Staffie off the lead and she disappeared around the corner into the darkness. I decided to take the direct route into the house. I had no idea who was inside, but I didn't care. I was going to get Fabienne out and then call the police. The fact that she was still alive would back up my crazy story; they would have to believe me. The Niners had brought her to the farm. I'd told them they met there and they'd obviously done fuck all about it. The Press had gone bananas for a while, but now the attention had shifted off the farm, they were back.

I used the butt of the shotgun to smash the window and then reached inside and ripped one of the curtains from its rail. I used it to knock out the large shards so that I could climb in without lacerating myself. I vaulted over the windowsill and landed heavily on the other side, aiming the shotgun at the open doorway. I was expecting the men to come running in, but they didn't. Wiping sweat from my eyes, I sprinted to the door and ducked into the hallway. It was empty.

The hallway was dimly lit by a low wattage bulb. Its glow couldn't illuminate the kitchen at the back of the house, but I could sense that there was nobody in there. A strong gust of wind blew through the broken window and chilled me to the bone. The draft opened a door beneath the staircase, and it creaked noisily before stopping against the frame. I froze and listened intently for the sound of footsteps coming, but none came. With my back to the wall, I slid along the hallway, keeping the gun trained on the doorway. As I peered into it, I saw a narrow wooden staircase leading down into the cellar. There was no way that I could creep down there unnoticed. I toyed with the idea of chucking a couple of pipe bombs down there and shutting the door, but Fabienne was there, too. Constance may be there. I was still debating my next move when a high-pitched scream echoed through the house. It was Fabienne.

I took a deep breath and ran down the stairs at full pelt. I had no idea what I was running into, but it was shit or bust time. I jumped the last three steps swinging the gun in a wide arc, searching for a target. I was looking at a dimly lit cellar. It was cavernous, but there was no one there. I peered into the dark corners, looking for anyone who was hiding from the light, but there was nothing there except shadows and cobwebs. I took a few deep breaths and walked to the far wall. From there I could see a narrow door at the one end of the cellar. It was fitted with two deadbolts and a padlock, which were all open. I realised that the men must have taken Fabienne through that door, which would explain why they hadn't heard me breaking the window.

I tiptoed to the door and put my ear against it. I could hear the low murmur of men's voices chanting. Fabienne was crying. I could hear her sobbing. I had no choice but to open the door and take my chances with whatever was on the other side. I swapped the shotgun to my right hand and stood back as I twisted the handle with my left. The handle turned, but the door wouldn't budge. I swore silently and looked at the doorframe again. There was a mortise lock fitted to it. The bastards had locked it behind them. I was at a loss. The door opened outwards towards me, so I couldn't kick it open. I had three shots in the Remington before it would need to be reloaded. All I could do was hope that the door was weak. Another piercing scream forced me to act.

Taking a few steps back, I fired three times. The gun roared, and in the confines of the cellar it sounded like a howitzer. I slotted three new shells into the breach before I'd assessed the damage to the door. Reloading the shotgun was my number one priority. Without a weapon, I had no chance. I needn't have worried; the blasts had blown a hole in the door the size of a dustbin lid. I bent low and looked through the hole. My stomach turned at the scene before me.

Fabienne had her back to me and she couldn't turn around. She was tied face down over an altar of some kind. A second narrow staircase climbed up the left-hand wall. I wasn't sure, but from the distance I'd travelled through the cellars, it probably led to the barn. Thick black candles flickered and cast an eerie amber glow on the bizarre gathering. Her underwear had been ripped, but it still hung from her body. The four men were positioned either side of the altar; two behind her and two in front of her. Their ridiculous chanting had ceased. One of them was trying to force her thighs apart with his hips. She was squirming and screaming, but there was nothing that she could have done. A few minutes later he would have penetrated her.

One of the men near her head was holding a boleen knife with a curved blade like a scythe. The blade was coated with dried blood. He was holding her by the hair and pressing the blade to the back of her neck, near the spine. The sick grin on his face disappeared instantly. The other two were still in the process of undressing, and despite the noisy entrance that I'd made, they looked genuinely surprised to see me. They looked shocked and pathetic in their socks and white Y-fronts. They were podgy, middle-aged men with saggy bellies and man boobs. Their milky white skin was almost translucent in the candlelight. They looked at me with hatred in their eyes, but I wasn't scared of them. I could have ripped them apart with my bare hands. That's what I wanted to do.

I shouldered the shotgun and aimed it towards them. There was a tense moment of silence as everyone weighed up the situation and then one of the men grabbed a second knife from the altar and pointed it towards me. It was an athame, a ritual dagger. One side of the blade was razor sharp and the other was jagged like a saw. The jagged edge would explain the wounds on the throats of Pauline Holmes and Caroline Stokes. They weren't caused by bloodsucking monsters drinking blood. They were caused by these idiots with their demonic dagger purchased from the Internet. Naked, they didn't seem scary to me at all, especially down the barrel of a pump-action shotgun.

'Put the knife down,' I said calmly. There was no way he could close the distance between us, but I was concerned that others might arrive.

'Every police officer in the country is searching for you,' he said, smiling. He stepped away from the altar and faced me square on. 'What are you going to do, shoot us, too? Do you think she's worth it?' He moved a step closer.

I wasn't there to mess around, so I squeezed the trigger. The man took the buckshot in the chest and the force knocked him backwards against the wall. He looked down at the holes in his chest in shock. Blood poured from them like red wine from a pepper pot. He left bloody smears on the wall as his legs sagged and he slid down into a sitting position. His legs began to twitch violently as shock spread over him. The other three men raised their hands in the air. I wasn't sure what to do as I didn't plan on taking any prisoners.

'Untie her.' I waved the gun towards Fabienne. None of them moved.

'I knew you would come.' Fabienne tried to look around, but she couldn't. 'Shoot these animals.'

'You don't understand what's going on here,' one of the men said quietly. 'This is not what it looks like to an outsider.'

'Shoot him, Conrad,' Fabienne shouted.

'Shut your face and untie her now,' I aimed the gun at the speaker. 'What's your name?'

'John,' he replied, but his expression told me that he was lying.

'Okay, John,' I said, nervously. My hands were shaking. I didn't care what his name was for now. 'Untie her.'

'Are you that stupid that you don't understand what's going on here? I'm not untying her.' He laughed and reached for his clothes. 'What are you going to do, take us prisoner or shoot us all?'

'That's really up to you.'

'I don't like either option.' He looked at the others for support. 'He can't take all of us at once.' That was a huge mistake.

I squeezed the trigger a second time and the shot hit him in the thigh. Arterial spray burst between his fingers as he grasped at the ragged wound. He screamed and turned to run for the door, but a second shot slammed into his lower back, ripping a huge chunk of muscle from his buttocks. The force launched him against the altar with a sickening thud. He rolled over, groaning in agony and his heels dug into the cellar floor as he tried to scramble away from me. I reloaded and walked closer to him. I glanced around to get my bearings. I was nervous of new arrivals sneaking up from behind me.

The room was empty apart from the altar. There was a screed floor; stains soiled it around the base of the altar. The walls were bare and newly painted. Apart from the bloodstains, the cellar was spotless. John was trying to crawl away. His blood was pooling around him. His friend was already dying; I could tell from his eyes. I felt nothing seeing death in their eyes. I walked over to the injured man and bent towards him. I grabbed his ankles and dragged him back towards the altar. He dug his fingernails into the concrete and groaned.

'Shut up,' I said. There was no sympathy left in me. There hadn't been much there to begin with, but now there was only hate. 'You untie her, or you'll get the same as he got.' One of the remaining men reached for the dagger and then thought better of it. He looked at me for permission. 'Pick it up and cut her free.' I pointed to the dagger.

He used the smooth side of the dagger to cut her bonds. 'He's telling you the truth,' he said, throwing the blade onto the floor. 'This is not what it seems.' Fabienne ran and stood behind me.

'I don't care what it seems.' I turned the gun on him again. 'Throw me your clothes, all of them.'

'What?'

'You heard me.' The two uninjured men exchanged concerned glances and gathered the four sets of clothes in their arms. 'Get their trousers, Fabienne,' I ordered. 'Get their wallets and their mobile phones.'

She paused momentarily before approaching them. She snatched the trousers roughly from them. 'Here,' she said. She held them out to me like a mother giving her child a birthday present.

'I knew you would come,' Fabienne said. Tears streamed down her cheeks and she turned to face me. 'They were going to rape me again.' She sobbed uncontrollably.

'Are you okay?' I turned to look at her. Her eyes were darker than ever, and despite her tears they seemed to sparkle. She didn't look scared at all. She just looked sad. I rummaged through the pockets and collected their personal belongings. I resisted the urge to look through them; getting distracted now would be a fatal mistake. I stuffed their keys, wallets, and phones into my haversack alongside my pipe bombs. 'This lot will open a few eyes when it lands on the superintendent's desk.'

'Thank you for coming for me.' Her lips quivered as she spoke. 'I'm okay, but they were going to hurt me again. Kill him, Conrad,' she nodded to the injured man. He cried out and tried to crawl away again, but a swift kick in his ribs from Fabienne stopped him. He curled up in the foetal position gasping for breath.

'No, Fabienne, don't let him kill me.' He begged. 'Tell him the truth. Tell him the truth.'

'You snivelling little shit.' She kicked him again as she spoke. He flipped over onto his back.

'You brought her here to rape her and now you want her to help you?' I asked.

'No,' he tried to speak, but she kicked him again.

I shouldered the gun and aimed at his groin. 'Is there anyone else coming here tonight?'

'No. Please listen to me,' he said.

'Kill him,' Fabienne shouted.

'Why is nobody else coming?' I didn't believe him.

'Kill him!' she screamed. Her voice resounded in my head. 'Kill him, kill him, kill him.'

'No one comes anymore because of you.'

'What are you talking about?' I asked.

'Listen to me, please,' he tried to explain again. I thought that he might be telling the truth. They were lying low because of the fuss I had caused on the Internet. They daren't meet while the focus was on them. 'I can explain this.' He babbled. 'Don't listen to a word that bitch says.'

'Kill him,' she screamed again. Her voice was piercing. Spittle flew from her lips. 'They raped me, Conrad. They raped my brothers and sisters. Don't let them do it to me again.'

'Fabienne, calm down.' I turned on her. She was becoming hysterical and her voice was grating on my mind. I was confused. 'Please, stop shouting.'

'Okay,' she said, nodding.

'Have you seen a young girl called Constance?' I asked. 'I think they've taken her.'

'They have taken her.' Fabienne's eyes lit up. 'Ask him where she is. That pervert there.' She pointed to the man who had cut her free.

'I don't know what she's talking about.' His lip quivered. 'I don't know anything about any young girls.' His voice was well-educated, and I thought that I recognised it from Knowles's recordings.

'He's lying, Conrad,' Fabienne snarled. 'She's been here for days.'

'Where is she?'

'Up there.' She pointed to a small cupboard door that I hadn't noticed. It was built into the wall at the top of the staircase. 'They keep them in there until it's playtime. Don't you, you bastards?' Her voice reached a deafening pitch. 'God knows what they've done to her already.'

I looked at the door and I could see that it was padlocked. I had a conundrum. Two of the men were badly wounded, one was nearly dead. The other two were unhurt and dangerous.

'Who has the keys to that door?' I asked the two men. One of them had dyed his hair black, which didn't match his grey eyebrows, and the other had a comb-over that Bobby Charlton would have cringed at.

'I don't know.' Comb-Over shrugged nervously.

'He does.' Hair Dye pointed to the man who was bleeding to death against the wall. I walked over to him and kicked his feet. He opened his eyes for a second and blood trickled from the corner of his mouth.

'Where's the key to that door?'

'He has it,' he gasped, pointing back to Comb-Over.

'I don't!' Comb-Over shouted in fear. 'He's lying.'

'Kill him.' Fabienne was cowering against the wall, covering her eyes with her arms. 'Kill him.' Her screams were driving me to distraction.

'Calm down, Fabienne,' I shouted. 'Last time, where is the key to that door?'

'She's not in there, you fool.' The injured man near the altar laughed.

'Where is she?' I pointed the gun at him.

'You're an idiot.' He spluttered. 'You have no idea what you're getting involved in. Your daughter is already dead and that's your fault. Either call the police or get out of here.'

'She's already dead?' I asked.

'Yes. And she suffered.'

I'd had enough. I pointed the gun at his face and squeezed the trigger. The gun kicked and his face disintegrated beneath the force of the blast. Flesh and blood splattered the two unhurt men. Comb-Over frantically wiped the viscera from his face and he made a strange mewing noise.

'Where's the key?' I asked again. They stopped smearing the bloody mess from their bodies and looked at each other. I shouldered the Remington and aimed at Hair Dye. 'Three seconds, two, one.'

'Wait, I'll check his clothes.' Hair Dye held up his hands and reached for the pile of clothes. 'He keeps it under his belt.'

'They raped me last night,' Fabienne spoke calmly this time. 'They were going to rape both of us again.' She nodded towards the locked door. 'Constance is in there.'

'What do you mean, 'both of us again'?' I asked the two men. Fabienne started screaming again and it was driving me to frenzy. I couldn't hear my own thoughts. 'Have you touched Constance?' I felt spittle spraying as I spoke. I felt the blood pounding through my brains, and I slammed more shells into the gun.

'Don't listen to her.' Comb-Over tried to scramble backwards, away from the altar. 'She's lying. We haven't raped your daughter.'

'How the hell do you know that she's my daughter then?'

'It's all over the newspapers.'

'He said she was already dead.' I was losing it.

'She probably is, but she isn't here.'

'Kill him!' Fabienne was screaming repeatedly.

'Did you rape her?' I was steaming. Anger was taking control and Fabienne was adding fuel to the flames.

'It isn't like that,' he tried to explain. 'It isn't like that; she insists that we do this; she demands that we come here and do this.'

'Who does?'

'Her,' he said, pointing at Fabienne.

'Don't listen to him,' Fabienne said. 'Shoot him.'

'She's lying to you.'

'Kill him or he'll never stop.' Her voice became a sickening wail. 'He's the one who tells them what to do. He told them to take Constance. I heard them talking.'

'Don't listen to her,' the man shouted. 'She's the cause of all this. She'll get us all killed in the end.'

'They did terrible things to her,' Fabienne said. 'I heard him bragging.'

'Don't listen to a word she says,' he said, panicking.

'Kill him, kill him, kill him, kill him,' she screamed as I reloaded the gun. She was frantic; the men were terrified. Something inside me took control and it was as if someone else was guiding me. I raised the barrel and fired two shots. His legs buckled while I reloaded and turned to the others. Nine shots later the men were dead. The walls were covered in blood and brains, and the smell of urine and excrement pervaded the cellar. The corpulent odour filled my senses and clung to me. I fought the urge to puke.

I looked at Fabienne as sweat mingled with my tears. They ran down my cheeks in warm rivulets. Her eyes rolled into the back of her head. I thought she was going into a fit. She grinned like a mad woman and she smiled at me as I bent to touch her hands.

'I knew you would come. I knew that you would come for me,' she shouted, but her tone was odd.

'I thought you were dead,' I said, confused. 'I came to the hospital and the doctor told me you were dead.'

'Thank you, Conrad.' She smiled as her hands became free. She stood up and flung her arms around my neck. Her mouth moved towards mine. As I looked into her eyes, I felt my strength waning. The need to unlock the door and search for Constance was replaced by a far more urgent desire. She pulled my head down and put her mouth over mine. She forced her tongue between my lips and gripped the back of my head as she probed my mouth. Her tongue felt hot and swollen. It filled my mouth, almost choking me, but it felt so good. I kissed her and waited for her to pull away, but she didn't. She pushed her tongue further into my mouth, withdrawing it to her lips before forcing it back again.

Unfamiliar lights and sounds filled my mind as she tore my clothes from my body. She literally ripped them apart and I shook them free as we writhed against each other. She pulled back, her mouth exploring my face.

'You killed them for me,' she gasped. Her breath was tainted with something rancid. I felt her teeth nipping and biting my ears and neck. Her nails scratched my back and chest, drawing blood where she raked deeply. She placed her mouth over my nipple and bit down hard as she took me to the floor. Her strength was incredible. I didn't fight her because I wanted her. Her body was lean and muscular, and she smelled musky. Images began to fill my mind, images of sex and of blood. As she lowered her body onto mine, I heard her howl with pleasure.

She howled like a dog, but the sound seemed to be so far away. I could feel her body grinding against mine. I could smell her sweat mingling with my own. The musky smell of her filled my nostrils and there was an uncontrollable urge to bite her hard and draw blood. Her body was becoming tense, hard, and taut. The muscles and sinews in her neck were protruding and they pulsed as she bit my face and neck. A deep growling came from her throat as her movement became more desperate. 'You're a killer, just like me,' she whispered.

I felt her nails ripping the flesh on my back and her teeth bit into the skin on my throat. I felt her tear a nick of flesh from my neck and a trickle of warm blood ran from the wound over my collarbone and onto my chest. And the pain increased. I tried to push her off, but she was too powerful. I felt that she would suffocate me. Part of me welcomed the pain. Part of me desired the intensity and the violence. She was right. I was a killer. I stopped struggling, opened my mind and let her take me away with her. I felt her in my mind again, leading me by the hand. I was scared now but I couldn't fight her.

The place she took me to was vile. It was like walking into a dream so real you cannot tell the difference between fantasy and reality. I've never tried drugs, but I can only imagine it's like tripping. I was suddenly aware that we were no longer alone. I saw images in my mind. They were terrible images. The cellar was full of people. The floor was a writhing, stinking mass of people dying in the vilest and most perverted ways imaginable. Men, women, animals, and demons were present at this orgy of violence. Many of the participants were bound and gagged, unwilling victims of the insatiable crowd. I heard women screaming and men crying. Men groaned in agony. Their screams haunt me to this day.

'Join us,' they screamed.

'Join us, Conrad. Be with me. Your heart is as evil as mine. You're a killer,' I heard her whispering in my ear. Men cried out in pain and animals howled. I heard Fabienne howling; I heard myself howling like a wolf and then there was nothing but pain.

I opened my eyes and looked for her, but she was gone. She was on the altar at the head of the room and the evil in the room seemed to magnetise towards her like smoke through an open window. She was the centre of the violence and the focus of their energy. Fabienne Wilder wasn't their victim, she was their princess. I could hear chanting. The frantic screams of the consensual and non-consensual were reaching a fever pitch. I heard them chanting 'Baphomet, Baphomet, Baphomet'. I remembered that Baphomet is a sinister entity and is depicted in their scriptures as a beautiful, mature woman, naked from the waist up, who holds in her hand the bloodied severed head of a man.

I watched as she walked across the altar to a spot where a man was being strangled by another dressed in a goatskin jacket. He was wearing horns on his head. The receiver was bound and the expression on his face told me that he wasn't consensual. Fabienne swung her arm once and a boleen flashed in the candlelight. As she raised the severed head in the air, the man in the goatskin laughed. I suddenly knew much more than I ever had.

Fabienne Wilder is the dark, violent goddess to whom human sacrifices were made. She ritualistically washed in a basin full of the blood. She wasn't a victim; she was the centre of their worship. She was their vampire princess; their goddess.

As the realisation hit me, the sick tableau vanished, and I was back in the cellar. Fabienne was on me and I could feel every nerve ending in my body tingling. I knew that letting her back into my mind would spell my death, I couldn't stop her. Her body tensed and she howled like a dog in pain. This time it was a high-pitched whine that cut through my brain. I heard a growling – the deep, ripping growl of an animal savaging its prey. I felt her pulling away from me, struggle was no longer against me. Her howling became more intense and the growling grew deeper and more guttural. I felt her letting go of my mind and my body. I reached up and moved from under her, tossing her aside. She screamed in pain and frustration as the Staffie savaged her.

Evie Jones had attached her teeth into her neck below her left ear. The Staffie was twisting and turning her body trying to maintain her grip. Fabienne stood up and ripped the Staffie from her throat.

Arterial spray exploded from the wound. Evie Jones bounced off the wall at the far end of the room, but she was up in a flash and she launched herself back towards Fabienne.

I dived across the concrete for the gun. I heard Evie Jones howl as I turned and watched Fabienne take her true form. She was no longer the helpless victim; she was an enraged animal. Her jaw opened wide, her lips curled and exposed her teeth, still stained with my blood. Her eyes were as black as the night and evil oozed from them. She snarled at Evie Jones and the Staffie stopped in her tracks, growling and barking, but obviously scared of the monster Fabienne had become. For a second there was a flash in my mind. She was desperately disappointed. I'd caused her kind no end of problems and she'd set the trap to lure me in and kill me. I was weak and I let her into my mind and surrendered to her.

Only Evie Jones stopped her from taking me. I grabbed the gun, but she moved like lightening. She was on me in a second. As I turned the gun towards her, she struck me in the chest and launched me across the cellar. I hit the wall and cracked my skull hard against the plaster. I squeezed the trigger and the blast hit her square in the face. A plume of red mist splattered the ceiling. Pain flashed through my brain and I crumpled to the floor as unconsciousness enveloped me.

CHAPTER 27

Aftermath

Where are we now? I can't tell you for obvious reasons, but we are safe. When I woke up, Fabienne – or whoever she really is – was gone. The Staffie was licking my wounds and the sun was coming up. She was gone, but the bodies of the men she used to trap me were still there and they were stinking. Sticky bloodstains congealed on the concrete around them. All the evidence of her being there was gone apart from a blood trail which ran from the cellar, up the staircase and into the hallway. Why didn't she kill me? I don't know. Maybe she was too badly injured. Maybe Evie Jones attacked again. I've asked the Staffie a thousand times what happened when she knocked me out, but she just looks at me and sticks her tongue out. I'll never know.

As my senses cleared, I gathered my tattered clothes and retrieved my bag. I found the key to the door at the top of the stairs, but all it contained was a water meter. The back of the door was scratched and there was a fingernail in the wood. They'd imprisoned some poor soul in there. We scoured the farmhouse; each and every room we searched was empty. There was another cellar beneath the barn, but that was empty, too. I couldn't find anything of use. The Mercedes was gone, and the outhouses held no clues. I thought about calling the police and waiting there for them, but the more I digested the situation the less the idea appealed. What was there to gain?

What would I tell them?

Hello officer, I've broken into this farm, shot another four men dead and had sex with Fabienne Wilder before shooting her in the face with a Remington. By the way, her body has disappeared, but there's plenty of blood on the stairs and carpet to back up what I'm saying.

The whole thing was madness. I decided that leaving the bodies and bloodstains there could only make my case worse. I placed my bag of pipe bombs onto the electric hob in the kitchen and switched the ring on. Evie and I were safely into the treeline when they exploded, and according to the pictures in the Mail, the place burned to the ground before a single fire engine attended. I know one thing for sure: they're still looking for me. They'll regroup and begin their insidious recruitment again. I can only tell the world about them and hope that someone listens.

The four men in the cellar were reported missing by their families. At first, their disappearances were treated as isolated until I linked them to the Niners on the Internet. I didn't explain how I knew; I just made enough noise for the Press to hear it, and they picked it up and ran with it. The police searched their homes, and lo and behold, their laptops contained thousands of pornographic images of abuse. No one alluded that their evaporation was my fault, which suited me. Fabienne Wilder was already *dead*, so nobody was looking for her.

Two months on and the weather has changed. Winter is upon us again. The wind roars around the caravan at night like an angry beast trying to break in. Things are very different now, though. I received a message which was posted on a book review site. Attached to it was a jpeg file. The photograph was the scan of an unborn baby. The message attached read,

'This is our child, your unborn son. I pray to Lucifer that his heart is as black as yours, Conrad. I may rear him to be one of us; or I may slaughter him as a gift to my dark lord. Either way, your son is a child for the devil, love Fabienne.'

I'm jumping at shadows. Every creak and groan makes me turn around fearing the worst. This book is about monsters and it's they who hunt me. I have to pinch myself to see if I'm awake. I wish it was all just a dream, but it's not. It was real, and although I've written many books, I couldn't have imagined this story in my most creative moments. This is a shocking tale; it may disturb you and make you question my grip on reality, and your own, too. You'll tell your friends it can't be real, but as I listen to the wind gusting against the windows and watch the lightning flashing against the blackness of the sky, I can still hear her screams in my mind.

I'm scared of the dark and scared of my own shadow. The Staffie is healthy and she eats lambs' liver every day because I never know if it will be our last. She gets tummy tickles at every opportunity because if it wasn't for her, I wouldn't be here. The Press has the identities of the men at the farm, but I have their contacts. I have their mobile phones. I'm working my way through them one by one and the body count is rising. Constance is still missing, but I won't stop looking for her until I know that she's either dead or safe. I'll never stop looking for her.

Eventually, one of them will lead me to Fabienne Wilder. If she is carrying a child, then I'll send them both to her demonic master. Until then, we'll travel and hide, and then we move on and start over. If you believe a single word that I've written, google them and read their websites. They're there and they're in the millions and they're hunting me.

The difference now is I'm hunting them, too.

Printed in Poland
by Amazon Fulfillment
Poland Sp. z o.o., Wrocław